Love
ON THE RUN

OTHER BOOKS BY RACHEL ANN NUNES

Love to the Highest Bidder

Framed for Love

Ariana: The Making of a Queen

Ariana: A Gift Most Precious

Ariana: A New Beginning

Ariana: A Glimpse of Eternity

To Love and to Promise

Love
ON THE RUN

a novel

RACHEL ANN NUNES

Covenant Communications, Inc.

This is a work of fiction. The characters, names, incidents, places, and dialogue are products of the author's imagination, and are not to be construed as real.

Cover photography by "Picture This . . . by Sara Staker"

Published by Covenant Communications, Inc.
American Fork, Utah

Printed in the United States of America
First Printing: February 2000

07 06 05 04 03 02 01 00   10 9 8 7 6 5 4 3 2 1

ISBN 1-57734-604-1

Library of Congress Cataloging-in-Publication Data

Nunes, Rachel Ann, 1966-
    Love on the run : a novel / Rachel Ann Nunes.
        p.   cm.
    ISBN 1-57734-604-1
    I. Title
    PS3564.U468 L55 2000
    813'.54--dc21   99-088762
                                  CIP

For Jared,
the best surprise ever.

PROLOGUE

Roger Edward Stanton III clicked shut his briefcase, satisfied that all he would need was inside. Not that it took much preparation. His client had been extremely organized and exact in her demands. He had long respected her for her clarity, as well as her sleek beauty. When he had first met her, he had entertained thoughts of pursuing a personal relationship, but he was quickly cured of the idea. She was hard, cold, and calculating—everything he admired in a business associate, but detested in women. And yet some longing inside him remained. Her beauty, brains, and—yes, he would admit it to himself—her amoral attitude had been compelling. She was much like himself.

His trip to the morgue yesterday had been unnecessary with the newspapers full of the account. But he needed to see for himself that she was really dead. And she was. With a bullet hole in her chest, right through her heart. Funny that the organ she had used so little in life had been the cause of her demise.

There were none to mourn her as far as Roger had been able to determine, though if there had been, it would have made no difference in her plans, updated for the last time early on the day of her death. Not that she had planned to die, of course, but there was always the possibility. And she had always covered every possibility.

Roger had fleetingly thought of searching out her promised fortune for himself—an idea that left his head as soon as it entered. If he went against his client's wishes, he had no doubt he would join her in the grave and another contingency plan would go into effect. He smiled. What a woman!

He took a plane to San Diego and then a taxi to his destination. Immediately, he was admitted into the mansion where a man waited. The crime boss had no knowledge of why Roger was there, but the well-known name of his law firm had been more than enough to gain him an appointment.

"Good day." Roger didn't sit, but opened his briefcase on the man's desk.

"Have a seat."

"No, thank you. This won't take long." Roger noticed two body-guards standing at a ready position. One stepped closer to make sure there was no gun in the briefcase. Roger cleared his throat. "Laranda Garrettson has a billion dollars in rare paintings and art objects stashed away in a safe place."

"I've heard that rumor," said the man. "The forty-million-dollar Van Gogh painting that was stolen a few months ago wouldn't have anything to do with this, would it?"

"I'm sure I wouldn't know," Roger said. "It doesn't matter. What matters is if you want this fortune and are willing to do what it takes to get it."

The man's eyes showed greed. "Of course I am interested."

Roger handed him a large eight-by-ten envelope. "My client is willing to give you this fortune, if you complete her wishes."

"Which are?"

Roger shook his head. "As you can see, the envelope is sealed. I do know some of the details, including the existence of a safe deposit box containing directions to the location of the art treasures. But what you must do to obtain the information is between you and Laranda Garrettson."

"Garrettson? But she's dead—or is she?"

"Is that important?" Roger knew his face was expressionless. He had practiced the facade many times in the mirror.

"I suppose not." The man hefted the thick envelope, and the heavy gold ring on his finger reflected the light. "So what if I choose not to fulfill whatever demands Garrettson has in here?"

Roger shut his case. "You have until tomorrow morning to decide. At that time I will be leaving for the airport." He turned to the door, then paused and permitted himself a tight smile. "But I think you will find that you will enjoy this little game. My client studied your organization well. Her purpose will most likely serve you both. However, I will await your call."

Without another word, Roger left. He knew the man would accept the challenge. Garrettson was anything but a poor judge of character. And whatever murder or larceny was involved, Roger was free of it and a million dollars richer, tax-free. Perhaps it was time to take the wife and kids on an extended vacation until his next big case.

* * * * *

The man opened the white envelope, fascinated despite himself. Inside was a sealed letter envelope, unaddressed, but attached to a photograph of Quentin Thomas Holbrooke, alias Big Tommy. A typed page gave a detailed explanation.

He chuckled. All that was left for him was to choose the means to carry the letter to Big Tommy and thus set the wheels in motion. Not too difficult. The plan certainly fit in with his own lust for revenge.

Behind the picture of Holbrooke was a set of keys clipped to two other photographs. One was of a beautiful brown-eyed woman with dark, tightly-curled hair. The second portrayed a man with medium blond hair and intense blue eyes. After the headlines in the paper, it was impossible not to recognize them: Cassi Mason and Jared Landine.

Behind the photographs was a clothes catalogue with two outfits circled in red. There were also two video cassette tapes. He watched them, all the time laughing aloud. This was definitely his type of game. Too bad Garrettson was dead. He would have enjoyed meeting her in person.

CHAPTER 1

Jared jerked suddenly from sleep. Cricket song and the sounds of other night animals echoed in the cool mountain air. He listened to their symphony and breathed in the fresh smell of pine from the forest. Nothing out of the ordinary. What had awakened him? Why did chills of fear ripple through his body?

Just a dream, he told himself. Since his release the week before, he had dreamed several times that he was still being held captive by his former boss, Laranda Garrettson, and Big Tommy, the mobster. But Laranda was dead and Big Tommy in prison; neither could hurt him or Cassi again.

Knowing this didn't prevent him from having bad dreams or from feeling angry when he thought of the danger and terror Laranda had put him and Cassi through. During the years he had worked for Laranda as a buyer for her art gallery, she had used him to smuggle goods into the country; and when he and Cassi had finally realized what Laranda was doing, the discovery almost cost them their lives. Only one good thing had come from the experience: he and Cassi had fallen in love.

Yet the problems had not ended with the miracle of love. Laranda had been wounded in their first encounter, but her injuries were largely faked. She soon escaped her hospital prison and joined forces with her nemesis, Big Tommy. She had many plans, among which was to take over Big Tommy's organization. But hate, jealousy, and revenge had also consumed her, and she had come after Jared and Cassi again with a single-minded vengeance. She had attempted to murder Cassi and to corrupt Jared's soul—that, or see him dead. He knew only a miracle had saved their lives.

Jared forced the unwanted thoughts away; it was all behind them now. Cassi slept next to him in the bed, her soft breaths coming deeply and regularly. He watched her for a moment by the light of the moon streaming in through the window, marveling at his good fortune. *Alone in a mountain cabin with the most beautiful woman in the world. What more could a man ask for?*

A two-week stay in this one-room cabin in the French Vosges had been her idea for the honeymoon. This was their second night together, and already it was proving the most exciting and profound time of his life. He loved being married to Cassi.

Thump! The sound burst through the calm of the night, a stark noise that didn't resonate with nature's simple music. Was this what had awakened him?

Jared slipped from the bed and went to investigate, his toes curling at the touch of the cold boards of the cabin floor. He cast a backward glance at Cassi, still lying peacefully on the bed. Even without the long hair he had so adored, he thought she was beautiful. The tight brown ringlets, lightly touched with auburn, splayed over her face as she slept, her lithe body curled in a loose fetal position.

Grabbing his robe from the table where he had left it earlier, Jared headed for the door, wondering who could be outside. The Perrault family, who had provided them with both the cabin and a vehicle for their stay in France, certainly wouldn't intrude upon their privacy so soon, if at all.

The noise came again. It was a dull thud, sounding as though something had been dropped on the porch.

Jared opened the door quickly, his eyes widening in surprise. A blond, tousle-headed boy stared back at him in the bright moonlight, his jaw clenched and his face sullen. On either side of the child sat two large, battered suitcases. A taxicab was heading down the dirt drive, away from the cabin.

"What are you doing he—?" Jared didn't wait to finish his question to the boy, but sprinted after the taxi. "Wait!" he shouted. The small, sharp rocks on the ground dug into the soles of his bare feet. "Wait! Ow! Wait! Ow! Ow! Wait!" But by the time he was halfway down the drive, the taxi had disappeared.

Jared stared after the vanished car for a full minute, shaking his head in frustration. The air was cool and fresh and uncluttered with smog, unlike the city of San Diego where he and Cassi lived. Nearby, he could hear a brook gurgling in its never-ending cycle of life. It was the perfect honeymoon retreat, far from the demands of the art gallery which Cassi had only recently inherited from her boss and mentor, Linden Johansen. But their retreat had now been suddenly invaded.

Jared started back toward the cabin, determined to get some answers out of the child. For the first time he noticed the coolness of the late September evening—or early morning, more likely. He pulled his dark blue robe more tightly about him and wished he had stopped for his slippers.

The child waited for Jared on the moonlit porch, his dark gaze sullen, his stature defiant. That made at least two of them who were less than happy about this situation. Who was this child? And why did he seem so familiar?

"Who are you?" Jared asked sharply. "And why are you here?"

"You're Jared, aren't you?" the boy said.

"Yeees." Jared elongated the word. "You seem to have an advantage over me."

"I'm here to stay. I don't like it any more than you do." The boy clamped his jaw shut and glared at Jared.

Jared glanced at the cabin door, wondering if the commotion might awaken Cassi. "Look, we got off on the wrong foot. I just want to know who you are and who I can call to get this straightened out."

"My dad's in jail. Like you didn't know."

"And your mom?"

The child's scowl deepened. "Dead."

Jared ran a hand through his blond hair. "It's not that I don't like kids. But I'm here on a honeymoon, you know? This is bad timing. We have to find out where you belong. You have to have a guardian, someone who's looking for you. They'll be worried."

"There's nobody. That's why I'm here. And like I said, I don't like it any better than you do. I'd be better off on my own. In fact, I'll be going now." The child reached for the suitcases that together must weigh more than he did, causing the small flight bag on his shoulder to fall to the porch. He picked it up and reached again for the suitcases.

"Wait." A suspicion formed in Jared's mind. There was only one child whose father was in prison, awaiting sentencing, and who was also remotely connected to him and Cassi. That dimple in his chin certainly looked familiar, and the large brown eyes as well.

The door to the cabin swung open. Cassi, dressed in her lace-trimmed red nightgown, yawned delicately as she stretched in the doorway. "What's going—" She stopped as she spied the boy. "Sampson! What are you doing here?"

Jared's suspicion had been correct. "This is Big Tommy's son?" he asked. Instinctively, he scanned the trees for hidden eyes. A mobster's son as a visitor was not a good sign, and Jared had seen enough guns and thugs to last a lifetime. He had hoped those days were behind them.

"Dad sent me. He said now that he was in jail, where *you* put him, you could take care of me."

Cassi hefted one of Sampson's suitcases. "Come on, it's a little cold out here. Let's go inside."

Jared stifled a sigh and picked up the other suitcase. This was not exactly how he had envisioned his honeymoon. He saw Cassi smiling; no doubt she knew exactly what he was thinking, and it amused her. Jared had to admit that if it had happened to anyone else, it would have been laughable.

"Did you just come from the airport?" Cassi asked as Jared lit the lantern. She swept up her sheer red robe from the chair by the bed and wrapped it around her.

"Yeah, in one of my dad's planes."

Jared caught Cassi's gaze again. What was so important that Big Tommy had wasted a huge sum of money on fuel to send Sampson to France? Jared doubted the reason had been to ruin their honeymoon.

"Are you hungry?" Cassi asked. "It's nearly one in the morning here, but it's still daytime in San Diego."

Sampson brightened. "I could eat."

In the cupboard Cassi found some boxes of cereal they had purchased in town yesterday, but Jared put them back. "I think this is a bacon and eggs story." Truth was, Cassi couldn't cook more than burnt toast, and Jared needed to do something to help him keep his emotions under control. Cooking was therapeutic. With one match, he lit the prepared fire in the wood-burning stove where they cooked their meals.

"So tell us what you know, Sampson," Cassi said, sitting at the small round table. "Why would your father track us down all the way in Europe and send you? I don't get it."

"It's for my protection." The careless way Sampson said the words showed Jared how little he thought of the idea.

Cassi passed out the plates Jared handed her. "Why do you need protection?" she probed.

"Because I'm the only heir. Dad just wants to make sure I'm safe till he gets out. When I'm old enough, I'm taking over."

"Taking over what?" Cassi asked. Jared knew that the innocence in her tone was faked. She was testing the boy.

"Over what my dad does. The family business. You know."

"I do. But I wonder . . . do you know what that really is?"

"'Course I do," Sampson said. His voice had resumed its sullen tone, but Jared noticed the boy still answered Cassi's questions, his eyes almost never leaving her face.

"So who do you need protection from?" Cassi's next question was one Jared really wanted answered. He left the bacon in the pan on the stove and approached the table to hear the answer.

"The competition, who else? Like, duh, with my dad *and* me outta the way, our guys'd lose heart and the competition could take over."

Cassi looked up at Jared, alarmed. He motioned for her to continue her questioning. "So your dad thinks you're in danger, huh?" she asked. "But instead of telling the police, he sends you to us. Why?"

Sampson stared steadily at Cassi before answering. "He said he could trust you to take care of me. He said you would do what was right."

Cassi's bewildered glance told Jared that she was as confused at this turn of events as he was.

"So don't you have any relatives who can do the job?" Jared asked. Sampson didn't reply.

"Tell us," Cassi urged. "Someone's taken over running the business while your dad's in jail. Who is it? And why aren't they taking care of you?"

"Dad has a cousin, but he died. I got an uncle, too. He's the one running the business."

"Why didn't your dad send you to him?"

Sampson gave a shrug. "Dad said he had his hands full enough."

Jared thought he heard a ring of truth in Sampson's words. The boy believed what he had been told. But Jared doubted it was the whole truth. "How old are you, anyway?" Jared asked.

"You tell me," the boy said darkly.

Jared hazarded a guess. "Eight?"

"No, older," Cassi said. "About nine, right?"

Sampson snorted. "You guys know nothing. I'm not some baby. I'm eleven now." He shook his head woefully. "And you're supposed to take care of me. What a joke! You guys know nothing about kids."

"You're right." Jared glanced at Cassi. "We'd better call Fred at the FBI and let him know what's going on."

"No!" Sampson protested. "I'll just run away."

"Look, we're not making any decisions right now," Cassi said. "At least not before we eat. Are you hungry, Sampson?"

Sampson sniffed appreciatively. "That bacon smells good."

Jared took that as his cue to return to the stove. In minutes he had eggs, bacon, and juice on the table. Before sitting with the others, he slapped thick slices of French bread in the pan to toast.

Sampson lifted his fork to dig into the meal, but Cassi's touch on his hand stopped him. "We give thanks first." It was Cassi's turn, so she offered the prayer. Jared thought it was just as well. Sampson didn't seem to mind anything coming from her.

"Mmm," Cassi said after taking a bite of scrambled eggs. "I don't know why, but it always tastes better in the mountains."

Sampson gave a grunt, but didn't pause in his hurry to down everything within reach. *Typical boy,* Jared thought.

"Jared's a great cook," Cassi said as Jared served the toast.

Sampson shot a deadpan glance at Jared. "My dad never cooks."

Jared laughed. "Your dad's a multibillionaire and an organized crime boss. I bet there are a lot of things he's never done. Not to mention a lot of things he's done that many people would never do."

Sampson dropped his fork onto his plate, as though unsure whether to take offense or not. Cassi offered him more bacon and the boy scooped up his fork and resumed eating, pausing occasionally to scowl at Jared.

After breakfast, Cassi took their dishes to the sink. Jared joined her, keeping an eye on their unwanted guest. "Do you want me to light the heater?" Jared referred to the small water heater that connected to large bottles of natural gas. The device heated the water almost instantly as it circled through the heater and out into the sink or the tub. An efficient and effective system.

"Thanks," Cassi said. She waited until he lit the heater and adjusted the temperature before she turned on the water and added soap.

"I don't like this," Jared said in a low voice over the sound of the water.

"I know it's inconvenient, but we'll take care of it." She gave him a seductive grin. "You've waited thirty-five years for a honeymoon and I've waited twenty-nine. What's a few more days?"

"It's not just him coming here now, it's him coming here at all. It doesn't make sense that Big Tommy would send him to us when he's got an uncle."

Her hands suspended motion, as though frozen in the warm water. "Unless he can't trust that uncle."

Jared's jaw dropped. Cassi's intelligence was one of the reasons he was so attracted to her. "Why didn't I think of that?" He rubbed a hand over his tired eyes. "But, Cassi, that only makes it even more important for us to report this to Fred."

"You're right, of course. We'll shower and get dressed and go into town. We'd better hurry, though. It's almost five now in San Diego. Isn't that quitting time for Fred?"

"Naw, Fred's always working, from what I've seen," Jared said. "But it's too bad this cabin doesn't have a phone so we could call him from here."

"Hey, we're lucky it has hot water. And I'd rather have hot water than a phone any day."

Jared grinned. "Count your many blessings, huh?" He gathered her into his arms.

"While we're at it, we can count the car, too. The Perraults are one nice family for lending all this to us."

"They are," Jared agreed. "But this just isn't the way I'd planned on spending my honeymoon. Three is definitely a crowd."

She gave him a wry smile. "Well, me neither, but here we are."

Jared kissed her, but a disgusted grunt near the front window cut short the fun. "I guess I'll go get ready," he said. "The sooner we get rid of our chaperone here, the better."

"He's just a kid. I'll bet he's had a hard life."

"With Big Tommy as a father, it's no wonder."

Cassi's dark eyes grew thoughtful. "Quentin loves his son, but I don't know what kind of father he's been. I suspect Sampson's been lonely since his mother died. Quentin told me she died from a tumor three years ago."

For a moment, Jared had forgotten that Big Tommy, a.k.a. Quentin Thomas Holbrooke, had any other name. "I'm wondering if old Big Tommy's motive for sending his son isn't twofold," Jared said. "The guy was half in love with you."

"Yeah, right," Cassi replied, her voice full of irony. "He was in love with me after meeting me only twice. That's why he almost killed both of us."

Once again she had a point, but Jared was too irritated to admit it. He loved Cassi more than he had ever loved anyone, and these two weeks had been their time to be alone. He looked over at Sampson. "Don't worry, I'll be nice. I like children, remember?"

She smiled. "I know you do. And you're good with them. But this little boy doesn't seem to like you too much."

Jared left her at the sink and went to stand with Sampson in front of the window. "It's pretty in the daylight."

Sampson gave a noncommittal grunt.

"Have you ever been in France?"

"Tons of times."

"Oh, yeah? Ever been fishing?"

Bored eyes focused on Jared. "Yeah, all over. My dad has more yachts than he has cars."

"Impressive." Jared had seen the huge garage on the Holbrooke estate. It could have easily held twenty automobiles.

"Well, have you been hiking?" he asked the boy next.

"In just about every country in the world. I like the Amazon jungle the best."

Maybe it was time to try a different approach. "Ever been to church?"

"Sure. I go to mass sometimes."

"Oh." Then Jared had an idea. "Ever been tracting?"

"What's that?"

Jared laughed. "Maybe I'll show you sometime. But right now I'm going to grab some clothes. We need to go into town."

The boy's eyes followed Jared as he went to the small bathroom. He hoped he'd made the boy curious enough to take him seriously. "Eleven going on forty," Jared muttered. "What's this world coming to?"

* * * * *

Supervisory Special Agent Fred Schulte hadn't expected the press would care much about Big Tommy's capture and pending sentencing. He was right. There had been a few flashy articles in the paper when the initial information was released, and then nothing more as either Big Tommy's friends bribed them into silence or other more pressing issues hit the headlines. Either way, it was all the same to Fred. In light of the evidence against him, Big Tommy, alias Quentin Thomas Holbrooke, had agreed to discuss a plea bargain to kindly save taxpayers the expense of a lengthy trial. Hah! Fred knew that more than likely Holbrooke was simply trying to save himself from extra time in prison. An unbought jury would have sent the mobster away for life. Now, if they were lucky, he might serve ten years. At least for the time being, he was out of Fred's hair.

For this reason, Fred wondered why Brooke Erickson of the San Diego Union-Tribune wanted to meet with him to discuss Big Tommy's case. She arrived promptly at five o'clock on Tuesday afternoon, the time Fred would have left for his apartment if he had ever gone home on time. He didn't know what he had imagined from her crisp, no-nonsense voice on the phone, but she wasn't what he expected. Brooke Erickson was beautiful. She had short-cropped golden blonde hair, striking pale blue eyes, and a figure that made men look twice. Or even stare. But like her voice on the phone, her manner was all business.

"How long do you think he'll be sentenced for?" she asked after hearing his brief, over-rehearsed statement on the events leading up to Big Tommy's capture.

Fred sighed, thinking of the stack of unsolved cases in his files that he could be working on. "It's hard to say. He deserves three or four life sentences with all the dirt we have on him—forgery, fraud, murder, and kidnaping, to name a few. But he's got money and expensive lawyers who don't care who they hurt as long as they get paid. I hear they're working out a plea bargain. Just what it is we'll find out at the sentencing—whenever that finally rolls around."

"I know. That's partly why I'm here. I'm amazed that they didn't stall the idea of a plea longer. I mean, I've seen these types of characters living months in freedom while their lawyers cause all sorts of delays."

"Well, part of that was because Big Tommy, or Quentin Thomas Holbrooke, was denied bail. Our guys proved that he'd skip town. He could work his brand of sordid magic just as well from some European country."

"Still, I'm surprised his lawyers didn't come up with something to get him freed."

Fred tensed and felt the ache from the week-old bullet wound in his upper right arm, suffered at the last showdown with Laranda Garrettson and Quentin Holbrooke. Or was the ache coming from his heart? "Big Tommy was responsible for the death of a very good friend of mine and others here at the FBI."

"An agent?"

"No. A guy who worked with us sometimes. Linden Johansen. We all pushed to get the ball rolling on Big Tommy. And go figure, this time it worked. Or started to, until this plea bargain stuff came up. I doubt Big Tommy will get half of what he deserves."

"I guess we'll have to wait and see," Brooke said.

"Well, you'll still see a lot of stalling, I'll bet," Fred continued. "Big Tommy's an expert at deals. No, this thing is far from over. We got him, and he'll have to serve some time, but before long he'll be my problem again."

"Yes, this isn't the first time you've been after this group," she said. "But it seems you've had a lot of success working with people who aren't FBI agents. That's amazing. I guess what really fascinates me is that the two people who were primarily responsible for putting Big Tommy in jail are Mormons."

"Oh, and why does that interest you?" But he knew before she answered. "You must be a Mormon-hater, huh?" *What these newspaper reporters will do for a story,* Fred thought. It rankled him that she would try to inflict damage on the reputation of those he considered his friends, albeit not very close friends. Jared and Cassi were two of the most upstanding people he had ever met. And their likewise Mormon friend, Renae Benson, the perfect image of womanhood, was still in Fred's thoughts far more that he cared to admit.

"No, actually, I am one." Brooke blushed, but didn't look embarrassed. For the first time her voice wasn't crisp and precise. "A Mormon, that is. Definitely not a Mormon-hater. And there are so many negative things about us in the papers . . . I guess I try when I can to give some of the good."

Fred felt himself warming to her. He was suddenly glad that last month he had quit smoking after a fifteen-year addiction. It was a dirty, smelly habit anyway. One that wouldn't impress this fine lady. "So how can I help you?" he asked.

"I want to know a little about Jared Landine and Cassi Mason."

"Both Landine now. They're married."

"Oh, I didn't realize that. And what about their friend who was almost killed? Is it true the doctors say his undergarment saved him?"

"Yes, it's true. The cloth stuck in the wound and helped stem the bleeding."

Brooke glanced at the tape recorder on the desk to be sure it was recording. "Interesting." Then she asked a few more personal questions about Jared and Cassi.

"Look," he said, "I'd feel more comfortable if you got your answers from them. They're on their honeymoon right now, but when they get back, I'll give them your card."

"Okay, thank you." But she didn't leave. "Do you think Big Tommy's in any danger?"

"I thought you were interested in the Mormons."

"Not just. After all, without Big Tommy, there wouldn't be a story." She gave him a slight smile. "I couldn't just write about Mormons, you know. I wouldn't last long on the paper."

"I guess not." Fred certainly admired her persistence. "Well, the answer is that of course he's in danger. He's a mobster. There's no telling how many people he's responsible for killing over the years, or how many fortunes he's stolen. And then there's the question of the plea bargaining—who's he planning to give up? It has to be somebody big. Yep, in all, I'd say there has to be a ton of people out there who'd be happy to see Big Tommy dead."

"So you think he'll be killed."

"No, I didn't say that." He leaned back in his chair and studied her, enjoying the puzzlement on her face. It wasn't often that he was alone with such an attractive woman. Her blonde hair reminded him vaguely of Renae Benson and the potent feeling she had evoked in him. Renae, of course, hadn't shared his feelings. She had been loyal to her husband, Trent, and Fred had worked hard to see that Trent was returned to her in one piece. The last time he had seen Renae was when he had put her and her baby on the plane to Portugal to be with her wounded husband. Later, after returning to California, she had sent him a polite thank-you note and a picture of her, her husband, and their five children. Fred was glad she appeared happy.

"Then what are you saying?"

Fred met the intense pale eyes and realized that Brooke didn't look anything like Renae. Her hair was shorter, blonder, and more artfully styled. And her figure—well, she looked like she had never given birth to one child, much less five. Was she even married? Involuntarily, Fred's gaze dropped to her left hand, where a simple gold band circled the ring finger. He felt a keen sense of disappointment. To cover the unexpected feeling, he pretended to smooth his moustache in deep thought.

"I'm saying, Ms. Erickson, that someone might try to kill him, but might not succeed. There will be just as many people trying to earn money by protecting him. And then there are the guards, of course, who try to watch both sides and keep order."

"I see. So it's like a game."

"Right." He rubbed gently at his sore arm. "A deadly game. And anyone could win."

"Or lose."

"Yeah," he agreed, liking her even more. "Or lose."

"Well, what about the rumor of a billion dollars in paintings and other art objects that Laranda Garrettson supposedly has stashed in another location apart from those found in Portugal?"

"I've heard the rumors, but I haven't been able to substantiate them. Holbrooke, of course, would be the one to verify any of this, but if they do exist, he probably will go after them himself once he's out. After all, any money that was used in acquiring the paintings had to have come from him."

"None of them could be stolen?"

"Well, yes. But Holbrooke would have still paid someone to steal them. Garrettson had a lot of resources, but not *that* many."

Brooke's next question was lost in the buzzing of Fred's intercom. "Excuse me," he said. "It must be important. I asked the secretary not to disturb us." He pressed the black button. "What is it, Cherral? Jared Landine? You've got to be kidding. No, put him through. Immediately. Thank you."

Brooke's eyes grew more interested, but Fred scarcely paid attention. Why would Jared be calling him? Certainly even Mormons had better things to be doing on a honeymoon than calling an FBI special agent. It could mean only one thing: trouble.

CHAPTER 2

In minutes Cassi and Jared were in their borrowed car, an older but well-kept Ford, and headed for the nearest town of Griesheim, a small town of fifteen hundred people. They passed deep forests and tall peaks of pink sandstone, barely discernable in the light of the moon and stars. They drove by vineyards and quaint farms that had been beautiful the day before, but now seemed to court danger by their very isolation.

The community of Griesheim was small by any standards, but filled with the fairy-tale image of old Europe. Cassi loved the half-timbered houses, the bunches of colorful flowers, the gabled roofs and chimneys, and the precisely set cobblestones. Yesterday, when they had come in for food and supplies, she had found the people friendly and helpful. She spoke little French, and Jared spoke even less, but they had learned quickly that smiles and cash spoke a universal language.

Everything was shut and quiet when they arrived, giving her an eerie sense of the place that she hadn't noticed by day. They parked near a pay phone on one of the deserted streets. Jared placed the call to the San Diego FBI office while Cassi hovered nearby with Sampson. The boy looked edgy, as though he wanted to flee. He seemed to have an unhealthy dislike of the FBI—a legacy from his father, no doubt. Cassi placed a hand on his shoulder. She was glad of the seclusion night offered from the curious gazes of people in this small French village.

"Yes, I need to talk to Special Agent Fred Schulte, please. It's urgent. I need to talk to him now if he hasn't left for the day. I don't care if he's in a meeting. Tell him it's Jared Landine. He'll talk to me."

As they waited, Cassi scanned the dark street for signs of trouble. To her it was no longer the sleepy Parisian town that she would remember with tenderness, but a place where danger could be lurking around every corner. Jared met her eyes and smiled faintly. His eyes flicked to Sampson. She could tell by the movement that he was also worried the boy might flee.

A white sedan drove by, all too noticeable in the stillness. Under her hand she felt Sampson's muscles tense. Before she could say anything, he ducked away from her touch and bolted. Jared shoved the phone into her hand and flew down the street after Sampson, his longer strides closing the gap.

"Hello, Jared," a voice said on the phone. "I'm in a meeting right now, but the secretary said it was urgent."

Cassi put the phone to her ear. "Fred, thank heaven!"

"Cassi? What's happened?"

By the dim rays of the single streetlight, Cassi saw Sampson turn down a side street. Jared was only an arm's length away. She knew he would catch the boy soon; there wasn't any place to hide in this small town, even in the dark.

"Big Tommy is what happened!" she told Fred. "We woke up in the middle of the night and found his son, Sampson, on our porch—with suitcases! Apparently, dear old Dad wants us to baby-sit while he's in prison. Sampson says that's because he's in some kind of danger. Needless to say, Jared and I are more than a little worried. So we called you."

"Where is Jared?"

"Chasing Sampson. He ran off a minute ago. Jared's probably caught him by now."

"Not exactly the honeymoon you envisioned."

"You can say that again. What should we do? Any minute now, I'm afraid someone will come after Sampson. Do you think there's any truth to his story?"

"I don't know, Cassi. Unfortunately, there's nothing I can do—yet. I guess we could make a case for abandonment, but you'll have to come back to the U.S.A. to do it. Still, I'll bet Big Tommy's planned for that option. Did Sampson have any papers on him?"

"I don't know. There hasn't really been time to ask. And what do you mean, you can't do anything about this?"

"Well, the FBI has jurisdiction when crimes are committed against U.S. citizens in foreign countries—in conjunction with the local authorities, of course. Like in a terrorist attack against a U.S. citizen or something. But so far in this situation, no serious crime has been committed. The way I see it, you have three choices: turn the boy over to the French authorities, take him to the embassy, or come back here and turn him over to social services, and so forth. But if someone started shooting at the child—"

"Then it would be your business? Come on, this is Quentin's son we're talking about. If he weren't in danger, why would Quentin entrust him to us?"

"Yeah, I already thought of that, and that's why I'm going to look into it myself. But we can't ask the French government to get involved. That's what it will mean if we call in our guys over there."

Cassi sighed in frustration. She knew Fred was trying to do his best, but it wasn't good enough. "So what if they come after us?"

"Look, there's a good chance that if someone is after Sampson, they won't know where you are. Presumably that's why he's with you, right? For protection. I'll nose around over here and see what's going on. I'll even go over to the federal prison and talk with Holbrooke. Meanwhile, you guys just sit tight. Do you have a number where I can reach you?"

"There's no phone at the cabin. We'll have to—" Cassi broke off. She could see Sampson and Jared coming back up the cobblestone sidewalk. Jared wasn't dragging Sampson along as she had expected, but both were running, side by side. Jared was yelling something at her. What, she couldn't tell.

Several doors down, a light came on and an old French lady came out of the door of her store where she sold fruit during the day. She wore a dingy white shawl, a long, shapeless nightdress, and tattered brown slippers. Staring at the running pair, she smiled a curious, toothless smile.

"Car!" Jared's voice came to Cassi urgently. "Hurry, get in the car!"

Then Cassi saw the white sedan at the end of the street, gradually gaining on Jared and Sampson. Cassi dropped the phone and crossed the few feet to the car, fumbling for the keys in her purse. Jared and Sampson opened the doors and threw themselves inside as Cassi gunned the engine, tires squealing in protest against the cobblestones in the road.

"They shot at us!" Sampson screamed from his place in the back-seat. "With silencers!" As if to prove his words, a gunshot shattered their back window. Cassi stomped harder on the gas pedal. In her mind, she remembered the last time she had made a run from thugs. She had been scared then, as she was now, but this time her mind was strangely clear. She had gotten away before . . . could she do it again?

* * * * *

"Cassi! Cassi! What's going on?" There was no answer. Fred stared open-mouthed at the receiver in his hand. The connection hadn't been broken, but now he could hear nothing from the other side. Seconds earlier, he had heard a car and shouting.

He buzzed Cherral. "Look, could you listen in on this line? Let me know if anyone comes back on." Fred waited for Cherral to pick up the other end before replacing the receiver.

Brooke's pale eyes once more became intense. "What happened?" she asked.

Because Fred was lonely and he liked the reporter, he switched off her tape recorder and answered. "Holbrooke had his son dropped off in France at a cabin where Jared and Cassi are staying. Apparently he wants them to look after his son while he's in prison. The boy says he's in some sort of danger."

"That makes sense."

"What?" Fred asked politely, but more than a little annoyed. What did this reporter know of such things? Cassi and Jared were obviously in trouble; he should be helping them, not wasting time with her.

"Well, one of the reasons I've been asking if you think Big Tommy is in danger is because right after his arrest, I learned that his cousin had a suspicious heart attack."

"Are you saying he was killed?"

"Well, my friend at the coroner's office said the evidence was inconclusive, but he'd bet the guy was murdered. But that's not all. Another cousin of Holbrooke's, a second cousin I guess, was killed two days ago in a car accident. And that man's only adult son is now missing."

"So you think someone killed them." Fred took another look at Brooke. She had obviously done her homework. "So who's next on the list?"

"There's a brother-in-law, TC Brohaugh. He's Big Tommy's wife's brother. And the boy, Sampson. That's as far as I got." She smiled. "I was hoping you could help me from there."

Fred sat forward, making a rapid decision. "Okay, we'll work together. But none of this goes public until I say so."

"Deal," Brooke replied. "As long as I get the exclusive."

"That can be arranged. But I want no playing hero here. You watch from a safe distance."

"I'll just be an observer," she said smoothly. Her eyes danced, betraying her excitement.

Fred picked up the phone. "Still nothing, Cherral? Okay, go ahead and hang up. They'll call again when they can." *If they can,* he added silently. "Meanwhile, get me our Legat's office in Paris. This has just become an FBI matter."

* * * * *

The car shot up the narrow mountain road, the trees a black blur on either side. The headlights of the Ford carved out a path in the dark. "Are they still behind us?" Cassi asked.

"Yes." Jared sat in the front seat beside her, but sideways to keep an eye on their pursuers. "But they aren't gaining. You're doing fine."

Cassi didn't reply. She was too busy searching for the small roads she knew were coming up soon, the ones leading to neighboring cabins.

"We can't go back to the cabin!" Sampson shouted. He flipped the locks on the back doors, as though that would save him. "They'll know where it is. They must have followed us! I saw them at the airport. I swear it!"

Cassi's head reverberated with his statements. It seemed that in his excited state, Sampson couldn't say anything without shouting.

"We're not going back to the cabin," Cassi said grimly. She glanced at Jared. "There's a road just after the bend, isn't there?"

"Yes, two or three, I think. And a few more after the next bend."

"Good."

"What are you thinking?" Jared asked, darting a look behind them.

"We go fast enough to get out of their sight and then hide up one of the dirt roads until they pass. Before they realize we're not ahead, we'll be on our way back down to the freeway toward Paris."

Jared nodded. "Good idea. We don't know where this road ends."

"Hopefully, neither do they."

Their eyes met briefly. "I'll tell you when they're out of sight," Jared said. "It'll be better if we do it right after the next bend. That way they might think we're ahead around one of the other bends. It'll take them longer to realize their mistake. Don't forget to turn out the headlights."

Cassi's heart thumped painfully against her chest. She wished she could let Jared drive, but she had no choice. To stop now would be suicide.

She whipped into the curve faster than she should have, barely keeping the wheels on the pavement. The road was fairly new, but along the edges there was a row of cobblestones where the past merged with the future. The idea had fascinated her during their first days in France, but now it held no pleasure. It might be the last road they ever saw.

"Now!" Jared said. "They're out of sight."

Cassi jerked the wheel to the left into the very first gravel road. She couldn't see a cabin, but knew there was probably one farther up in the trees. If only there was enough time to get out of sight. She flipped off the headlights.

"Did they go by?" Sampson asked.

"I thought I saw their lights," Jared said.

Cassi hadn't seen them. She had been too busy driving.

"They should have passed by now." Jared peered into the night. "Come on, let's turn around."

Cassi put the car in park. "Okay, but it's your turn to drive. I'm shaking too much."

Jared took over the wheel and nosed the car up to the paved road. There were no cars in sight, only the dark road, lit by a benevolent moon and a flurry of bright stars. He drove quickly back down the mountain road the way they had come. They didn't go back to Griesheim, but headed directly to the road that would eventually lead them to the freeway.

Cassi felt Jared's gaze and looked over at him. She had finally stopped shaking, and her heartbeat was almost normal. "Where did you learn to drive like that?" he asked with a grin. "I thought my heart would jump right out of my chest."

"Oh, around," she said, faking nonchalance. "You know, the last time I was chased by mobsters on my way to Utah."

Jared's grin vanished. "I'm sorry, Cassi. It seems that even beyond the grave, Laranda haunts us."

Laranda was Jared's former boss, and it was she who had first involved them with smuggling, forgery, and organized crime. She had been killed in their last run-in with Big Tommy, but apparently her legacy lived on.

Cassi gripped Jared's knee. "We'll get through this," she said. "We will. But first we need a plan. I have my purse with my credit cards, the money we exchanged, and our passports. With my inheritance from Linden, we aren't going broke any time soon. But where will we go?"

Jared didn't take his eyes from the road. "My first instinct says that we should definitely leave France."

"I agree."

"But all my stuff is back at that cabin," Sampson protested.

"We'll send someone for it later," Cassi said. "Until then, we buy what we need."

"I'll buy it." Sampson pulled out his wallet. "See? I got a Visa card. It can get us anywhere. Dad gave it to me. Said for you guys to buy whatever you want."

Cassi exchanged doubtful looks with Jared. Sure Holbrooke would provide for his child, but with a credit card?

"Really," Sampson said. "I'm not lying. And I've four Swiss bank accounts, too—with passwords." He shoved four more cards under Cassi's nose. "I have more money than that old dead guy who left you his gallery. It's part of *my* inheritance."

"How did you know about Linden's gallery?"

"Dad told me."

"Why would he give you so much money?"

Sampson's face grew sad. "He said it was just in case. No one else knows about it." He silently put the cards back in his wallet and shoved it in his pocket.

Cassi met Jared's eyes again. Like her, he didn't seem to know what to make of Sampson's revelations.

"Look, I don't need you two," Sampson said crossly. "I have enough money to make it on my own."

Cassi reached across the seat and touched his arm. "Everything's going to be all right, Sampson, but let's stay together, huh? Who knows? It could be fun."

"You want me to stay?" His face was expressionless, but his eyes begged for confirmation.

Cassi saw Jared nodding, urging her to comfort the boy. "Yes, Sampson," she said. "I do want you to stay. We both do. We need to find out what's going on before we know where you really belong. Until then, we'll hang out, okay? And you don't have to worry about using that credit card. I have enough to take care of all of us."

"But Dad sent it for you. It's payment."

Payment for baby-sitting. Cassi sighed. "Look, Sampson, I don't know what your father has planned, but I do know that you are our responsibility for the time being. Will you promise to stay with us? It has to be on your honor. I know your dad has taught you about your word. Don't give it to me if you don't mean it."

"Okay, I'll stay," Sampson said.

"That reminds me of a story about a servant named Zoram," Jared said. He briefly told Sampson the story of Nephi going to Jerusalem to get the brass plates, and how Zoram had ended up going with them to the Promised Land.

"So what happened?" Sampson asked.

"Well, Zoram kept his word, of course. He married and had a happy life."

"Do you keep your word?" Sampson asked.

"Of course."

"So do I." He paused, thinking. "I wonder where I could buy a sword like that guy who cut off the bad guy's head. That was cool."

Cassi laughed, and Jared made a face at her. "It'll have to wait," she said. "Let's find a place to get some gas and food."

"Are we going to stay at a hotel?" asked Sampson.

"That's what I was thinking," Cassi said. "But I've just had a better idea of where we can go."

"Where?" Jared and Sampson asked together.

"To England. We can drive into Paris and take a train to the English Channel. We'll cross by boat. My guess is that whoever is after us will check the airports first. By the time they realize we aren't going that way, we'll already be in England."

"Yeah," Jared said. "We were going to visit your friend, Grant Truebekon, on the way home anyway. So what if we show up in England a little early?"

"I don't think Grant will mind. He'll give us a place to stay until we find out what's going on. Maybe Fred will find some answers."

"He's probably worried."

Cassi gave a mirthless laugh. "Well, at least with people after us, it does seem to be a police matter, an FBI matter too, since we're out of the United States."

"You're not giving me to the FBI, are you?" Sampson asked.

Cassi glanced at Jared, this time willing him to speak.

"No, Sampson," he said. "We're not handing you over to the FBI."

"Promise?"

Jared's face was solemn. "I promise, Sampson. You have my word. Until we hear from your father, we're in this together—even if we *all* have to hang out with the FBI for a while."

Something in the boy relaxed, although not completely. Cassi saw a very lonely, lost child behind his sullen exterior and wished she could do something more for him. Maybe in time he would trust them.

And then what? her conscience asked. Sampson was destined to be a mobster. Could anything save his soul before it was too late? Looking at the too-knowing eyes in his young face, she had to believe it was possible. Maybe Sampson's coming to them wasn't only Quentin Holbrooke's latest whim. Maybe it was more than that. Maybe his mother was looking out for him. Or maybe the Lord had sent Sampson to them for a reason. Cassi vowed to do the best she could with the time she had with the boy.

"Why did you run off in the first place?" she asked. "You said something about recognizing the car."

"I remembered the driver's face from the airport. I saw him watching, and I knew he was coming after me."

"Well, he didn't succeed," Jared said. "He's probably lost in the mountains by now." Despite the pressure, they all laughed.

Cassi and Jared drove for the next seven hours, taking turns at the wheel, stopping only for gas and food. At the first place, they bought a map and learned that Sampson was a great navigator. In the glove compartment, Cassi found two worn Books of Mormon—one in English and one in French. The find wasn't very surprising, considering the Perrault family were members and Zack Fields, an American, had married into the family. They let Sampson read for himself the story of Nephi and Zoram. The boy asked endless questions and showed a surprisingly good understanding of the Biblical vocabulary.

"I'm a good reader," Sampson said. "But I like science fiction and fantasy the best." He held up the Book of Mormon. "This is kind of interesting, though."

Cassi and Jared were relieved when daylight came, the sun seeming to chase their fears away. By ten o'clock they had reached Paris, and both Jared and Cassi were exhausted. Even Sampson had begun to doze in the backseat. They couldn't find the train station and stopped to ask for directions at a gas station. Thus far in their journey they had always found someone who had spoken English reasonably well, but to their frustration, this attendant spoke only French. "Too bad we left the phrase book back at the cabin," Jared said. "Hey, maybe he sells one here." He looked around, but to no avail.

"Daughterrrr speak Engleesh. Not herrrre," the silver-haired man said for the third time. Apparently, it was the only English he knew.

Sampson approached the man and spoke to him in French. The man smiled and pointed down the street, saying something Cassi couldn't begin to fathom.

"Merci beaucoup," Sampson said. He turned to Cassi and Jared. "He says if we turn left up there and go down two streets and then turn right, we'll find it."

They nodded at the man in thanks and climbed back in the car, with Cassi at the wheel. "You know French?" Jared asked Sampson as Cassi concentrated on finding the station.

"Yeah, so what? I speak Spanish, too."

"Isn't that unusual for a boy your age?"

"I don't know. But I had a nanny who spoke Spanish when I was little, and now we almost always have at least one Spanish or Mexican maid. I like to practice with them. And my mom taught me French. We used to spend about four or five months each year here. She was half French, you know. In fact, my parents met on the Riviera. Dad bought a place here since she loved it so much, but we haven't been there since . . . well, for three years. When we come now, we stay at a hotel. I wish we'd just go to the house. It's better than staying at a hotel for three weeks."

"You miss it," Cassi said softly. There was a lot they had yet to learn about this child.

Sampson clamped his mouth shut and picked up the Book of Mormon, pretending to read. Jared opened his mouth to voice another question, but Cassi spoke first. "There's the station."

"It's big," Jared commented.

Sampson shut the book and stared out the window. Once again, his face was sullen and closed.

Cassi glanced at him. "You think you can get us some tickets?" she asked. "In case they don't speak English?"

"Sure," Sampson said, his features relaxing. "Piece of cake."

Then Cassi caught sight of a white sedan in the rearview mirror. When she turned her head to take a better look, it was nowhere to be seen. Was it the same one that had been following them earlier?

CHAPTER
3

Fred looked up as Justin Rotua, one of the special agents under his command, came into the office. Justin was his favorite of all of the special agents under him, and he was good at what he did. The men worked well together and had spent many nights at the office—like tonight. Fred knew their days together were numbered. Justin was a rising star; it was only a matter of time until he was promoted.

Before Fred could form a question, Justin pulled a small notepad from his front pocket and launched into the information Fred had asked him to find. "The local authorities arrived at the cabin first. They found a couple of suspicious characters inside, but they got away into the woods. Probably had their escape planned. The police let our boys search the cabin, but the only thing of interest they found were some documents in one of the boy's suitcases. One was a legal document giving Jared and Cassi Landine temporary custody of Sampson Quentin Holbrooke." Justin folded his tall, lean frame into one of the chairs in front of Fred's desk, the same chair Brooke Erickson had sat in four hours earlier.

"And get this: in exchange for the baby-sitting, the Landines are to receive a half-million-dollar allowance per year until the boy reaches eighteen or until Big Tommy is released, whichever comes first. Collectable on a Visa credit card—"

"Is the number included?" Fred interrupted. If Jared and Cassi used the card, they might be able to be traced—if it became necessary.

"No. And I suspect the funds won't be coming from the United States."

"Did they find any credit cards in the cabin?"

Justin ran a hand through the extremely short brown hair on his head. "No. Either those two thugs took it, or the boy still has it. Or maybe Cassi or Jared."

"Could be. Well, tell our boys to hold on to those papers. We might need them."

A slight smile creased Justin's face. "I did."

Fred laughed. "Of course you did."

A knock at the door interrupted their conversation. "Come in," Fred said.

A man Fred vaguely recognized from another department entered. "Sorry to bother you," he said, "but there's a guy downstairs demanding to see you. We told him the office was closed, but he seems to know you're here. I'm not sure what you want me to do. He's got two guys with him. They look like bodyguards. He's a mobster type if I ever saw one."

Fred exchanged glances with Justin. Given the latest developments, this was obviously no coincidence. Justin stood, stretching slightly as though in need of sleep. "I'll see this man up," he said. "But his friends will have to wait outside."

Fred smiled; it was exactly what he would have done.

Justin returned minutes later with a man dressed in a suit Fred knew cost more than an FBI agent earned in a month. He was of average height and build, with dark-brown eyes, dark-blond hair, and a receding hairline. At first there was nothing to mark him as different—except the clothes—until Fred recognized the hard, expressionless face and eyes that he had seen on so many men before. There was no doubt in his mind that this man was connected to organized crime.

"TC Brohaugh, I presume," Fred said, standing to meet his guest. He had learned early that it was always wise to be courteous to these kinds of people. It appealed to their civilized sides—or at least the part they considered civilized. To Fred, they were little better than hunters who preyed upon the weak. He despised them.

"And you are Fred Schulte," Brohaugh said with a nod in greeting. "I would have preferred to speak to you under other circumstances, but it seems you don't intend to return to your home tonight."

"No, there is pressing business here," Fred said, glad now that he had stayed. A meeting alone in his apartment with Brohaugh and his two goons was not high on Fred's list of preferred activities.

"That's why I've come. I believe you have news of my nephew."

"Some," Fred replied warily. He glanced at Justin, who studied the man in silence. Later they would exchange impressions. "But some of it may be classified. I will try my best to help you, however."

"I thank you," Brohaugh said. "You will see I am not unreasonable."

"What would you like to know?" Fred sat and motioned toward a chair for his guest, but Brohaugh gave a slight shake of his head.

"I want to know if the boy is safe, and when he can be returned to me."

"Well, I can't answer either of those questions, as much as I would like to," Fred said. "I did have contact with the couple and the child, but it was broken, and currently I know nothing of their whereabouts."

Brohaugh stared at Fred for a full minute before speaking. "You're talking about the Landine couple. So they do have the boy. Oh, you don't have to answer, I already know. My brother-in-law thought turning him over to the Landines was best for Sampson, given the untimely demise of his two cousins. But I would like the boy with me so that I can protect him."

"So you think someone is killing off your relatives." Fred smoothed his moustache in thought.

Brohaugh gave a short, dry laugh. "Not my relatives, Quentin's. I'm a brother-in-law, not blood-related."

Fred leaned back in his chair and asked very slowly, "And who is running the business while Big Tommy's in jail?"

"I really don't know or care." Spreading his hands out before him, Brohaugh shrugged. "It is none of my concern. My only concern is my sister's child. I need to know where he is."

"Once again, I can't help you," Fred said. "To tell you the truth, I don't even know if this is an FBI matter. No reported crimes have been committed against any of the U.S. citizens involved. The cabin where they were staying was searched, that much we do know, but that could have been a one-time occurrence by common thieves or directed toward the French family that owns the cabin. Until we hear from the Landines, or find other evidence, we can't assume anything. I also know that the Landines aren't exactly anxious to keep the boy. In fact, they are rather disturbed by the whole situation. They're on their honeymoon, you know."

"I'll bet. But half a million would sweeten the deal," Brohaugh said dryly. "Maybe even convince them to overcome their disturbed state." He leaned forward, shifting his weight to the balls of his feet. "If you hear from them again, tell them this: I will give them two million dollars myself if they will return the boy safely to my custody."

"Two million, huh?" Fred didn't try to hide his surprise. Brohaugh wasn't joking around.

Justin cleared his throat, and the other two looked at him. "Tell me, Mr. Brohaugh," he questioned, "with such resources, can't you find the boy yourself?"

"I will find the boy, make no mistake," Brohaugh said. "I am here simply to try to facilitate things. In fact, I have operatives in France even now who hopefully await me with better news than you have." He approached the desk and laid down a card. As he did, a thick gold ring on his finger caught the light. "Please contact me if there are any new developments. The bottom line is that I care about Sampson. I want to protect him. And I can do that better than anyone else." Without another word he left, and Justin hurried to escort him out of the building.

When Justin returned and settled again in his chair, Fred spoke. "Interesting fellow, Brohaugh."

"He wants that boy badly."

"Yeah, but why?"

Justin wrote something on his ever-present notepad. "He seemed sincere when he said he loved Sampson."

"Yes, but he lied when he said he didn't know who was in control of Big Tommy's organization. He's in it big time, if not the top man. I'm sure of it."

Justin drew one long leg up and set the edge of his foot on Fred's desk. It was his ultimate thinking pose. "Brohaugh already has men in France looking for the boy," he said. "For all we know, they were the ones at the cabin. We can't overlook the fact that if Sampson and Holbrooke are out of the way, this guy stands to inherit big."

"But Holbrooke isn't dead."

"Not yet."

Fred met Justin's steady gaze. "Good point, Justin. And one has to wonder why Holbrooke didn't leave his son with his own brother-in-law. I think early tomorrow morning we had better take a little trip to visit Quentin Holbrooke. Maybe he can give us a clue as to why he trusts this TC Brohaugh enough to run his company, but not to watch over his son."

* * * * *

TC Brohaugh left the FBI offices fuming inside the calm outer shell he had shown the special agents. They knew more than they were telling, he was sure of it. And he also knew by studying their reactions that they didn't believe him.

Well, no matter; he *was* lying, after all.

He approached the limo where his men waited. Something moved in the shadows, and TC instinctively dived toward the car. That move saved his life. He felt a bullet rip into the back of his left arm, tearing apart skin and muscle, pummeling deep into the bone. Pain filled his senses.

In an instant, his men returned the near-silent fire, dull thuds in the dark night. One pulled him inside the limo and hit the gas.

"You okay, boss?" Baker asked.

"Yeah," TC grunted. "I'm going need to see the doc, though." He held his handkerchief over the wound.

"Right away." Baker spoke into his cell phone, directing the doctor to meet them at the house. TC knew he wouldn't grumble—not at the rate they paid him to keep his mouth shut.

"Any idea who they were?" TC asked.

"Didn't see 'em. But it's got to be Donelli." Baker motioned for one of the other bodyguards to hand TC a glass of wine to dull the pain. TC gulped it down and indicated that he wanted more.

"So the Donellis are involved," he mused aloud, his anger almost making him forget his pain.

"They'll want Sampson, too."

"But I'll get the kid first." Silently TC cursed Quentin for complicating matters. Why couldn't he have left Sampson in town? At least now that the cousins were out of the way and TC was in charge, things would go more smoothly.

"Get the jet ready for tomorrow night," he said through gritted teeth. "After we see the doctor and tie up a few loose ends, we're going to France to clean up that little mess. It seems our men there haven't been doing their duty."

TC sat back in the seat, satisfied that he had things well under control. It was good to be in charge.

* * * * *

Nicolas Donelli glared at his nephew, Giorgio, and two other men. "Outside the FBI offices! Don't you think that was a risk? I'm as upset as you are at that idiot Brohaugh. Who would have guessed that he'd end up in charge? But we have to move more carefully now. Stay away from the FBI. We've got enough trouble as it is. Don't worry; we'll take care of Brohaugh in time. And Holbrooke's going to regret the day he decided to take over my territory." He laughed and rubbed his hands together, realizing that he sounded obsessed. And he was. With Big Tommy in jail, Nicolas intended to get everything back that was his own. He would stop at nothing. Revenge was sweet.

"Heard anything from France?" he asked into the awkward silence.

"Yeah. They—"

"Wait. Have a seat and taste this wine. It came from France, you know." As he poured the liquid into a glass, the heavy gold ring on his finger glinted. "Before we begin, I want to tell you about this idea I've been working on. An idea as delicious as this wine. I think you, my dear nephew, will approve. I'm even going to let you be the one to carry it out."

* * * * *

Dennis Faron was hauled out of his house through the back door, taken quietly from bed where he had lain next to his sleeping wife. He struggled soundlessly, to no avail. *A burglar,* he thought, expecting they would kill him. Instead, they took him in a car to a dark part of the local playground. Bright light shone into his eyes, making his captors murky shadows in the night.

"Who are you? What do you want?" Dennis asked desperately. He shivered, though the September night air wasn't cold. Wracking his memory, he still could think of nothing he had done that would have brought this terrible occurrence upon him.

There had been many prisoners over the years at the federal prison where he worked. As a guard, Dennis had always treated them with respect—unlike many of the others who laughed and jeered or even tortured their prisoners when they thought no one was looking. So what had he done to deserve this? He thought of his beautiful wife, Gloria, and their two children. Would he ever see them again? Tears gathered in his eyes, and he couldn't blink them away.

"Do you know Big Tommy?" a hard voice asked.

"Who?" Dennis was genuinely confused.

"Quentin Thomas Holbrooke," another voice said. Or maybe it was the same voice. Dennis couldn't be sure. "The mob boss awaiting sentencing."

"I know him," Dennis said, collecting his wits as best he could.

"We have something we want you to pass on to him."

"What?" Dennis' voice came out as a squeak.

"Look here, either you do it, or we'll get someone else. It's all the same to us. It's just a letter, nothing more." A gloved hand entered the light and waved an envelope for emphasis.

"Plans for escape?"

"No, just a personal letter. No escape, nothing for you to concern yourself over. You deliver it and we'll pay you well. One million dollars in an account of your choosing. Tomorrow morning we'll transfer half the money, and you'll get the other half after you give him the envelope."

"That's all?" It seemed too simple. An envelope delivered, and Dennis and his family would be rich. Voices inside him battled to be heard. It was against the law, and failing that, there had to be a catch. He should refuse and keep his honor clean.

But then, with the money they could take that trip to Spain Gloria had been longing for. She had sent for the passports already, hoping to convince him. He could also pay for his children to take whatever lessons they wanted and buy them the things they had always asked for. No more making excuses, no more scraping by from paycheck to paycheck. And best of all, no more patronizing statements from Gloria's brother. Dennis didn't have to do anything really illegal, just pass on a sheet of paper that Holbrooke would most likely dispose of quickly. No one would ever have to know.

I'd know, he thought. But maybe with the money, he could live with the knowledge. There were many things much worse.

And did he really have any choice? The guard in him thought not. If he refused, his life would probably end as a headline in the local newspaper: *Prison guard found murdered in local park.* No, there had never been a choice for him, not really. Not since they had taken him from his bed. His honor wouldn't do his children and Gloria much good once he was dead.

"I'll do it," he said.

"Good." The envelope was shoved into his hands. "We want it done tomorrow. And don't try to open the envelope. We'll be watching."

Dennis had toyed with the idea of seeing what was inside the envelope, but now he wouldn't open it for anything. He just wanted the whole thing to be over.

"Call this number tomorrow morning and tell us the bank and the account number. We suggest overseas."

Dennis knew all about that. His brother-in-law had bragged for years about his overseas account that yielded high interest and no federal government looking over his shoulder. Dennis had secretly hoped he would be caught, but now he was grateful for the knowledge.

The men took him to the back of his house and ordered him to count to a hundred before removing the blindfold. When he did, they were gone, and there was nothing to remind him of their visit except the blindfold and the thin white envelope. Dennis breathed a silent prayer of relief. The envelope shone in the moonlight and seemed to burn his hand. He went inside and shoved it in his top drawer under his wallet and checkbook. Gloria was still sleeping peacefully.

For the first time in his life, since they were babies, Dennis checked the kids as they slept. Their chests moved up and down at regular intervals. Dennis clenched his jaw. "They're okay," he whispered. "They're okay."

* * * * *

On Wednesday morning, Dennis Faron put on his guard's uniform with less will than normal. Gloria looked at him strangely, and he hurriedly pulled on his socks. He was already late, having taken an early drive to the gas station where he had exhausted his supply of newly purchased phone cards making telephone calls. But the bank end was all set up. The only thing left was the letter.

"Is something wrong?" Gloria asked. Worry lines creased her forehead, and for a moment Dennis wished he could tell her everything. He wished last night hadn't happened. He wished he could just walk away.

But he knew if he did, he would die. Or Gloria would, or his children. Likewise, if he told the police he was a goner. There was nothing to do but pass the envelope to Holbrooke and pray that it was nothing more than an innocuous letter from a business partner or a girlfriend.

Yes, a love letter, he thought. *That's what it is.*

He gathered Gloria in his arms and kissed her as he hadn't for a long time. Her long blonde hair smelled clean and fresh. He reluctantly let her go and kissed the kids, who were still in their pajamas eating breakfast cereal at the table.

"Yuck, Dad!" said his son. He was twelve and not used to such remonstrations from his father.

The wrinkles in Gloria's forehead deepened. "Are you sure you're okay?"

He forced a smile. "Just a little tired. I've been thinking we need a vacation. What about making that trip to Spain? I think we could swing it now. I've got some time coming, and I've heard that airline rates have gone down."

Gloria's face lit up. "Do you mean it?" she asked. He nodded, and she threw herself into his arms. "Oh, it'll be wonderful!"

He kissed her again. "We'll talk about it when I get home."

Before leaving the house, he slipped the envelope into his chest pocket. It seemed to burn his hand and then his chest through the fabric, but it was only his imagination.

Once in the car, he carefully cleaned the envelope of fingerprints, wrapped it in a cloth, and hid it in his sock. That should get him past the cursory search at the prison that had been instigated to screen out guards who sold drugs. Of course, the few guards who were involved in a drug ring found other methods, but they were always eventually caught. Dennis had never been a part of such activity. Until now.

He made every green light and arrived at the federal prison on Union Street only fifteen minutes late. He passed inspection with barely a second look. Everything was made too easy. The men knew him and his sterling character.

Earl looked up from some papers as he came in from the locker room. "That book Holbrooke wanted came in. Why don't you deliver it? Nobody else can stand the guy."

"Okay." Dennis picked up the book. He went down on one knee to tie his shoe, and with the edge of his handkerchief slipped the envelope into the middle of the book. He saw the title, *The Faulkner Reader.*

"Why the man'd want to read that junk is beyond me," Earl said, leaning back in his chair. "I read a few pages and couldn't understand a thing. Give it a try."

Dennis opened the book, but was unable to focus on the words. "I see what you mean."

"Reading mixed-up stuff like that's probably what got him in such big trouble in the first place. There's such a thing as being too literary. They get so they think they're better than the rest of us."

Dennis didn't reply. In seconds he was walking down the corridor to Holbrooke's cell, feeling the ever-present camera burn into his back. "Here's your book," Dennis said. He didn't toss it as was his inclination, but slipped it carefully through the bars.

"You have a kid?" Holbrooke asked, accepting the book as though it were something special. He had dark hair and the kind of dangerous good looks women adored—the kind everyone adored. Dennis bet he wouldn't serve much time, despite his serious crimes. Holbrooke was too much in control.

"Two," Dennis replied. "A boy and a girl. Twelve and ten."

"My son's eleven," Holbrooke said.

He had known the mob boss had a son, but the poignancy in the man's voice brought it home. Holbrooke obviously missed his son and was worried about him. "You'll be with him soon," Dennis said.

"I hope so. And thank you. You're a nice man. Not like the others."

Dennis' face burned, thinking of the envelope. When Holbrooke found it, would he think Dennis had been bought? Well, he had, in a manner of speaking. But he really hadn't had a choice. He wondered if the mob boss would expect more favors.

"Well, have a good day," Dennis said. He left quickly, relief flowing through him. *Now back to normal,* he thought. *I'll pretend it never happened.*

Of course he would now have a million dollars sitting in a Swiss bank account, or at least a half million if the owners of the envelope didn't follow through with the second installment. But Dennis knew they would. When he called later, the money would all be there. But he wouldn't spend it. No, he would give it to charity. All of it—except enough to take Gloria to Spain and give his kids the karate lessons they had been wanting. Nothing for himself.

Feeling much better, Dennis went about his work.

* * * * *

Quentin Thomas Holbrooke watched the guard leave. He had made a fortune from studying people, and he could tell there was something different about the man this morning. Dennis was scared almost to the point of breaking. Odd. He looked at the thick book in his hand. Printed in 1946, it had a blue cover and the title was in gold lettering, framed by rectangles of black. Very simple. Nothing to be afraid of.

He wondered what Sampson was doing. If he were here, Quentin would read aloud to him from *The Sound and the Fury* and then discuss it. The boy had inherited his mother's love of reading, and the old classics had been family favorites. Quentin had been interested in the classics himself when he was younger, but now read them only when he missed Maura . . . or Sampson.

It won't be long now, he promised the boy who could not hear him. *If I have to use my whole fortune to get free, or at least all that Laranda left intact, I'll do it.*

TC, of course, wouldn't like it. Quentin knew he enjoyed being in charge. But it was Quentin's empire, after all. He could always build another, but he couldn't replace the years of Sampson's childhood. He had to be there for that, especially since Maura couldn't be.

How he had loved her! She had been the only pure thing in his life. What's more, she had loved him in return. Yet even with all that love, she had not been able to withstand his corruptness—the secret murders, the bribes, the questionable business ventures. She had planned to take Sampson and leave, and Quentin would have let her rather than see her hurt. Then came the tumor, and not all the money in the world could save her. He would have lost her either way, but he would have rather had her live. Sampson needed her.

Which was another reason why he had sent Sampson to Cassi. She was much like Maura. Not in the way she looked or acted, but in spirit. Quentin knew Cassi would care for Sampson until he could be reunited with his family—or at least until Quentin found out who was killing his relatives. His suspicions pointed to TC, but he hoped he was wrong.

Thumbing through *The Faulkner Reader*, he was surprised to see an envelope tucked inside the pages. What was this? Could it be the reason for the guard's terror? Quentin felt a surge of hope. Maybe there was some way out of this hole. If the guard had been bribed to carry this note, there could be others. The man had children and would not refuse.

Smiling darkly, Quentin broke open the seal to the envelope. The inside was lined with a thin plastic sheeting. Top of the line. Which of his allies had sent it? What was the plan?

He pulled a single sheet of thick paper from the envelope. As he unfolded the letter, there was a soft pop and a cloud of something floated into Holbrooke's face. He scarcely had time to view the short note before the symptoms began.

Bang! I win after all. You're dead.

Quentin's breath came rapidly, and he gasped for each breath. He tried to call out, but he couldn't make a sound. The room seemed to spin at high speed around him. He felt his face flush, and a horrible pounding assaulted his skull. Dropping the letter, he fell heavily to the floor. His heart sounded loudly in his ears, beating much more rapidly than it should have. He couldn't breathe or focus on anything in the room.

Who had done this to him? Could it have been TC? Or was it Donelli, his major competitor? Or perhaps someone else entirely? In the end, it was all the same. He would still be dead.

His body began to convulse. As unconsciousness took over, Quentin's last thought was of Sampson.

* * * * *

"We're here to see Quentin Holbrooke," Fred said to the man at the desk. He and Justin took out their FBI identification. "We need to see him privately. It's been cleared through the warden, if you want to check."

The man checked. He had a disgruntled look on his face, as though he had been interrupted at something important. *Probably a nap*, Fred thought uncharitably.

He was in a lousy mood. He had slept last night in his office at the Federal Building, waiting for a call from Jared and Cassi. None had come. Where were they now? It was already early Wednesday evening in France, about fifteen hours since he had talked to Cassi. Had they been captured by whoever had chased her from the phone? No, he had to believe they were still free. They would call him when they could. Meanwhile, he would find his own leads.

"You can see him," the man said, putting down the phone. "But we're at full capacity right now, and it'll take me a while to find a room." He lifted the phone.

Fred saw Justin roll his eyes. Even if they were at full capacity, there should be plenty of rooms for an FBI interrogation.

The guard suddenly turned white and nearly dropped the phone. "He's what!"

"What happened?" Fred demanded, thinking that in spite of the extra security measures he knew the warden had ordered, Holbrooke had somehow escaped.

"He's—they say he appears to be—uh—dead."

"Take me to him. Now!"

Fred forced his way through the mill of guards into the cell, where he found Holbrooke lying on the floor. His body was curled as though it had suffered convulsions, and his skin was abnormally pink. "Get a homicide team in here on the double!" he growled. "And don't touch anything. It looks like poison."

Well, Cassi and Jared, he thought. *Someone has just upped the ante. That little boy with you is now a multibillionaire target.*

CHAPTER 4

At a pay phone, Jared called Zack Fields, who had arranged for them to stay at his in-laws' cabin. "Something's come up, and we have to leave France now. We've left the car here with plenty of money to pay for the parking. And, uh, there's a broken window and a few holes from some bullets. We left you a check to pay for it. You can exchange it at your bank, can't you?"

"Sure; it takes a few weeks, but I've done it before. And don't worry about the car. It's old and can be fixed. But what happened? The police called and said something about a break-in. Are you guys okay?"

"Well, sort of." Jared gave a brief explanation, thanked him profusely, and hung up.

"How'd he take it?" Cassi asked.

"Well, it seems he received a call from the police about a break-in at the cabin. He was worried about us. He asked me when we were going to learn to stay out of trouble."

"Seems like never," Cassi said. "Maybe we really should move to a deserted island like Carl suggested." Carl Boyer was a friend who lived in Los Angeles, and who had helped them during their last run-in with Laranda.

"Too late now," Jared said wistfully. He kissed her, and Sampson rolled his eyes.

"Would you two quit that? You're embarrassing me. We're in public, you know."

They still had some time before their train left, so they walked until they found a store to buy toothbrushes and a few other essential items. "In England, we'll do some real shopping," Cassi told Sampson. Jared hoped whatever store they visited didn't have swords.

The train ride took several hours, but was uneventful. Jared even managed to doze part of the time. Sampson was asleep the second the train pulled out of the station, his head falling first against Cassi's shoulder and then coming to rest on her lap. Cassi stroked the boy's cheek and blond hair, humming a little song under her breath. Jared thought it was a lullaby.

They arrived in Calais and waited for nearly an hour for the ferry to arrive. Once aboard the *SeaFrance,* they dined in style at La Brasserie. "This is good stuff for a ferry," Sampson said. Sampson with his father's connections would know, but Jared ate without tasting the food, feeling too tense to enjoy himself.

It took an hour and a half for the ferry to cross the English Channel to Dover, as opposed to some of the hovercraft which took about a third of the time. This belated discovery, made only once they were on board, worried Jared. He hoped that no one would be waiting for them in England. A headache began to plague him.

"Look at those beautiful cliffs," Cassi said, pointing at the English coast. Jared saw long cliffs of white shadowed by fluffy clouds, white on top and an upswept gray on the underside. It was an impressive sight, and his headache lightened considerably.

In Dover, Cassi exchanged some French francs for English pounds and placed a call to her friend Grant Truebekon. He was a reclusive member of the Church who also happened to be one of the foremost authorities on Indian art. Cassi had met him while serving a mission in England and had later studied with him. Under other circumstances, Jared would have been pleased about the meeting, but this wild trip was not exactly how he had expected to meet the renowned art connoisseur.

They had to wait another thirty minutes for Cassi's friend to arrive at the ferry station. Jared studied each passerby as they waited, expecting at any minute to see their pursuers. But he saw no one who appeared threatening.

"There he is, I think," Cassi said at last as an older man parked and came around the car to greet them. "Grant! Hi!" Cassi hugged him.

"It's so good to see you, Cassi," Grant said, returning her embrace.

"You too. It's been a long time. Thanks for coming. Grant, this is my husband, Jared Landine."

"Nice to meet you." Grant shook his hand. The man was very tall and lean, except for a modest bulge around his middle. He had brown eyes, dark gray hair, and thick eyebrows of the same color. His presence was commanding, but not overbearing, and Jared liked him at once.

"I've heard a lot about you," Jared said. "It's nice to finally meet you in person."

"And you, too. Cassi has been like a daughter to me."

"I think she feels the same way."

Cassi's smile grew. "I certainly do." She touched Sampson's shoulder. "This is Sampson. He's staying with us for a while."

"Some honeymoon," Grant murmured with a grin. "You never did like to do things in the usual way, Cassi. But it is good to see you again. Sophie's looking forward to your visit."

On the drive to Grant's house outside Dover, they explained their troubles and the reason for the sudden change in their visiting plans. Grant shook his head in disbelief. "I'm really sorry, Cassi. Trouble seems to follow you."

"Yeah, you'd think we'd get used to it," Cassi said wryly. "But it's a little too exciting for us."

"Now that it's over, it was kind of fun," Sampson put in. "When they were chasing us, Cassi drove the car like a wild woman. You should have seen her! It was like being in a movie. If it wasn't for her, they would have caught up with us and shot us through the heads. And then thrown us into the ocean or something. Nobody would have ever known."

"Yeah." Cassi's smile was grim. "Some fun." She looked at Jared as though wishing for a change in subject. Like him, she knew their troubles weren't over as Sampson had suggested.

"So tell me, Grant," Jared interjected. "What are you up to now?"

Grant laughed. "Would you believe I'm starting a publishing company? There is so much filth being published out there that I thought it time I used some of my money to help change the tide."

"That's a pretty risky venture, isn't it?" Jared asked. "There aren't too many people who are interested in reading Indian art books."

"You're right, and that's why I'm doing fiction. Only the best drama and adventure. Something that will either change lives for the better, or simply give people a chance to relax with a good clean book instead of being inundated with filth." He paused, then added, "But you guys certainly don't need any adventure added to your lives. You seem to find enough. Whew! And I thought the world of fiction was interesting."

Cassi sighed. "Well, if I ever write a book, I'll let you know."

The sun had already begun to set over the countryside when they arrived at the quaint cottage surrounded by magnificent ash trees and smaller maples. Neatly trimmed hazelnut shrubs lined the cobbled walkway where they were greeted by two sheepdogs and Sophie, Grant's wife of thirty years. "I wasn't expecting you so soon," she said, enfolding Cassi in a warm embrace. "So the rooms aren't quite ready. But I'm so glad you're here." She hugged Jared next, as enthusiastically as she had Cassi. Sophie had blonde hair, kind blue eyes, and a vibrant face. Much shorter than her husband and only slightly plump, she reminded Jared of his own mother.

"And who is this young man?" Sophie asked, eyeing Sampson. She didn't try to hug him, probably a good thing from his expression. "Why, you're very tall, aren't you?"

Sampson wasn't exceptionally tall, but at her words he smiled for the first time since they had arrived in England.

"I do declare you must be about thirteen, by the looks of you," Sophie continued.

Sampson beamed further. He cast a look at Jared and Cassi that said, "This woman knows children."

"He's eleven," Jared said.

Sampson scowled.

"Well, come on in. You must be hungry. I'll bet you haven't eaten much of anything, and I have dinner all ready." She sounded so content that Jared hadn't the heart to tell her they had recently eaten.

"She's a great cook," Cassi whispered to Jared. "But don't get used to it."

"Maybe she could give you lessons."

"Ha!"

While the others helped bring the food to the table, Jared called Fred in San Diego. The secretary told him that Fred was at the jailhouse checking up on some things. When Jared mentioned his name, she forwarded the call to Fred's cell phone. No answer. Jared left a message saying he would call back later.

Before sitting down at the table, he slipped outside and walked around the house, checking for anything unusual. The house was not really a cottage, and it was much larger than it appeared from the front side. The air of it appealed to Jared. He would hate their trouble to mar the atmosphere or to affect their hosts. As soon as he talked to Fred and made plans, they would leave.

Just to be sure, he walked up the long drive. Nothing looked out of the ordinary. Maybe they were safe. But then, how long would it take whoever was after Sampson to trace them? It wouldn't be too hard for experts, he knew. No, they would have to move on tomorrow, even if he didn't talk to Fred.

"Where have you been?" Cassi asked when he arrived back at the house.

"Taking a little walk. I just wanted to be sure."

"They're going to find us, aren't they?" Her voice was low and intense.

"I think so. But we should be safe for tonight."

"I'll let the dogs out," Grant said, coming from the kitchen. "They'll let us know if anyone comes. And it might just be harder to track down this place than you think. It's not listed in any phone book, and when I have visitors, we usually have them at the apartment in London. Come on now, eat. You did right in coming here."

The meal was everything Cassi had promised. Thick beef stew with fresh herbs, a chicken casserole with broccoli, lightly steamed vegetables, and fresh-baked bread. Jared found himself asking about the recipe for the stew.

Sophie blushed. "Oh, I just threw that together with whatever I had on hand. And the casserole—well, that's left over from last night. I didn't know you were coming, or I would have had something better."

Cassi helped herself to another slice of homemade bread, and Jared followed suit. Sampson downed two more thick slabs and another bowl of stew. At the rate he was eating, Jared was sure he would grow two inches by the next day.

While they helped Grant clean up the remains of the meal, Sophie made their rooms ready. "I'm sorry the rooms are so far apart."

"Anything will do." Jared thought the farther apart, the better. After all, they were still on a honeymoon of sorts.

Sophie showed them first to the room on the second floor that she had prepared for Jared and Cassi, then took them to the small room on the main floor near the library where Sampson was to stay. There was a single bed and a low dresser topped by a lamp, the only light in the room.

"Well, I'll leave you to get settled," Sophie said. "Let me know if you need anything. Otherwise, I'll see you tomorrow morning."

Sophie and Grant withdrew, leaving Jared and Cassi alone in the small room with Sampson, who was already making himself at home on the bed. Jared put his arms around Cassi. She kissed him, stirring him more than he cared to admit, then gently disengaged herself from his grasp. "I'll see you in the morning."

"What?" He had just been thinking of being alone with her in the other room.

She looked pointedly at Sampson on the bed before dragging Jared into the hall. "We can't leave him here alone," she whispered. "What if he runs off again?"

"He promised he wouldn't."

"And you believe him?"

"Yes." But Jared admitted to himself that Sampson might not keep his word. He wondered how many times the boy's father might have broken his promises because of business interests. Did Sampson know what true honor was, taught as he was by a mobster? Thieves' honor wasn't exactly the same thing.

"Well, even if he keeps that promise, what if someone comes in? We have to protect him. I'd stay with him myself, but it hardly looks right."

"But . . ." Jared took her again into his arms. She seemed to melt into him. For a long moment neither said anything, but let their bodies communicate their love and commitment to each other.

Finally Cassi pulled away. "I know it's tough—it's my honey-moon, too. But like it or not, that child is our responsibility."

"I know." Jared sighed with defeat. "But once this is over . . ." He left the sentence unfinished.

Cassi laughed, giving him an impish grin. "As you are fond of saying, we have an eternity, don't we?"

He tried to kiss her again, but she flitted up the stairs. It was just as well. If he held her again, he might not let her go.

After peeking in to see if Sampson was all right, Jared used the Trubekons' phone again to call Fred. Still no answer on his cell phone. Where was that guy? What was he doing? Well, there was nothing for it but to try again tomorrow.

He found a heap of blankets and pillows on the floor by Sampson's bed. The boy leaned up on his elbow, looking inordinately pleased. "In the doghouse, huh?"

Jared sighed. He couldn't tell Sampson the real reason he wasn't sleeping with his new bride. "Something like that," he muttered. "It's just us guys, I guess."

Sampson chuckled, obviously finding the whole situation very amusing. "Yeah, good night."

* * * * *

The forensic team arrived quickly. It was all Dennis Faron could do to show them to the scene. He was shaking badly. What had happened to Holbrooke? The envelope and its contents were in plain sight for everyone to see.

"Don't touch it or get too close," one of the FBI agents had told him. "You might end up dead."

Dennis felt sick. Had he unwittingly killed the mob boss with the envelope? He knew he had. *A love letter*, he thought bitterly. *No one pays a million dollars for a love letter. But a death, yes, that's worth a million.*

"Hey, Dennis, phone's for you," Earl said. "It's Gloria."

He was grateful to leave the appalling scene. "Hi, honey."

"I just wanted to make sure you're all right."

"I'm fine. How's everything there?"

She laughed. "I called the travel agency. Are you sure you mean it?"

"Yeah, you deserve it, honey."

"The kids are so excited—especially about missing school."

He forced his laugh to sound natural. "That's kids for you. But we'll talk about it later, okay? There's some stuff going on here, and I've got to get back to work." That "stuff" he knew would be all over the evening news.

"Okay. I love you."

"I love you, too." Dennis hung up the phone, wondering if he had been right to insist that Gloria didn't work. He loved the idea of her being home waiting for him. The house was always spotless and dinner ready. Gloria said she enjoyed being at home, but she could have been earning money, now that the kids were in school. Maybe then he wouldn't have accepted a million dollars to kill a man.

I didn't know! he screamed silently in his own behalf. *It could have been a love letter, couldn't it?*

Ultimately, it didn't matter if Gloria worked or stayed at home. He hadn't had a choice in what he had done. It had come down to Holbrooke or his family. He had made the right choice—the only choice.

* * * * *

Fred was busy the rest of the morning and into the afternoon. By the time he left the jail, he had talked to several other prisoners and most of the guards. The only clue was the envelope. He was awaiting results on that now.

Outside the prison, he found Brooke pacing. He wasn't too surprised. "Did you follow me?"

She smiled. "No, your office told me where you went—I can be very persuasive. Besides, you didn't tell your secretary not to tell me. I've tried to see Holbrooke myself, you know, and they wouldn't let me. So I thought I'd pop on over to see what you found out—about his cousins. And then suddenly this place started hopping. Wow!"

"Holbrooke's dead," Fred stated, leading her to his car.

Brooke's smile faded. "I was right, then." She didn't look happy.

"Yeah, you were right. And now Jared and Cassi and that child are in bigger danger than ever."

"Who would kill a child?" Brooke looked at Fred, but it was Justin who answered.

"Money does strange things to people." He pulled a pad from his pocket and began writing. Fred knew that before the day was out, Justin would have doubled-checked every area of the investigation.

"Your phone was ringing like crazy earlier," Brooke said as Fred opened the door. "While I was waiting for you, I checked the parking lot for your car—just to make sure you were here. I had it down to this one or that gray one on the far aisle. You know, you really shouldn't leave your cell phone out on the seat like that. Not only could it be ruined by the sun, it invites crime."

"It must have fallen out of my pocket on our way over. It does that sometimes." Fred knew he should put it in his suit coat pocket instead of in the front pocket of his pants, but the truth was that his favorite suit had a hole in the suit coat pocket, and he hadn't taken it in yet to be fixed. He would do it soon.

Fred checked the caller ID and the message screen. There were several calls. "Looks like Cherral called about Jared. Oh, and here's another message from Jared himself." He started to mutter a curse, but thought better of it. *It's not Brooke,* he thought. *It's my blood pressure. Swearing's not good for my blood pressure. Darn Mormons, anyway.*

Justin slid his tall frame into the car, looking up expectantly at Fred. "I have to get back," Fred said to Brooke. "I hope Jared's left a number with Cherral."

Brooke hesitated. "Look, can I go public with this murder thing? I mean, the media's going to be all over this one."

"Go ahead," Fred said. "Just don't mention my name."

"How about 'a high FBI source'?"

"That's good." His phone rang and Fred answered it. Brooke started to leave but he touched her arm, asking her to wait. The contact was even more pleasant than Fred expected.

"I suspected as much," he said into the phone. "Poor guy. Okay. Well, let me know if you find anything else. Thank you."

"It was the fellow who's heading up the police side of the investigation," he told the others. "They found a cyanide derivative saturating the note. Inside, there was a thin capsule rigged to emit a cloud of gas as the letter was opened. It was potent enough to kill within a minute. I'll bet the autopsy will confirm the cause of death."

"That means the envelope was probably given to him this morning," Brooke said. "Or he would have opened it before."

Justin wrote on his pad. "Well, it certainly didn't go through regular channels."

"No," Fred said. "Or they would have found it and had it opened by professionals. My guess is that one of the guards gave the letter to Holbrooke."

Brooke's eyes widened. "Bribery?"

"Yes, or coercion. They're going to question all the guards tomorrow and give them a lie detector test." Fred smiled at Brooke. "But that has to be off the record, or our deal's off."

"Got it. I'll mention the cyanide but not the guards," Brooke said. "But you'll let me know when I can print the rest."

"That's our deal, isn't it?"

She pulled her own cell phone out of her pocket. "Look, is it okay if I drop in later today? I just may have some more information then. I'm going to make an appointment with someone who might be able to help."

There was nothing out of the ordinary in the way she said it, but Fred felt an odd sensation creep up his spine. *Who was she going to see?* He didn't like the idea of her nosing around. *What if she gets hurt?* But then he couldn't exactly tell her how to do her job, and she had promised him she'd be careful. He watched her leave, feeling disgruntled and upset. Why did he care so much about Brooke Erickson?

"She is one good-looking woman," Justin said. "Smart, too. And I think she likes you."

"Huh?" Fred said, turning to look at his friend in amazement.

"Oh, yeah. I can tell all right. Look at her body language."

Fred had been trying *not* to look at her body. He stifled a sigh.

"You should ask her out."

"I don't think so," Fred said shortly. "I'm a little busy with this case." Justin didn't say anything, and Fred felt obligated to add, "Maybe later."

"Yeah," Justin murmured. "When dogs fly."

Fred pretended not to hear.

* * * * *

TC Brohaugh watched the woman as she came into the study. She cut an exceptional figure, and he allowed his gaze to linger over her suit coat and skirt, not finely tailored but modest and very becoming to her slender curves.

"Thank you for agreeing to see me," she began.

"You *were* a little persistent."

She smiled, and he noticed that the action made her more beautiful. Brohaugh sat in a plush chair, motioning for her to do the same. As he sat, his elaborate house jacket slid off one shoulder and revealed his sling.

"You're hurt."

He shrugged and pulled the jacket up to cover the shoulder. "Pulled a muscle, that's all. Now, you said you had some important information?"

"How do you feel about the latest developments in your brother-in-law's case?"

"Latest developments?" He smirked. These reporters. It was always the same thing. "I'm not sure I know what you're talking about."

"Well, with Holbrooke's death, I guess the question is who is next in line for his fortune?"

TC's smile vanished. "Excuse me? Did I hear correctly?"

"You didn't know Holbrooke was killed in jail only this morning?" The reporter put on a concerned face. "I am sorry to be telling you this. I thought the police would have contacted you by now." She stood. "I should be leaving."

"No, stay," TC said forcefully. "Please. Tell me what happened."

"He was murdered. I really don't know the details."

"How?"

She met his eyes and her expression changed, as though she saw something that didn't agree with her. "Maybe you can tell me," she said coldly.

"Are you inferring that I had something to do with my brother-in-law's death?"

"Of course not. But what the public will see is who is next in line for Holbrooke's fortune. With two cousins dead, another disappeared, and the child missing in Europe, there seems to be only you and a few odd relatives left holding the bag. Do *you* know who could be responsible?"

"I assure you I have no clue," TC said. "But I will, of course, cooperate with the police in their investigation. Now, if you will excuse me . . ."

"Of course."

TC pushed a silent buzzer, and a servant appeared in the doorway to show the reporter to the door. He looked at the card she had given him. *Brooke Erickson, San Diego Union-Tribune.* "I want her followed," he said to Baker, who stood like a shadow by the window. "She knows more than she's letting on."

"I'll get right on it. But it looks like the police are here to see you."

"Better show them in."

As Baker left, TC laughed softly to himself. So, Quentin was out of the way permanently. Things were getting better and better. Now to find Sampson.

* * * * *

Fred was relieved when Brooke showed up again in his office. Justin was off checking on a few things, so Fred was alone.

"I went to see Brohaugh," Brooke said without preamble. "Boy, that guy makes my skin crawl. When I talked to him about Holbrooke, he acted really odd. But the thing was, I could tell he didn't give a hoot about his brother-in-law dying like that. Not one tiny little bit. There was absolutely no sorrow in his eyes. I think he was even glad. It was a terrible feeling." Brooke shivered.

"You shouldn't have gone there." Fred looked at her sternly.

She laughed. "What, I can't interview the relatives? But I have to. It's the news. People want to know."

"You said you'd stay on the sidelines."

"No, I promised to do nothing dangerous. Going to see Brohaugh wasn't dangerous, although if you ask me, I'll bet he's the one who killed Holbrooke. The guy's as unfeeling as a doorknob."

"That's exactly why I want you to stay away from him."

"Well, you don't need to worry about me. I've had my fill of the man."

"Good." Silence grew between them, and Fred wished he hadn't been so gruff. He also wished he had the courage to ask her out. She was an incredible woman, and for some reason her presence daunted him. Fred had never thought of himself as ugly, even though he didn't think he was anywhere near her league. But what if he just asked her out for coffee? No, she didn't drink coffee. Soda?

"Uh, Brooke, I was wondering if after work . . ."

"Yes?" Her eyes danced as though she knew what he was going to say.

Fred suddenly found it difficult to breathe. Not even when facing deadly criminals had his heart leapt so curiously. But then there was the matter of the ring she wore. Was she really married? She had never mentioned a husband. "Well . . ."

There was a brief tap at the door before Justin walked in, carrying his pad of paper. "Oh, sorry, I didn't know you had company."

Fred stifled a grimace. "Brooke was just telling me she went to visit Brohaugh."

Justin raised one eyebrow. "Ah, you must be the woman the police are a little peeved with. They didn't like you telling Brohaugh about Holbrooke's murder. They wanted to see his reaction."

"Then they should have told him earlier," Brooke said without remorse. "But he could have done it. I was just telling Fred that Brohaugh is definitely glad Holbrooke's dead. He could be responsible."

A stickler for facts, Fred noticed that for the first time she had called him by his given name. He liked the sound of it.

"But he's not the only one," Justin said, waving his pad of paper. "In fact—" he broke off, looking at Fred. Obviously he had some information he didn't know if he should share with Brooke.

"Someone else?" she asked eagerly. She craned her neck as though trying to see what was written on Justin's pad. Justin put it in his shirt pocket. "Who?"

"Look, Brooke," Fred said. "Remember when I told you Holbrooke was trying for a plea bargain? Well, I thought if—"

"If you found out who he was going to give up, then you might have his murderer!" she finished.

"Exactly. But I can't tell you who it is. I'm sorry. FBI policy."

"But I thought we were working together!"

"We are, sort of, but this has to be kept quiet until we're sure."

"I wouldn't tell anyone." Her eyes challenged him.

"I know, but you might go see them." Fred looked at her, expressionless, until she smiled in defeat.

"Okay, I see your point. But surely there's *something* you can tell me."

Fred smiled back, glad that she could see reason. "Holbrooke has a step-cousin who died yesterday in a fire. Another cousin, a woman this time, is missing. Three other distant relatives have also disappeared. That leaves absolutely no one except Brohaugh and the child."

Brooke whistled. "You've got to find him."

"Yes, we do. Unfortunately, Jared didn't leave a number, and he hasn't called back—yet. I'm sure he will soon. But if you're into praying like all the other Mormons I know, now would be a good time. Jared and Cassi need to be warned before it's too late."

CHAPTER 5

Dennis Faron knew he would never pass the lie detector test, planned for Thursday morning. He would be caught and put in prison. As a former guard, he would suffer terrible indignities at the hands of the other inmates. Worse, his wife would have to bear unkind comments from neighbors and reporters, and his children would be taunted at school.

He made a decision. Before going home Wednesday evening, he made last-minute reservations to Rio. An inmate he had once known said that anyone could disappear in Brazil. Then he went home and told Gloria everything. Now the choice was hers.

She was devastated. But through her tears, she showed courage and understanding. "You had no other choice. They would have killed you . . . or us."

"Everything will be okay," he told her. "Please come with me. I couldn't bear it without you and the kids. We'll get new names—any name you want. We'll have enough money for whatever we need."

"I never did like the name Gloria," she said with a sniff. She arose from the couch. "If you help me, we can pack what we need tonight. We'll tell the children tomorrow on the way to the airport."

Dennis hugged her and went to find the suitcases in the garage. There was something else he was going to do before he left. He was going to write a letter explaining everything. Maybe someone would understand that he had made a necessary choice.

* * * * *

"Sleep well?" Cassi met Jared outside his room the next morning.

He grimaced. "As well as can be expected for a man who slept alone on his honeymoon, I suppose."

Cassi put her arms around his neck and gave him a solid kiss. "You don't look like you slept very well." She wondered if he'd had the dream again and shivered. What would it have been like to have been kept a prisoner for days, knowing you were the only thing standing between your friend and death? But Jared had stood up to Laranda; and in the end it was she who had died, not their friend Trent. "I love you, you know."

"I know," he said, kissing her back.

Sophie came into the hallway where they stood. "Breakfast is ready. Hope you're hungry. Where is that boy, anyway? I'll bet he could use a good old-fashioned English breakfast."

Jared thumbed at the door. "Still sawing logs. I'd better wake him."

"Shouldn't we call Fred again?" Cassi asked as Sophie disappeared into the kitchen.

Jared looked at his watch. "It's the middle of the night there. Let's eat, do a little shopping for something to wear, and then we'll call him. This place is out of the way; I think we're pretty safe."

The cabin had also been out of the way, but Cassi didn't bring that up. How had Quentin found them in the first place? And those who were after Sampson? "You know, we might want to go into London," she said as they went into the kitchen. "The FBI is sure to have a field office or something attached to the Embassy. We could pick up the things we need quickly and go there to contact Fred."

"Good idea," Sophie said. "There's better shopping in London, anyway. And we have the apartment there, if you need somewhere to stay."

After breakfast, Grant and Sophie drove them to London. There, they bought one suitcase each and several changes of clothing. Sampson insisted on paying for everything. "Your card could be traced," he said. "Mine can't. Or at least not very easily. My dad said so."

Cassi looked over at Jared with a silent question in her eyes. "Let him pay," he said quietly. "I think he really needs to feel a part of all this. And after all, it is his father who is responsible for putting us in the middle of this mess."

"Okay, Sampson," Cassi agreed. "Go right ahead. Buy it all." Sampson gave her a smug grin and presented his card. Cassi watched the money add up and hoped the card really was active and had a high enough limit to pay for everything. She soon found she had worried for nothing. Quentin had obviously taken steps to make sure his son would be well cared for.

Why?

The question kept coming back. Why was someone after Sampson? With Quentin alive and Sampson's uncle in charge of the business, killing Sampson would benefit no one. Unless Sampson's uncle had decided to take over his brother-in-law's business. Cassi felt sick at the only logical explanation.

At that moment, Sampson met her gaze. He appeared for all the world like any other young boy. His face resembled his father only in his chin, but even that fragile connection was enough to bring Quentin's face to Cassi's mind. At one time she had thought Quentin was a friend, but he had ordered the death of her friend and mentor, Linden Johansen. In the end, he had almost killed her and Jared.

"Are you okay, Cassi?" Sampson asked.

Quentin's face vanished, and once again Sampson became an innocent victim she wanted to protect. "I'm just hungry," she said with a smile. "Shopping takes a lot out of a person. What do you say we dump this stuff in the car and get to the Embassy? Fred should be awake soon."

"But I'm hungry," Sampson complained.

Jared laughed. "With all you put away at breakfast?"

"That was hours ago."

"A growing boy needs lots of food," Sophie said. "My two boys used to eat more in one meal than I'd eat in two days."

Grant put his arm around his wife's plump shoulders. "There's a good restaurant a few streets over. We can grab some take-out. That won't delay us much. And I'm sure whoever is looking for you hasn't come this far yet."

"Can I pay?" Sampson asked, flourishing his card.

Cassi sighed. How did Quentin ever expect to teach his son the value of money? Sending him off to Europe alone with an apparently limitless credit card was not a good start.

"We'll see." Cassi picked up a stack of purchases and watched as the others did the same—except Sophie, who fished in her purse for the keys and led the way to the car.

The streets were busy but not overcrowded. Ordinarily Cassi would have felt content, but the overcast sky added to her unease. She searched the street, looking for someone who did not belong. *Relax,* she told herself. *They couldn't have followed us here. We've been too careful.*

Near the car, Sophie pushed a button on her keychain. A chiming noise signaled that the alarm had been deactivated and the doors unlocked. Grant opened the trunk and began to supervise the package placement, while Sophie headed toward the passenger side door. As she opened it, there was an explosion that blew her short frame backward into the street. Cassi gasped as she struggled to maintain her own footing. Sampson cried out.

Grant stumbled to his wife's side as she lay motionless on the street, her face and clothing blackened from the blast. Cars backed up behind them.

"Over there!" Jared said, pointing. Two dark-haired men had appeared in the doorway of a small shop about a hundred feet down from the front of the ruined car. As Cassi glanced at them, they each raised an arm, holding what appeared to be guns. "Get down!" Jared shouted. Cassi grabbed Sampson and scrambled with him for the pavement behind the car. She was too late. Something sharp and painful pierced her upper chest. Her vision grew dim. Her last sight was of Grant, clutching his wife to his chest while tears rolled down his pale cheeks.

* * * * *

Jared watched as Cassi grabbed Sampson and hit the pavement. The boy cried out in fear, but stayed under Cassi where he had fallen. Jared also ducked behind the car, hoping it wasn't on fire in some place he couldn't see. Would it blow up and take them all with it?

Jared dared a peek at the men who had fired, and with terror saw them approaching. Grant was still in the middle of the street with

Sophie, yelling for someone to call an ambulance. One or two people had stopped to stare, but the shots had driven them back into their cars or the nearby buildings. There was no one to aid them.

Helplessly, Jared glanced at Cassi. She still lay on top of Sampson, unmoving. "Cassi!"

No answer.

"Cassi?"

Sampson slid out from under her. "She's not moving. Her eyes are closed. I think they hit her."

Rage boiled up in Jared. Was Cassi dead or dying? A heavy load of agony fell upon him, and he shut his eyes momentarily with the pain.

When he opened them, the men had moved closer. Sirens filled the air, overshadowing the sounds of the halted traffic around him. The men increased their pace. "You get him," one grunted. "I'll get the woman and the boy."

The words chilled the rage into something more dangerous inside of Jared. He was not going to let anyone mess with Cassi's life again. He crouched closer to the ground, taking stock of the approaching feet. Two sets. If he could knock out one on the first rush, it would be a fair fight.

Wait, he told himself. *Not yet. Let them come closer.* In one more second they would reach the back of the car.

Jared shot out of his hiding place, hitting both men and knocking them off balance. Rapidly, he brought up his foot in the most deadly kickboxing move he had ever learned. The man he hit crumpled to the cobblestone sidewalk and lay motionless.

The second man stepped back and pulled out a gun. On his rounded face was a mocking grin. His watery brown eyes showed anticipation. Jared didn't wait, but launched himself at the man's feet. He didn't realize how large the man was before he felt the impact throughout his entire body. Still, the thug fell. A shot rang out and hit the car. But the sound was odd to Jared, not like the bullets he had heard on other days. *Yeah, like you've heard so many.* But the truth was, he had heard more than enough in the past three and a half months to last him a lifetime.

A police car rushed up to the scene and the man on the sidewalk cast Jared an ugly stare, jumped to his feet, and was gone. Jared thought about following, but turned back to Cassi, needing desperately to see if she was alive. How could he face life without her? *Please be all right!*

Sampson had rolled her over onto the blacktop. Her face was pale and inert, her eyes shut and shadowed by her dark lashes.

"Look!" The boy held something in his hand, shaped like a dart. "It was in her chest," he said. "I tried to wake her, but she's not moving."

With a raw cry, Jared fell to his knees by her side.

CHAPTER
6

Fred looked up as Justin came into Fred's office Thursday
morning. He could tell his friend had news. "One of the guards at the
jail didn't show up for his job this morning or to take the lie detector
test. There's no answer at his house, and his children haven't been in
school. A friend of his at the prison received a faxed confession. Here's
a copy." Justin slid it onto the desk. "I've done some checking, and I
believe he's headed to Rio. I can have our people pick him up when
he arrives."

Fred read the guard's confession thoroughly before replying. "He
seems very sincere. I think he's telling the truth."

"Poor unlucky sucker."

"Yeah, what would you have done under the same circumstances?"

"I don't know."

"Me either." Fred stared at the paper for another minute. "About
Rio . . . could you be mistaken?"

Justin hesitated. "I guess there could be another Dennis Faron
traveling with his wife and two children."

"There's nothing more he can add," Fred said. "He doesn't know
who did it. He was just a poor unlucky guy who was in the wrong
place at the wrong time."

Justin ripped a paper from his small writing pad. "It's our call. If
we delay, he'll have time to hide. Perhaps he's suffered enough."

"Oh, he'll suffer more," Fred said. "That's not a good life, always
looking behind you. Wondering how long until you're discovered.
Picking up and moving every time someone suspicious looks your way."

Justin tossed his pad onto Fred's desk and crossed to the paper shredder in the corner. He put the sheet of paper he had torn from the pad into the opening. "At least he'll be free and with his family."

The men stared at each other for a long, silent moment as the shredder hummed quietly.

The intercom buzzed and Fred answered it. "Yes, Cherral?"

"Brooke Erickson here to see you."

"Send her in."

Justin didn't hide his smile. "I tell you, she likes you."

"What she wants is a story. Besides, she wears a wedding band."

"Maybe it keeps the creeps away."

"Maybe she's married."

Their conversation broke off as Brooke came into the room. "Hi," she said cheerily. "Have I missed anything? Have the Landines called?"

"Not yet. But we're hoping they reach us soon."

"What about the guards? Did they all pass the lie detector test?"

Fred exchanged an amused glance with Justin. There was certainly no fooling this woman.

"Come on. You know I'll find out soon enough. Give me the scoop first." Brooke sat down on a chair and crossed her shapely legs. Fred focused on her face.

"The police department will make a statement."

"But I won't hear it. I'm here with you."

She had a point. "Okay. One of the guards didn't show up. We think he's the one who—"

"Passed the envelope. Of course, it had to be! You guys knew it even yesterday. So did you get him?"

"Nope. Just his confession. You can read it if you'd like." He handed her the faxed paper Justin had given him earlier. "It makes you feel sorry for the poor fool." Fred glanced again at Justin.

"What aren't you telling me?" Brooke's eyes seemed to delve into his soul.

Darned Mormons. What do they have—a radar for the exact truth? "The rest is confidential."

Two spots of red appeared on Brooke's cheeks, marring the porcelain skin. Her jaw was set in determination. Fred had never been much of a praying man, but he prayed now. Anything to change Brooke's focus. The FBI letting a guilty man go, despite extenuating circumstances, wouldn't go over well in the legal circles, even if public opinion supported the gesture.

The phone rang. Maybe there really was someone up there after all.

* * * * *

Cassi opened her eyes and saw nothing but a white mist. Was this heaven? She searched the white but couldn't see anyone she recognized. On the other side of the veil, Linden at least would come to meet her, wouldn't he? And her grandparents. She closed her eyes, too tired to search any longer.

"I think she's coming around." The voice belonged to a stranger.

"Cassi? Cassi?" Now that voice was familiar—and very worried. Someone clutched her hand.

She opened her eyes again. "Jared?" Was he dead, too?

The fog slowly dissipated and Jared's face appeared, wavering slightly. Around her, she recognized the familiar furnishings of a hospital room—white sheets, monitors and equipment, and three other beds, currently unoccupied. A uniformed nurse watched her from a distance.

So she wasn't dead. Relief swept through her. It wasn't that she feared death, but she wanted to make more memories with Jared. She wanted to have a family. "What happened?"

Jared stroked her hand. "You were hit. But it was some kind of sleeping drug. The police arrived just in time."

"Did they catch them?"

"One, but he's not talking. And he's got a very high-powered lawyer on the case."

"A drug." Cassi's thoughts returned to that first bit of information. "Then they didn't want to kill us. Not right away."

"It seems that way. But they did find a real gun on the man . . . and there was the car bomb."

Cassi struggled to sit up, her memory raging back. "Sophie! Is she all right?" Dizziness flooded over her.

"You need to lie down for another hour or so until the effects of the drug wear off completely," the nurse said. Her British accent made her voice clipped, but she looked at Cassi with a warm smile.

Cassi lay back on the bed. "Is Sophie okay?" she asked more calmly.

Jared's face tightened with worry. "They don't know yet, but Grant and I gave her a blessing. She's been holding on all day. I think she'll pull through."

"It's all our fault. We shouldn't have come and dragged them into this." She swallowed hard. "Where's Sampson? They didn't . . . ?"

"No, he's waiting out in the hall. When the dart caught up with you, you passed out on top of him. He's been worried."

"Well, send him in."

"Are you sure you're—"

"I'm fine. Really." She glanced at the nurse. If the woman hadn't been in the room, she would have tried to sit up again. "Doesn't this bed move? I'd like to be propped up so I can see." Jared worked the controls and Cassi once more felt a wave of vertigo, but it passed quickly.

"Look," he said, "before the boy comes in, I wanted to talk with you about something."

"We can't leave him."

"It's not that. Grant says he knows some people who know some other people who have a friend who has a little cabin by a dam in Portugal where we can hide out. He says there's no way it could ever be traced. Apparently, they rent out the cabin to recommended strangers for vacation. I'm thinking we'll call Fred, or contact the FBI field office, and then we hide there while Fred and his crew find out what's going on. We'll be safe, Sampson will be safe, and we could get in a few days of peace."

"They could give us some guards, couldn't they?"

Jared's face darkened. "After all that's happened, they'd better."

"What about Sophie?"

"There's nothing we can do now but pray. And staying here will put her in more danger. The police said that only the front doors of the car were wired to blow, and they would only go off when triggered by remote control. I think whoever did it was watching us this morning, and they knew that Grant and Sophie were riding in the front. When Sophie tried to get in, boom, they had the distraction they needed. They didn't care what happened to Grant and Sophie, just as long as we were vulnerable."

Cassi let out a long sigh. "How could we have been so stupid? We should have gone straight to the FBI. We didn't need clothes, not really."

"We thought we wouldn't be found."

"Did we?" She met his eyes, searching for something to assuage her guilt. His understanding was enough. "I guess I did hope we'd lost them. But I just feel so bad about Sophie."

"We all do."

"I know." She squeezed his hand. "You go call Fred now. But send Sampson in, okay?"

"Okay." Jared leaned down and gave her a gentle kiss on the mouth. Her arms went around his neck.

"Oh, Jared, how did we get caught in this again?"

He shook his head grimly. "I don't know. But maybe Fred does."

She let her arms drop and watched him walk out the door. The nurse approached. "Your vital signs are completely stable now. But that wasn't always the case. There was a lot of the drug in your system." She motioned toward the door with her head. "He was beside himself, you know. You have a great man there."

Cassi smiled faintly, love filling her heart. "I know. Thanks."

Sampson shuffled slowly into the room. The nurse turned to leave. "Push the red button there if you need anything. I'm just down the hall. You slept through supper, but I can bring you something whenever you want." She was gone before Cassi could reply.

Sampson's eyes fixed on Cassi's face. "Come closer," she said. "I'm all right. Just a little dizzy."

"I thought you were dead."

"Naw. I'm tougher than I look." But Cassi knew that if a bullet had hit her chest instead of a dart full of drugs, she might well have been dead. "How're you holding up?"

"I'm fine," he said without expression. He slumped down into the chair next to the bed.

Cassi wished she could wipe the blankness from his face. He was too young to be so determined not to show his emotions. "How would you like to go to a cabin where there's a nice dam?"

"Is there a boat?"

"Probably. And I'll bet there's swimming, too. Can you swim?"

A little of the old arrogance showed in his eyes. "Of course. Who can't? I swim great."

"We'll have a race, then."

"Ha! I'll beat you."

"No one can beat me," she said. "It's because of my runner's legs. They're strong paddlers."

"Well, *I'll* beat you."

"Maybe."

Silence fell between them. Then, with no warning, Sampson looked at her. "Do you think my dad's going to be long in prison?"

"I don't know." Cassi couldn't tell him that she hoped Big Tommy would be put away forever. Obviously Sampson loved his father, and the poor child seemed to have no one else except an uncle who was possibly trying to kill him. "But we can go and visit your dad. Just as soon as we figure out who's after us."

"I wish my uncle were here. He would find out."

"You like your uncle?"

"Yeah. We get along. My dad never liked him much, though. I think it had something to do with my mom. But I think he's a nice guy."

Cassi opted to say nothing. Sampson had little enough to believe in as it was.

* * * * *

Jared walked by the intensive care unit before going to the phone. The nurse went to get Grant. "How is she?" Jared asked.

"Still breathing, thank heaven. And the internal bleeding has slowed. I keep praying."

"I'm so sorry. If I had known . . ."

Grant waved the words aside. "You couldn't have. But what about Cassi?"

"She's a little disoriented, but she's going to be fine in an hour or two, once all the drugs are out of her body. They gave her something to speed up the process."

"Did you leave her alone?"

"Sampson's with her. And there's a policeman outside the door. I told her about the cabin, and I'm going to talk to the FBI about the idea now. I think it'll work. But Cassi will want to see you and Sophie before we head out."

Grant shook his head; it appeared much grayer to Jared than it had that morning. "They don't want anyone in to see Sophie except me until she's stable. But I'll go to Cassi's room before you leave and say good-bye."

"Thanks." Jared watched Grant walk away. His heart grieved for the older man as he recalled all too vividly his own agony when he had thought Cassi was dying. To be robbed of a companion so senselessly was a burden no man should have to bear. Jared bowed his head and said a silent prayer on Sophie's behalf. Like Cassi, guilt lay heavily upon his shoulders. Why hadn't he called Fred sooner, or the local FBI field office? Another question also tortured him. Why couldn't people just leave Cassi and him alone to live out their lives?

At the pay phone, Jared made the connection to America and Fred's office. *Please let him be in,* he prayed again. The secretary answered and immediately put Jared through. His hopes soared. Maybe now he could get some answers.

"Jared, where are you?"

"England. I—uh, there's been a problem." He quickly explained about the car bomb and all that they had been through in the past two days.

"I want you to stay right there," Fred said. "We'll have some of our boys there within the hour to give you some protection."

"What's going on, Fred?" For a moment, Jared felt his fear return. He hadn't felt it so strongly since Laranda had held him prisoner. But she was dead. He had seen her shot, and had later visited the morgue before she was cremated, just to be sure. He had thought being sure would help the nightmares.

"Holbrooke's dead. Killed right in his jail cell. Poisoned. A guard took in a letter for him, apparently without knowing what was in it."

Holbrooke dead, Holbrooke dead. The words reverberated in Jared's mind. "Who?"

"We don't know yet. We do have some suspicions, but the bottom line is that it could have been anyone with a grudge. And that's only the beginning. A total of eight relatives of Holbrooke's have died or disappeared in the last week. The only relatives we believe left are Sampson and his maternal uncle."

"Could he be the one who's behind it?"

"Yes. He is one of the suspects. He could definitely have been clearing the way for a permanent takeover. You know, offing the relatives who might object. However, it could be the competition as well, or some other relative we don't know about. It could even be someone else altogether. We don't have enough information to know yet. But one thing for sure is that the boy isn't safe, and neither are you while you're with him."

Thoughts of Sampson engulfed Jared. The boy had lost his father—perhaps because of his uncle, his only remaining close relative. How could Jared pass on that terrible news? The boy seemed to dislike Jared enough as it was, and this information would certainly not gain his trust. "No matter what, we want to stay with the boy," he said. "He trusts Cassi, and she won't desert him now. Besides, when they attacked us this afternoon, they didn't try to kill Cassi and me, they tried to drug us. Why would they do that if they were only after Sampson?"

"You have a point," Fred said. "Look, is there something you haven't told us?"

"Like what?" Jared let frustration enter his voice. "Fred, I've been honest with you down the line. I really don't know why these people are after us."

"Okay, relax. I just wanted to be sure you weren't keeping anything back. You know, there's that rumor of the paintings that were never recovered."

"I don't know anything about them. But you know, if I hadn't seen her cremated, I'd almost believe Laranda was behind this. It's her style."

"Impossible."

"I know."

There was a brief silence, and then Jared began to explain about the dam and the cabin. "Grant assures me no one could ever connect it to him. And we need to go somewhere we can feel safe."

"Where is it?"

"Portugal."

Fred chuckled. "Thought you'd had enough of that place."

"As long as Laranda isn't there, I'd love to go. It's a beautiful country."

"Yes, and out of the way enough not to be suspect. Okay, look, give me a few minutes to arrange things. Someone will be there shortly."

"I'll need a key word, a signal," said Jared. "They can show their badges, but I want to be sure they're from you."

"Hey, the leaks are sealed at this end," Fred assured him.

"I trust you. It's everyone else I have a problem with. How about this? The phrase, 'the Mormon temple.'"

"I'll pass it on." There was a trace of amusement in Fred's voice.

"All right." Jared paused. "And that reminds me, have you read that book I gave you?"

"The Book of Mormon? Well, Jared, I would, but you and Cassi have been keeping me too busy to read."

"Yeah, sure."

There was another long pause. "Take it easy, Jared. Be careful. I'd like to see you back here in one piece. And keep in touch. If you need me, call."

"Will do." Jared hung up the phone and made his way slowly back to Cassi's room. When he entered, she smiled at him and held out her hand. Sampson only glanced briefly in his direction and looked away again without acknowledging his presence.

"Sophie?" Cassi asked.

Jared shook his head. "She's not awake yet, but the internal bleeding has slowed. Grant says he'll come down to say good-bye."

"Is he all right?"

Jared understood the anxious question. "He's holding up."

"So are we going to the cabin?"

"Yes. Fred's going to send some guys from their office here to stay with us." He hesitated. "There's a lot more going on." Jared looked pointedly at the back of Sampson's head.

Cassi paled, and Jared knew she wondered if there was anything worse than what they had already been through that day.

"Sampson, would you mind getting me a drink of soda or something?" Cassi asked.

The boy glared sullenly at Jared. "I know you want to be alone, so just say it."

"Cassi and I have to talk over some stuff. You know, married people stuff."

Sampson jumped to his feet and stomped to the door. "I'm not getting a drink."

Jared watched the door close behind him.

"We shouldn't leave him alone."

"There's a policeman out there. I asked him to keep an eye out for him."

Cassi's eyes never left Jared's face. "What is it?"

"Holbrooke's been murdered."

Cassi gasped. "Oh, no! Poor Sampson. How?"

"Poisoned in his cell. I don't know the details, but it was definitely murder. How are we going to tell him?"

"I wish we didn't have to—yet. But he has the right to know. I'll tell him." Cassi's voice was resolute, and Jared was tempted to let her do just that, but his conscience refused to go along.

"Maybe I'd better do it," he said. "After all, the child already hates me."

"I think he's just a little jealous, that's all. But maybe we can tell him together. It won't be easy for Sampson to learn that his father is dead, especially if his uncle was the one who killed him."

There was a gasp at the door, and they both turned to see Sampson staring at them, his face white. He held a can of soda pop in his hands, which fell to the floor with a crash. "No!" he shouted. "No!" In an instant he was out the door. Cassi tried to rise, but fell back weakly.

"I'll get him." Jared ran for the door. They had made a serious mistake by not being careful to make sure Sampson didn't overhear. *Another mistake in a series of mistakes,* he thought. And now he had to stop the boy before he ran into the wrong hands . . . and ended up in a grave like his father.

CHAPTER 7

The policeman stood uncertainly by the door to Cassi's room, as though not knowing what to do about Sampson's departure. "He went down there," the man said with relief when he saw Jared.

Jared ran down the hall and turned the corner, catching sight of Sampson as he ducked into a room. At least he hadn't run outside the hospital where anyone could be waiting to abduct him or worse. He thought of Holbrooke being murdered in his cell. How could it have happened?

The room Sampson had chosen was dark and apparently empty. Glancing at the vacant beds, Jared knew they were in a patient room that was currently not in use. How many rooms had the boy looked into before he found this one?

"Sampson?" Jared whispered. There was no answer. "Look, I know you're in here. I saw you open the door and come in. Now, come on out so we can talk about it."

Still no answer. "Sampson, please. I know it was a shock finding out about your father that way, and I can't begin to imagine what you're going through. But can't you let me talk to you? Don't you want to know what happened?"

A sob erupted from the far side of the room. Jared took a few steps, grateful that his eyes were quickly adjusting to the shadows. A shuttered window in the far corner allowed a few rays of evening light to filter into the room. In one of these, Jared spied the edge of Sampson's tennis shoe. The boy was under the bed nearest the window. Jared approached cautiously. When Sampson didn't move, he knelt down and peered at the boy.

Sampson was curled into a tight fetal position, his hands clamped over his ears. Jared couldn't be sure, but he thought he saw a gleam of dampness on the boy's face. Soft, racking sobs came from Sampson's chest.

What should I say? Jared didn't know how to give him comfort. Cassi would know. What would she do? Jared lowered himself to his belly. "Sampson?"

"No! He's not dead! You're lying!"

At least the boy could hear him. "I'm sorry. Cassi and I are both sorry. We would do anything to give him back to you."

The hands fell from Sampson's ears. "You were the ones who put him there in the first place. And you're liars. You said you were going to talk about married stuff. But you lied."

Jared was surprised. "It may seem that way to you, Sampson, but that's what married couples do. They talk things out before they talk to their children or other people. We only wanted to tell you in the best possible way. We care about you."

"Ha!" There was a weight of hurt and anger in the boy's utterance. "When I tell my dad what you—" He broke off with a tortured cry. "Oh, Daddy, Daddy." The moaning chant was too painful for Jared to hear. How much more the child must be feeling!

Jared scooted closer to Sampson. He reached out and gently placed a hand on the boy's shoulder, but Sampson recoiled at his touch. "I know it doesn't make much sense, Sampson, but your father isn't gone forever. There's a place a person's spirit goes after death, and he's there waiting for you."

According to Jared's belief, the mobster would eventually receive his earned reward, which, given the terrible things Holbrooke had done during his lifetime, wouldn't make his future very promising. But Sampson couldn't possibly understand that at this minute, could he? And if he did, the understanding wouldn't bring comfort. In Holbrooke's favor, Jared did believe strongly that he had loved his son, and that Sampson would have the opportunity to see his father again one day. It might not be the reunion the boy would dream about now, but perhaps an older and wiser Sampson could come to terms with what kind of man his father had been.

"You see, Sampson," Jared continued, "this isn't the end of life. It's only the beginning."

The boy's sobs halted momentarily. "Mom used to say that. And I can think of her in heaven. But Dad—" The tears were back in full force. "Dad did things Mom said weren't . . . I heard him talking sometimes with people—" Again he broke off, and Jared felt his pain. Jared had underestimated Sampson. He understood, better than Jared had expected, the concept of death and hell. And while Sampson admired his father and craved his love, he knew deep inside that his father hadn't been a good person.

Thoughts rushed through Jared's head. How long had the child battled with these contending emotions? Hadn't Holbrooke seen the internal conflict? How had he felt about what he was doing to his son? Had he hoped that age would blot out his innocence and win him over to the dark side? How could any man want that for his son? Perhaps only someone who denied God. And perhaps such a person was better gone from the boy's life.

Jared felt pity and compassion fill his heart. "Sampson, it's going to be all right. I promise. You will see both your parents again. Beyond that, it's hard to say. But you *will* see them. And until then, Cassi and I are here with you. We're not going anywhere without you." Jared tentatively reached out to Sampson again. This time the boy didn't draw away. Jared pulled him to his chest and together they lay under the bed and held each other, Sampson's tears wetting Jared's shoulder.

"How—how did it happen?" Sampson sobbed.

Jared told him the scant details that he knew. Sampson cried harder, but continued to let Jared comfort him.

"It wasn't my uncle. It wasn't! He doesn't like Dad, but he wouldn't do that."

"I don't know, Sampson. I hope you're right. I really do."

Gradually Sampson's tears eased, and his slight body stopped shaking. He pulled away from Jared, but slowly as though reluctant. Without putting it into words, Jared knew something had changed between them—something for the better.

"We'd better go see Cassi," Jared said. "She'll be worried. Besides, you and I have some fishing to do in that cabin by the dam. What do you say?"

They crawled out from under the bed. For Jared, maneuvering the tight space was more difficult, and Sampson was already opening the door to the room before Jared made it to his feet. He followed the boy down the hall and around the corner. Sampson didn't look at him. Jared sensed he was still close to tears—and slightly embarrassed by his newfound trust in Jared.

Sampson stopped abruptly. "That doctor going into Cassi's room. I don't remember seeing him, but he looks familiar."

Jared gazed down the hall and saw the man in the doctor's smock. He also looked familiar to Jared, though he was too far away to pinpoint the memory. Before entering the room, the man nodded to the policeman, who was talking with a nurse by the door. Jared sprinted down the hall, Sampson on his heels.

He entered the room just as the doctor pulled something from his pocket. Jared saw the gleam of a needle as the door closed behind him. "Stop!"

Cassi looked up, startled. "He's just giving me something for the dizziness. Jared, what's . . .?"

At that moment the doctor whirled on Jared, raising the needle between them. Recognition filled Jared's mind: it was one of the thugs who had drugged Cassi earlier! The one who had escaped!

Jared dodged the attack. From the corner of his eye, he saw Cassi struggle to her feet and slump to the floor. Had the thug already given her another dose of the drug? One more potent than a mere sleeping mixture? Jared also caught a glimpse of Sampson frozen in terror against the door, his white face splotched by red from his earlier tears.

The thug's grin mocked Jared, and the watery eyes promised revenge. Jared tried to call out, but the thug's fist met his stomach, silencing him. The shiny needle came down for another pass. Jared jumped, kicking the hand holding the needle, and heard the syringe land somewhere in the room. Then the man was on top of him, easily outweighing him by fifty pounds. Jared tried to fight, but obviously the attacker had been better trained. Whoever had sent him knew that Jared had learned kickboxing and had made sure the thug knew all the counter moves. On the street Jared had been lucky, but now surprise wasn't on his side.

Again Jared tried to call to the policeman outside the door. Just one scream and the man should come running, despite the pretty nurse who conversed with him. Was she in on this attack? But the thug punched Jared each time he opened his mouth, and the air rushed out of him, leaving enough for only a weak gasp.

Jared broke away from his opponent long enough to land a solid kick on the man's knee. He heard a crunch, but the man didn't falter. What was he made of? Steel?

Glancing sideways, Jared saw Cassi struggling to her feet. She must not have received the new drug! Hope surged in his heart. There was still a chance to get away. She raised the plastic pitcher of water from the table by the bed and flung it at the thug. The plastic split on the back of the man's head, and the water soaked him, but he didn't appear fazed. One foot shot out and slammed into Cassi, knocking her into the wall. She slid to the floor and sat without moving.

Enraged, Jared fought harder. He jabbed his fist at the man's face and again heard something crack. Hoping it wasn't his own fist, he punched again. A cut appeared on the man's cheekbone, dripping blood. *There, he's not a machine,* he thought. A second later pain exploded in Jared's shoulder where months ago he had been shot. Another pain discharged in his head, and he lost his footing and fell. The thug jumped on him, fists swinging. Jared held up his hands to ward off the blows, praying for relief.

The man raised a massive fist, and Jared knew this one might be the last he could take. Abruptly, the man's mouth opened and the fist fell, but missed Jared completely. The thug slumped forward, sprawling on top of him.

Behind the limp body, Jared saw Sampson. The boy was trembling; in his hand he held the needle, its syringe now empty of fluid. Tears flowed down his face.

Jared saw Cassi moving in the corner. "Cassi?"

"I'm fine. And you?"

"All right." Jared heaved the stocky body off him and climbed to his feet, his moves deliberate and exhausted. He pried the needle and syringe from the boy's fingers. Then he hugged him. "You did good, Sampson. You just saved all of our lives."

"Is—is he dead?"

"I don't know."

The boy's voice turned ugly. "I want him to be dead. I bet he killed my dad." Underneath the ugliness in the childish voice was a terrible emptiness that Jared knew the boy needed desperately to fill. He hugged Sampson more tightly. "Come on, let's go call the policeman."

Jared walked weakly to the door and opened it. "Come in here! There's been an attack."

Surprise covered the policeman's face. He stared at the pretty nurse suspiciously before hurrying into the room. The nurse followed him. The policeman bent to check the thug's pulse while Jared gathered Cassi in his arms. She clung to him, and Jared uttered a silent prayer of thanks.

"I'd better call a doctor," the nurse said. She ran out the door and returned in less than a minute with a doctor and two other nurses.

"He's alive, but barely," Jared heard someone say. "Find out what was in that syringe."

Sampson sat on the bed, looking scared, alone, and more than a little defiant. Cassi motioned toward him, and Jared helped her sit next to the boy on the bed. She hugged Sampson, and tears began again on the already blotched face.

They watched as the doctor and his crew worked on the thug for what seemed an eternity. Jared prayed the man wouldn't die—not only for Sampson's benefit, but so that perhaps finally they would have some answers. At last someone brought in a stretcher and they took the goon away, still breathing. Sampson began to relax, but his face was dark and sullen.

The policeman stayed in the room. "I'm sorry. I really am. He looked like he belonged, like he was a doctor."

"It's all over now," Jared said. His initial anger at the man had faded. He kept an arm around Cassi. "Are you sure you're all right?"

"Yes. I knocked my head on the wall, but I'm not so dizzy anymore. But your face looks like it could use some stitches."

"I'll be all right."

A nurse they had seen before came in with the doctor who had been taking care of Cassi. Jared waved the nurse's ministrations aside. "We're leaving," he said to the doctor. "I've talked to the FBI, and we're going with them."

"In that case, I'll release her." The doctor glanced at the policeman. "Is that all right with you?"

"Yes. We'll work it out with the Americans." He looked at Jared. "I'll be out in the hall if you need me. I have to call this in."

The doctor looked at Jared's forehead. "You'd better let me stitch that for you."

Jared sighed. "Might as well. It seems we have the time."

Another hour passed before two well-groomed men in suits showed up at the hospital. One had pale blond hair, the other light brown. Both had blue eyes and were tall and built like runners. "Jared and Cassi Landine?" the blond man asked. At their nods, he continued. "I'm Special Agent Anderson and this is Special Agent Worthington. We're from the FBI's Legat office here in London. We've been briefed on your case and have cleared things with the local authorities. We can leave whenever you're ready."

"What's the code?" Jared asked.

"Well, we thought we might drive by the Mormon temple on the way to the airport."

Jared relaxed. "We're ready now."

Sampson made a move as if to speak, but said nothing.

"How's that guy?" asked Jared, guessing at the boy's unvoiced question.

Agent Anderson responded. "The one who attacked you here? Well, he seems to be in stable condition, but he's still out, so we haven't learned anything from him yet. He has a broken knee and a very damaged cheekbone, but the doctors say he had so many drugs in him to enhance his strength that he wouldn't have felt the pain at all. He would have kept at you until he succeeded or died trying." The agent's face turned grave. "There was enough sleeping drug in that syringe to put you both completely out. If he had given it all to Cassi, she would have died. He didn't die when Sampson gave him the drug simply because of his size and the contrasting drugs already in his system. We think he meant to give a portion of the drug to each of you, contact some hidden associates, and get you out of here."

Jared had been watching Sampson as the FBI agent spoke. At the news of the thug's survival, Sampson's dark expression lightened. But Jared also saw the guilt in his eyes that testified of conflicting emotions. Was he relieved the man hadn't died, but also feeling guilty for not managing to kill a man who might have been responsible for his father's death? What a terrible burden for a child!

There would not be much time now to help Sampson deal with everything that had happened. But perhaps at the cabin they could talk things out. For the first time since he had met the child, Jared found himself needing to help him. But how could he? What about the uncle?

I won't let him hurt Sampson, Jared vowed. But he didn't know how he could stop the uncle from taking legal custody now that Holbrooke was dead. He worried that after the transfer was made, Sampson would have an "accident" like the ones that had already claimed many of his relatives. Barring that terrible thought, would his uncle raise him to be a hardened criminal like his father? Jared found he couldn't deal with that idea either. A child should be loved and nurtured in truth. Sampson deserved at least that much.

Jared pulled his mind away from that poignant thought. "They certainly aren't giving up easily," he observed.

"No, they're not." Agent Anderson checked his watch. "That's why we're anxious to get you out of here."

"Well, what are we waiting for?" Cassi asked. With a hand on Sampson's shoulder, she arose. She stood unsteadily, but with the same determination Jared had seen when she had thrown the pitcher at the thug. "I'm ready. But I'd like to say good-bye to Grant first."

"I'll bring him here," Jared said.

Agent Worthington raised a hand to stop him. "I'll do that, if you don't mind. We aren't letting you out of our sight."

Jared watched the man leave. He put his arm around Cassi. "Some honeymoon."

Her dark eyes regained a spark of amusement. "It'll be something to tell the grandkids."

She was trying to be positive. Jared hugged her, but in his heart he wondered if they would live long enough to have children, much less grandchildren. Someone had it out for them and Sampson— someone who knew them very well. But who? And why?

CHAPTER 8

"So they're heading to Portugal!" Brooke exclaimed as Fred hung up the phone with Jared.

Fred looked up at Brooke in surprise. She peered over his desk at the notes he had written on a sheet of paper. He hadn't even realized that she'd left her chair in front of the desk. Her motions had been too fluid, too subtle. He placed his hands over the information, sighing in exasperation. "It's supposed to be top secret. If this information got into the wrong hands, do you realize how much danger Cassi and Jared would be in?"

"At least explain what happened to them. Did you say a car bomb?"

"Brooke, it's off the record. And you have no idea how many regulations I've broken even letting you hear part of the conversation at all."

"But we're partners."

"We're helping each other out, that's all." Fred saw her defiant expression and relented. "Look, since you already know most of it, I'll tell you what happened in England. But not a word to the papers yet. And certainly nothing about that cabin in Portugal. We're trying to keep them safe, not advertise their whereabouts to whoever is trying to kidnap them."

"I promise. It's for the book, that's all."

"For the book?" Justin cast an amused glance at Fred. "I thought you wrote for the paper."

"I do. But later on, this might make a good book." She brought out her tape recorder and turned it on. "Now, did you say someone tried to kidnap them?"

Fred turned the recorder off. "I did. But it's off the record."

"Well, in that case why don't we talk about it over at the café? It wouldn't take more than a minute to walk over. I haven't had breakfast yet, and I could eat something." She smiled at him and he felt himself smiling back. There was nothing more he would like to do at that moment than go somewhere alone with Brooke.

But there was the ring.

"I'll take care of things here," Justin said. He didn't laugh, but looked as though he might. "I'll work things out with the guys from London and call you on your cell phone if anything happens."

Fred knew Justin would have everything under control. "Okay. But they'll need the password, or Jared won't go with them."

"I don't blame him."

The matter settled, Fred walked to the door. Brooke caught up with him and put her hand on his arm. As they walked through the Federal Building and rode down the elevator, Fred felt people watching them. Or rather, watching Brooke. And probably wondering what she saw in him. *Let them wonder.*

At the café, they both ordered pancakes, bacon, and eggs—the true American breakfast. The waitress recognized Fred and winked at him. Fred nodded.

"It's nice being here with you like this, Fred," Brooke said. "I don't know what I expected when I first walked into your office, but you're different. I mean not bad different. But nice. I enjoy being with you." She looked away as though she had said too much. Fred felt a heat begin in his gut that had nothing to do with the warm food he had swallowed.

"You're different than I expected, too," he admitted. In fact, her presence was more intoxicating to him than any wine he had tasted. "But you are rather insistent." They laughed together, and an odd sensation of comfort spread through Fred. He relaxed as he had never been able to do completely with a woman. All at once he wanted to know Brooke. He wanted to find out her deepest thoughts. He wanted to learn what moved her, what was important to her.

All these things he communicated to her silently. He thought he saw in her eyes an echoing desire. Given time, perhaps they could become more than good friends.

There was still the ring.

Before he could ask, she smiled and spoke. "So tell me what happened."

Fred swallowed. The other question could wait.

* * * * *

Brooke Erickson whistled as she left the café. She had gathered more information than she had expected to find that morning. Too bad her promise to Fred wouldn't let her use it—yet.

In her car, she pulled out the small notepad she had seen on Fred's desk. She was sure it was Justin's pad from the day before—the one where he had written the name of the person whose organization Big Tommy was going to turn over as part of his plea bargain. Why it was on the desk she didn't know, but she hoped Justin wouldn't miss it soon. Maybe later, when she talked Fred into going out to dinner, she could throw it under his desk or behind a chair.

Guilt washed over her, but she shoved it away. It wasn't as if she was going to sell the information. She only wanted to help solve the case as soon as possible, and she knew she could get into places where the FBI wasn't welcome.

She flipped through the pad, and almost immediately found the name she was looking for: Nicolas Donelli. She knew the name as anyone interested in organized crime would. He wasn't as important as Big Tommy had been, but then he wasn't as free to act because people knew who he was and where he lived. Big Tommy, on the other hand, had been an ingenious front for Quentin Thomas Holbrooke's operation. Only his closest associates had ever known the identity of Big Tommy, and anyone else unlucky enough to stumble over the information met a sudden demise. After the case had been broken, the world had been shocked—for one day at least—to learn the man's true identity. For some, like Brooke, who had read about his public persona and ample donations to charitable causes, it had been difficult to believe.

Is that why I am so fascinated with this case? Perhaps partly. If she could be the first one to print the story of who was behind Holbrooke's murder, it would most likely make her career. But even more than with Holbrooke, she was intrigued by the woman who had engineered the whole disaster. Laranda Garrettson—what a mind! And she was also fascinated with Cassi and Jared, the Mormons who had saved the day.

Brooke suddenly found her thoughts going in quite another direction. Fred Schulte was a nice man, one that she found herself strongly drawn to. In the café, she had felt something she had never before let herself experience when it came to a nonmember. Of course, there was no question of a serious relationship between them, given their religious differences; but for a moment there, she had wished otherwise. Then again, maybe he would be receptive to learning about the gospel.

Regardless, she wasn't going to sit on the sidelines, safe and sound, while so much was at stake. No, she would go and see Nicolas Donelli herself and offer him this slim piece of news in exchange for any light he could shed on the situation. Brooke didn't feel guilty for planning to tell the mob boss that Holbrooke had been about to turn over enough evidence to destroy him. The FBI would confront him about the matter soon enough. At least this way, she might possibly find out something that would help the case. She would prove to Fred that she could pull her own weight.

* * * * *

"Any news from England?" Nicolas Donelli was usually assured of success from his best operatives, but this time the trail had been rather cold. They might just be on another wild goose chase.

"No news—yet," his nephew told him. "I should have gone with them."

Nicolas looked at the boy fondly. If he could have chosen a son, it would have been Giorgio. He was a little hot-headed, but that was to be expected, given his youth and his Italian blood. Giorgio had every quality that would make a good leader—unlike Nicolas' four daughters. Of course there was still time for a son from his new, younger wife; but if that never happened, he would be satisfied with Giorgio.

Nicolas rubbed his fingers under his tired eyes. "Don't worry, Giorgio, you will go in the next phase of my plan." He permitted himself a smile. "Meanwhile, with Holbrooke finally where he belongs, we have a lot of work right here to take care of."

There was a knock at the door. "Enter," Nicolas said.

One of his bodyguards appeared in the doorway. "There's a woman down at the gate. She says she needs to talk to you. Says it's urgent. About Holbrooke."

"Who is she?"

"A reporter. And a real gorgeous one at that."

Nicolas sighed. "Send her away. We don't give interviews."

"She doesn't want one. She says she's been working with the FBI and has some information for you. About who might've killed Big Tommy."

Nicolas rubbed his chin thoughtfully. He glanced at his nephew, whose heavy-lidded eyes were bright with the desire to act. Nicolas now had the chance to show him firsthand how to deal with the annoying press. Perhaps the display would temporarily satiate Giorgio's eagerness.

"Send her in, then," he directed. "We'll see how much she has to offer us. But I doubt it'll be worth the time."

They received their guest in the drawing room, but did not offer her a drink. "Thank you for seeing me," she said, sitting gracefully on the black leather sofa. "I'm Brooke Erickson of the San Diego Union-Tribune."

The woman was indeed beautiful. Her short, golden-blonde hair was well-groomed, her skin smooth and flawless, the large pale-blue eyes intense, her figure perfect. Nicolas noticed Giorgio's interest. How old was the boy now? Thirty? Perhaps it was time to find him a wife.

"You said you had information for me."

The reporter smiled. "I do indeed, but I would like an exchange."

"How do I know it's worth my effort?"

"The FBI has important information regarding Holbrooke's death. I tell you how that affects you, and you tell me what you know about the poisoning."

As Nicolas stared at her, an idea crept over him. If his operatives in England succeeded, she would be perfect for part two of the plan. The hair was right, the bearing perfect. Of course the eyes were wrong, but that could be fixed. In fact, she was much better for the part than any of the other women his men had turned up. How convenient for her to come to him like this, asking for a deal. He could certainly use her.

"I think, Ms. Erickson, that something could be worked out between us. In fact, we may be more beneficial to one another than even you might imagine. But first, may I offer you a drink?"

"Oh, no thank you." She twirled the wedding band on her finger. "I'm working."

Nicolas frowned at the ring. If she was married, that might cause problems. But she was so close to perfect for the job that a husband might be a mere inconvenience. "So am I. But I do understand how important it is to keep a clear head. How about juice?"

"Well, all right. Thank you."

Nicolas looked at his nephew and made a swirling motion with his hand, a signal for the special addition to her drink. It was odorless and tasteless, and she wouldn't realize what was happening until it was too late. "Perhaps you could see to it, Giorgio."

If the reporter noticed anything odd about their exchange, she said nothing. Giorgio smiled, his teeth showing white in his dark face. "Sure, I'll take care of it."

* * * * *

Fred hung up the phone after talking to the Legat office in London. In England it was very late, past midnight, but they were also still working on the case. They had traced the thugs from France, but still knew nothing of who hired them. Fred worried that their lawyer would be able to free them before they spilled the information. Once out of custody, he knew they would immediately disappear.

At least he was satisfied that Jared and Cassi were on their way to the safe house in Portugal. Somehow he would get to the bottom of this mess. He would begin by confronting Nicolas Donelli this afternoon. There was no way the man could know how much Holbrooke had talked before his death, and they might be able to use that against him.

Justin came in the door, fingering the pocket in his shirt. "Have you seen my notepad?"

"You don't have it?" It was uncharacteristic of Justin to lose or misplace anything.

"No. The last time I remember having it was this morning, when we shredded the information about that guard. I set it on your desk. Then Brooke came and Jared called . . ."

Fred and Justin searched the room. "It's not here," Fred said. "Are sure you didn't take it?"

"Yes."

Fred sat in his chair. "Brooke!"

"You think she took it?"

"Yes. I think she may have." His heart sank as he spoke. Had he only imagined there was something special between them at the café? "She's all too eager for information."

"Did she leave a number?"

"No." That in itself was odd. What reporter didn't have a slew of business cards to hand out? "Let's try to find her. If she did take that pad, we're going to have a serious discussion."

"I'll call the paper." Justin looked up the number and placed the call. "Yes, this is Special Agent Justin Rotua with the FBI. I'd like to speak to one of your reporters, a Brooke Erickson. Yes, that's right. Or if you have a cell phone or pager number, I'll take that. What? Are you sure? Could you check again?"

Justin hung up the phone. "She's not there."

"You mean she hasn't checked in with the paper?"

"No. They claim no one by that name works there. I'm sorry."

Fred stifled his irritation. Why should Justin be sorry? That a beautiful woman had lied to him? It wouldn't be the first time. But why had she done it? And where was she now?

He mentally kicked himself for trusting her. Why hadn't he checked up on her in the first place? Just because she came touting a good story didn't mean she was legitimate. It was one of the first lessons he had learned in his short stint as a police officer.

"Let's do a complete background check on Brooke Erickson," Fred said. "I want to know where she lives, what she really does for a living, and even what she eats for lunch."

But hours later, they still knew little about Brooke Erickson. National phone records placed a woman by that name in a town called Lehi, Utah. Local driver's license records showed she was near the same age as the Brooke they searched for, though the picture was too poor for proper identification. Using that woman's social security number and digging deeper, they found that she had worked until two months earlier at the *Tribune*, a newspaper in Salt Lake City. The surrounding counties had no record of a birth certificate, meaning that she was most likely born somewhere else. She had no debts or outstanding warrants, or anything to mark her as unusual. Local police failed to contact her after repeated tries, nor had they been able to contact friends or relatives in the area. It was as if that Brooke Erickson and all she held dear had dropped off the face of the earth two months ago.

Fred wondered if this could be the same woman. But what if Brooke wasn't her real name at all? They would have to continue the search until they found a positive identifier.

"Utah is Mormonville," Justin said. "It could be her."

"But why lie to us? What's her game?"

"Maybe she'll come by tonight and we can ask her."

Brooke had said she'd come by after work. Fred had hoped to ask her out to dinner, and then to casually mention her ring.

"There were no marriage records for her in either Utah or Salt Lake counties," Justin said, as though reading his mind. But the words weren't convincing. Justin knew as well as Fred did how hard those things were to track without central records. It would take time to follow the paper trail backwards to find out who she really was. If there *was* a paper trail. People who didn't want to be found usually avoided anything on paper. Even with all the resources of the FBI, finding a person was sometimes very difficult. A needle in the proverbial haystack.

Fred sighed in frustration. "Let's put one of the guys on this and go back to work. Jared and Cassi are our priority now."

"What would you like me to do?"

"Check out Brohaugh again. See what he's been doing these last twenty-four hours. Meanwhile, I'm going to pay Donelli a personal visit." He wanted specifically to see if Brooke had visited him. It would have been just like her.

Nicolas Donelli was a big man without being fat. He had a square, fleshy face, a large nose, and exotic Italian features that exuded confidence. He had the servants usher Fred into his house without hesitation. Fred took the proffered seat on a sleek black leather sofa. "I'm here because of Quentin Holbrooke's sudden death," he stated without preamble.

"Yes, I read about it in the papers," Donelli said.

Fred thought about how Brooke had pretended to be planning to give that information to her paper. What kind of scam was she running?

Donelli poured himself a glass of red wine from the coffee table between them. He didn't offer any to Fred. There were a few used glasses already on the tray. Had Brooke taken a drink with him? No, she didn't drink alcohol—or was that, too, a lie?

"But what I don't understand," Donelli said into the silence, "is what Holbrooke's death has to do with me."

Fred smiled without mirth. "He was going to put you out to dry. He had enough dirt to completely sink your organization." Now the gamble. "I've seen enough that he would have done it, too."

"So you think I killed him." There was no surprise in Donelli's eyes or voice. Someone had already told him about Holbrooke's plea bargain. Brooke? Fred winced inwardly at the possible betrayal. *Take it easy,* he told himself. Donelli could just as well have gleaned the information by other means. That was Fred's premise, after all: Donelli had to know what Holbrooke planned before deciding to kill him. *If* it had been Donelli who ordered the murder. That was not yet certain.

"I assure you, I had no reason to kill Holbrooke," Donelli continued. "He was safe enough in prison, in my opinion. Besides, I have nothing to hide. He couldn't hurt me."

Well, he can't now, that's for sure. Fred forced a smile. "The FBI has been speaking to a few reporters. One was headed over here. A woman. Brooke Erickson."

"Yes, she was here. A very insistent, beautiful lady."

"That's the one."

"She left about an hour ago. I didn't have anything to tell her, just as I don't have anything to tell you."

There was a movement at the door, and for the first time a frown passed over Donelli's dark features. "What is it, Giorgio?"

Fred craned his neck around to see a young man with a strong family resemblance. There was a fresh scratch across the man's right cheek. Giorgio glanced at Fred, then away quickly. "It's done."

"How long?" Donelli asked.

"A few days, maybe longer."

"Okay then, you know what to do."

The younger man left and Fred stared at Donelli, a clear question in his eyes. "Business, huh?"

"Yes. My nephew is young, but he has a good head on his shoulders. That's vital in the importing business. Now, was there anything else, Mr. Schulte?"

Fred stood. "No. Nothing. Thanks for seeing me." He crossed to the door. "And what was it you said you were importing?"

"I didn't." Donelli's smile was like ice. "But since you are so curious, we import wines. Mostly from France. I suspect you already know this."

Fred had known, but it didn't hurt to pry. "Oh, right. Well, have a good day."

A servant appeared to show Fred to the front door.

The day progressed, and there were no leads on the case or news about Brooke. Dinnertime came and went. Fred began to worry. He had a feeling in his chest that told him something terrible had happened to her.

"Well, what did you find at Brohaugh's?" Fred asked Justin.

"He wasn't there, and they wouldn't tell me where he went. The men he left in charge seemed very uneasy."

"You think Brohaugh's disappeared like the others?"

"No, it wasn't that. But when I asked them about Brooke, just to see if she'd been around, I got the feeling they were definitely hiding something."

Fred had suspected that something bad would come out of Brooke's impulse to visit Brohaugh. "I wonder if she upset Brohaugh yesterday." She certainly seemed to have a way of upsetting people. "I wonder if he decided to do something about her. He could have easily had her followed and abducted."

"I don't know."

"Better check the morgue."

Justin nodded and set about that grim task.

Fred called to see if the agent he had assigned to the case had found more information on Brooke. He hadn't. But one thing seemed to be sure: Brooke—if that was even her name—was definitely missing.

CHAPTER
9

Cassi relaxed between Jared and Sampson in the backseat of the car. They had taken a commercial flight late Friday morning, and were now driving in a rented car toward the Alvito Dam. The dam was farther south in the Alentejo than Laranda had taken them in their previous visit to the country, and they had been assured by Anderson and Worthington that the weather would be great for fishing, boating, and swimming.

Anderson was at the wheel and Worthington studied a map. Cassi was glad to leave it all to them. At least if they were in another car chase, they would be protected by the men's weapons.

Sampson was sound asleep, his head in Cassi's lap. In repose, the child's face looked calm instead of tortured as he had since learning of his father's death. She stroked his blond locks and hoped the cabin really was the safe haven they expected. Sampson needed time to heal.

At least there seemed to be no chance that someone would find out where they were, even in the case of a leak at the FBI. After the last incident with Laranda, Fred had gone to extreme measures to make sure his office wasn't bugged or his phone calls overheard. And not even Anderson and Worthington had been given the exact location of the cabin until they had arrived in Portugal. Both Jared and Cassi had insisted on total secrecy.

If only I had been so smart when it came to Grant and Sophie! Regret knifed through her. Why had they gone to England at all?

She had tried to tell Grant how sorry she was, but words hadn't been adequate. "I don't blame you, Cassi," he had said when he had come to say good-bye.

"No, but I'm responsible all the same."

He had hugged her like the second father he had always been. "I love you, Cassi, and that will never change. And I love Sophie. Even if I lose her now, the hardest thing I can imagine, it won't be for forever. The gospel is still true." His words of strength temporarily lightened her guilt, but if Sophie died, Cassi didn't know if she could forgive herself.

Sighing softly, she bowed her head in prayer. Jared had his arm behind her back, and now Cassi felt it tighten around her. He bent and kissed her cheek. She leaned into him, enjoying the contact. "I thought you were asleep," she whispered.

"I was trying, but my mind is too busy thinking. I keep wondering who's behind all of this. The only one I can think of is—" His voice lowered. "—Sampson's uncle or another Mafia guy. But even in that case, I don't know why they want us. Anyone who knew where to look for Sampson would have known we weren't responsible for his being here, and we should just be someone to get out of the way. But that's not the case. Whoever was after us in England wants us, but doesn't want us dead. Why?"

"I've been thinking too," Cassi said. "What if there's more than one group after us? I mean, those guys in France shot real bullets, didn't they? The bullet holes in Zack's car certainly looked real."

"They were," Jared said grimly. "I don't know what to think."

"At least we're safe now."

"But I keep coming back to the fact that the only person who holds such a terrible grudge against us is Laranda. If I didn't know better, I'd say it was her."

Cassi felt her heart beat faster. "But she's dead! We both saw her."

"And I went to her cremation. But none of it makes sense without her."

"It's just because of Sampson and Quentin," Cassi said. "Maybe now that he's d—" She broke off, glancing at Sampson. "Maybe now it'll be over. Still . . . I wonder. Could Sampson have a tracer bug on him?"

Jared shook his head. "One that works over such distances? Hardly likely."

"They did it before. Remember the bug Carl found in the phone card Quentin gave me? That was a pretty strong one."

"Yes, but they must have had people spread out looking for you everywhere in order to catch the signal. They knew that if you had the envelope, you would go to France. I'll bet they were watching all the international airports, waiting for you to get close enough for the signal to work. And when you first disappeared, I bet they followed you out of sight, just in range of the signal. That would explain how they followed you to Provo."

"They could be doing that now with Sampson. Maybe that's how they found us in England."

Jared looked at the sleeping boy. "His clothes are all new. Except his shoes."

Cassi eyed the tennis shoes on the carpeted floor where Sampson had discarded them the minute they settled in the car. She picked them up, but didn't see anything unusual.

Jared raised his voice. "Hey guys, at the next town, find a shoe shop, would ya? I think Sampson needs some new shoes."

If the FBI agents thought the request odd, they didn't say anything. And Sampson, once awake, was only too eager to use his credit card again. For the first time, Cassi was glad Quentin had equipped his son with a credit card that would be difficult to trace. Even if someone very powerful were looking for them, they would never connect the number to Sampson or them.

While Jared and Sampson were in the small shoe store with Anderson, Cassi stayed by the car with Worthington. She went through all of the clothing in Sampson's new suitcase—only slightly damaged from the car explosion—and then hers and Jared's, just to be sure. She even thumbed through the Book of Mormon Sophie had given her the day before. When Sampson returned to the car, she asked to see his wallet.

"Come on," she said when he balked, "I just want to see those Swiss bank account numbers you said you had."

To her surprise, Sampson cracked a smile. "Okay." He handed her the wallet, and Cassi made a point of exclaiming over everything as she thoroughly searched for a bug. She saw nothing but papers, several credit cards, and a wad of American greenbacks—all apparently given to Sampson by his father.

Satisfied, she sat back and relaxed for the rest of the drive. Lush green trees and meadows lined the side of the freeway. They often went miles without seeing another car. "Look, those are olive trees," Jared pointed out to Sampson.

"Cool," he said. "I don't remember seeing one before."

Cassi was surprised. Maybe the little know-it-all was finally willing to learn something from Jared. She was glad their relationship seemed to be changing. From the grin on Jared's face, he was, too.

They stopped to eat in a restaurant in a city called Évora, then continued on to their destination, arriving well before dinner. The cabin had two rooms, a main one with an old woodstove and another that had been used as a small bedroom. "Not much room for privacy," Jared whispered in her ear.

At least the cabin was clean and the main room spacious. There was a square table and a worn sofa that was actually a double bed. Cassi saw no sink or running water, but the pump outside seemed new enough and the water flowed clear. Mismatched dishes sat stacked in a worn freestanding cupboard. Buckets were piled by the door, inside a large metal bin that looked as if it might serve as both a bath and a sink for dirty dishes.

The cabin had two windows, one near the front door and the other facing the body of water behind the cabin. Only a glimpse of the blue water could be seen through the thick trees.

Sampson spied the water and took off running. The adults followed just as quickly. "Look! A boathouse," Sampson yelled. "A boathouse!"

"Wait!" shouted Worthington. He sprinted up to the tiny, rough-looking house near the lake. His hand was on his weapon, but he didn't draw. As with the cabin, the door opened with one of the keys Grant had given them. Worthington was back outside in less than a minute. "All clear," he said. "They have some cots inside, if we need them."

"Neat. I never slept on a real cot before. But what about a boat? They've got to have a boat." Sampson shot inside before the agent could answer.

Cassi heard a loud metal clang. "We'd better go help him," she said.

"We'll check out the rest of the area," Anderson stated. He motioned to Worthington, and the two walked into the trees. But

Cassi noticed that at least one of the agents kept them in sight at all times. As soon as they returned, Sampson insisted on putting the canoe he had found into the water. Jared, Cassi, and Anderson helped him lug the canoe down the short dock to the water. Sampson jumped inside.

"Wait, you need a life jacket," Cassi said.

"I told you I know how to swim."

Cassi met his defiant stare. "Look, I once had a friend drown in waist-deep water when he was jet-skiing. He was twenty years old and over six feet tall. A real strong guy. He still died. Now, make up your mind. Are you boating with a life jacket, or are you not boating?"

Sampson's gaze wavered. He jumped out of the canoe and ran up the dock. In minutes he came back carrying an arm load of orange life preservers. Cassi and Jared each put one on.

"I'm going to find a town to buy groceries," Worthington said. "Any requests?"

When he was gone, Sampson threw Anderson a life jacket. "That canoe doesn't look big enough for more than three," said Anderson. "I'll watch from here." He settled against one of the huge posts that held up the dock, his blond hair reflecting the late afternoon sun.

The canoe could have easily fit one more, but Anderson was kind to let them have a few moments of privacy. Cassi climbed into the canoe and settled in the middle. Still feeling weak from the trip and from her ordeal the day before, she was content to let Jared and Sampson use the oars. Jared also looked weary, his face sporting stitches on his brow. Cassi knew he had numerous bruises from his fight with the thug the day before and must be in some pain. That didn't stop him from having a contest with Sampson to see who could row the strongest on their side of the canoe, turning the boat. Jared won, but eased up to make the victory not so apparent.

The day was beautiful and peaceful, the air clear. Birds called in the trees, and occasionally Cassi caught glimpses of other small animals. She could almost believe that the past few days had simply been a bad dream, and that this peaceful reservoir was the only thing real.

"Let's go to the other side," Sampson urged.

Jared gazed at the far shore, dismay on his bruised face. Cassi squinted through the sunlight reflecting off the water. Even the trees

looked small. She knew from the map that it was not the other side of
the dam they were looking at, but the other side of one of the fingers
of the dam. Not the thinnest part to cross, but much closer than actually rowing all the way to the other side. She wasn't about to enlighten
Sampson. "Maybe we should go back and see if Worthington's come
with the food. I'm hungry."

"Me too," Jared said.

Sampson darted one last longing glance at the other shore. "Well,
I guess we can do that tomorrow. I could use some food."

Jared gave Cassi a pained look, as though he wasn't looking forward
to such a long row. His muscles must be more sore than he was letting
on. She hoped Worthington remembered the Tylenol she had
requested, since Jared would be needing it. From experience, she knew
that practically every European country sold that brand of painkiller.

"And tomorrow we'll also go swimming. And fishing—I saw some
poles in the cabin. My dad and I—" Sampson broke off, the terrible
loss and pain returning to his face. He looked away and put his effort
into rowing. Cassi wanted to reach out to him, but refrained. Better
to let him recover on his own for a few minutes as they went toward
the shore.

At the dock, Anderson moored the canoe and Sampson jumped
out. "Help me, Sampson," Cassi said. The boy held out a hand, and
Cassi grabbed it and stepped onto the dock. Her motions almost
made the canoe tip.

"Whoa," said Jared. "Are you trying to knock me into the water?"

Cassi laughed. "No, that's for tomorrow."

"You have to keep your weight centered on either side of the
canoe." Sampson jumped back inside to show her. He walked up the
length of the canoe, hardly rocking it at all.

Cassi already knew that. Hadn't she been to girls' camp with the
Young Women? But she smiled. "That's great, Sampson." He
jumped back on the dock and Cassi put an arm around him. "I'm
glad you're here."

He flashed her a grin, and Cassi saw that his pain had faded once
again.

They left the oars on the canoe, and the life jackets as well,
tucking them into a small tarp they found in the boathouse. Grant

had told them that there was little or no theft in the quiet community, which was just as well since they didn't look forward to hauling out the heavy boat each time they wanted to use it.

The sound of a car cut through the peaceful silence. Cassi instinctively froze, her heart racing. In a minute, they saw Worthington coming down the trail.

"He's back. Yeah, food!" Sampson said. The boy took off at a run.

Cassi breathed a sigh of relief. Why was she so worried? This was supposed to be a safe house.

Jared moaned softly. "I hope he brought the Tylenol." Cassi put her arm around him and together they walked up the path, Anderson trailing them.

They helped bring the groceries into the cabin. Only the few packages of meat and cheese needed refrigeration, and for these Worthington had purchased a chest and several blocks of ice. He and Anderson lit the stove and began frying steaks, while Jared gratefully took two Tylenol.

They ate out on the porch, lounging on the few chairs or on the steps. A slight breeze began, but it wasn't uncomfortable. "I could get used to this life," Jared whispered. They sat apart from the others on an old wooden bench near the left edge of the porch.

"Me too. But I do miss the gallery." Now that Cassi had inherited Linden's gallery, she was anxious to try some innovations that she'd had in mind for years—including free art classes for young children.

"Yeah, I know what you mean. But things at the gallery are fine. They aren't expecting us back for another week and a half."

Cassi knew their manager was competent, and she had promoted one of the other buyers to take her old position as head buyer. Yes, things were under control and would go on without them. But she missed the work. Most of all, she missed the ordinariness of her old life. Why couldn't people leave them alone?

"That was a great story you told Sampson about the life jacket. I'm sorry about your friend. But at least maybe his death taught people to use their life jackets."

"But that's just it," Cassi said, her voice low. "I didn't tell the whole story. He *was* wearing a life jacket. They still had to drag the lake. He was found in a large area where the water was only waist deep. He was trapped under. I don't know how. It was such a waste."

Jared put his arm around her. "Sometimes it's so hard to understand why things happen."

Exactly. For instance, why was this happening to them now? She looked at Sampson's face in the fading light. Was it all because of him, or was there some other reason?

"It's getting dark," Worthington said. "We'd better go inside and get some sleep."

"Aw, didn't you get marshmallows?" asked Sampson. "The guys at school say they always get marshmallows when they go camping."

"They don't have marshmallows in Portugal," Worthington said. "At least not at any of the stores I've visited."

"And he's the Portuguese expert in our office," Anderson said, climbing to his feet. "You notice that he was the one who went in for the groceries. Me, I know England. They speak my language."

The others laughed. Cassi stood and picked up her plate to go inside.

A snapping twig was all the warning she had that something was amiss, and then two armed men sprang up on either side of the porch. "Hold it right there. No, don't reach for your guns or you're dead."

* * * * *

When the man with the dark blue jacket came from the back of the room, Brooke looked up from the video. He must have shown it to her a hundred times in the past twenty-four hours. She had it memorized, but even so the desire to see it again had been ingrained into her subconscious.

The man switched the large-screened television off, and the image faded. "So let's try it again," he said. "Stand up and walk across the room."

A part of Brooke rebelled, but her body arose from the hard chair and crossed the small room, which was dark except for the single spotlight above the TV. One, two, three—she counted the paces, already knowing that there would be twenty before she had to turn and walk back across the bare hardwood floor.

The man watched her. She knew he was a doctor, and with his help, she was becoming better than she had been before.

No! No! a voice inside screamed. Brooke's step faltered. In a moment the doctor was at her side, and something sharp pierced her arm. The voice inside faded.

"Don't listen to that person," the doctor told her. "You have been very sick. But you can conquer that other voice. It only wants to bring you down. You know who you are. You know what you have to do."

His voice went on, explaining things over and over again, reasonably, comfortingly. Vaguely, Brooke knew that hours had passed. Her stomach complained. "I'm hungry," she said.

"We'll eat soon. Just one more time. Listen to me."

Brooke listened. She had done well to employ him last year. Strange that she couldn't remember doing it. But he remembered, and he was helping her to remember, too. The attack had been severe, but she had recovered. And there would be revenge.

Again the internal voice surfaced, screaming denial. Brooke's breath came fast and hard.

"Just look at me," the doctor said. "Breathe deeply. Everything is okay." Again he injected something into her arm, and she sighed with relief.

The doctor's comforting voice droned on. "You'll be strong enough soon. And then tell me what you'll do. Use your old voice when you talk. Don't let that inner person take over. You are in control."

"And then I'll go to Portugal. To the cabin or thereabouts," Brooke said. Her voice was soft and subtle as silk. She caught and held the doctor's eyes, seeing that he was pleased with her words.

A door opened, and a slice of light came into the room from the corridor outside. "The clothing lady's here, and the hairdresser."

Brooke couldn't see the speaker, only his silhouette, but she was glad the hairdresser had been called. Her hair needed rearranging, and her fingernails were too short. She wanted them painted a bright red, with lipstick to match. And what was this thin band on her finger? She wasn't married, and if she had been, she would have insisted on at least a three-carat diamond. Slipping off the gold ring, she dropped it under the chair. It made a slight tinkling sound, but no one noticed.

The newcomer stepped into the dark room and shut the door behind him. Now she could see that he had olive skin and black hair and eyes, which seemed to never leave her. A large scratch covered his right cheek. "How's she coming along?"

"Better than expected," the doctor said. "It's good she hasn't built up a tolerance to drugs of any type. The ones I'm using work much better that way. And I don't have to give her too much—that could damage her permanently. These are, after all, experimental drugs."

The olive-skinned man shrugged, his dark, glittering eyes still on Brooke as though entranced. She abruptly recognized him, knowing that the scratch on his cheek had been caused by her own hand when he had tried to become too friendly. *Stupid,* she told herself. *I shouldn't have reacted so strongly.* He was attractive enough to look at, with that beautiful skin and those heavy-lidded eyes, and he obviously held some high level of esteem in his organization. She could put him to good use in time. Brooke waited for the voice inside to protest, but the doctor's needle had silenced it. She smiled. She was in control.

"Are you sure she's given you all the information she has?" the man asked the doctor.

"Yes. She doesn't know the address to the cabin, just its general whereabouts."

He rubbed his hands together. "It shouldn't be too hard to pinpoint. We have the boy's uncle under surveillance, and if he goes to Portugal, he'll lead us right to them. We will soon be ready to act."

"Not yet," protested the doctor. "It's too soon. Better I have six months. Then we could be assured of success."

"We don't have six months," sneered the other. "You were recommended because you could get the job done in a short time. You have two days left, at most."

"I will have to use more drugs. And more severe methods of hypnotism. Her spirit is strong."

"Use them."

Brooke knew they were discussing her. But she was really in control. Hadn't she herself made the video and set everything in motion? They acted now only as she directed. With fluid movements that were becoming more and more natural to her, she took a few steps until she stood in front of the dark man. Their bodies almost touched. Her arms went around his neck, and she kissed him slowly and deeply.

For a moment he didn't return the kiss, but then she felt him weaken. *Yes, he will be easy to control.* She drew away with a promise in her smile. His face was expressionless, but the turmoil in his eyes was easy to read. Child's play. She kissed her finger and gently touched the scratch, her lips drawn into the pout she had seen on the video. His jaw tensed as though he made a great effort at restraint. If the doctor hadn't been present, he would surely have put his arms around her.

"It seems she will be ready," the doctor said. He wore a small, amused smile.

Brooke laughed, a light, sultry sound that she had heard more than a hundred times in the past day. The tenseness in the olive-skinned man's face increased. "What is your name?" she asked him, ignoring the doctor, who after all was only a simple employee.

"Giorgio. And who are you?"

She laughed again, enjoying the way he reacted to the sound. It maddened him, made him want to hold her, to kiss her again, despite the doctor's presence. She had always had such an effect on men. She had always been in control. "Don't you know? Then it's high time we meet. I'm Laranda Garrettson."

CHAPTER 10

"Who are you?" Agent Anderson said to the men with the guns. The men looked into the dark, waiting. Neither spoke. Obviously they were hirelings.

Sampson looked at the men and backed away slowly to stand beside Jared and Cassi, fear written on his face. Jared put a reassuring hand on his shoulder. He pushed the boy slightly behind him. "If you get a chance, run to the canoe," he said softly. "We'll catch up with you. But don't wait for us. If we get separated, call Fred Schulte at the FBI." There wasn't time to tell the child how to go about doing that, but Jared knew the boy was resourceful and would find a way.

Anderson and Worthington had their hands poised, as though at any minute they would reach for their guns and pull them on the intruders. Jared exchanged a glance with Cassi. They would both be ready to escape if the chance came.

Lifting her head slightly, Cassi spoke. "What do you want with us?" Her voice was soft yet firm. Jared saw the lines of determination in her face.

"I want what is mine," came a voice from the dark.

They turned toward the new figure, nearly obscured by the increasing shadow. The man had dark-blond hair and hard, dark eyes. Draped around his shoulders was a long black coat, despite the warmth of the evening. He was about Jared's age but of average height and build. Jared knew he could take the man in a fair fight, but the gun he carried in his right hand didn't leave him that opportunity.

"Uncle!" The shout came from Sampson. He darted around Jared and threw himself in the man's arms. The coat slipped aside to reveal a sling around the man's left arm and shoulder.

"Are you all right, son?"

Sampson nodded. "Yes. I knew you'd come. Dad's dead, and . . ." Tears started down Sampson's cheeks.

"Yes, he's dead, but I'm here. I'll take care of you. We're family. We will go on." His voice was hard, yet Sampson still clung to him.

"Who are you?" Jared asked.

The man's hard eyes fixed on them. "I'm TC Brohaugh, Sampson's uncle. His mother was my sister. And now it appears that I'm the boy's only living relative."

"His father left him in our care," Cassi said. She didn't flinch under Brohaugh's glare.

"His father is dead, and any arrangement he had with you for temporary custody died with him. I am Sampson's legal guardian now."

"What if he doesn't want to go?" Jared knew the words meant nothing. Sampson obviously wanted to be with his uncle.

"Of course he does. We're family."

But would you give him what he needs? Jared desperately wanted to grab Sampson and run. In Cassi's eyes, he saw a similar emotion.

"How did you find us?" she asked. Jared knew she was stalling for time.

"We've been following you. My boys did lose you for a time in France after you left the cabin."

"You're the ones who shot at us?"

He shrugged. "I gave orders for my men to get Sampson at all costs. If you had turned him over, they wouldn't have tried to hurt you."

"Yeah, right," Jared murmured under his breath.

"Luckily, my brother-in-law had set up a way to track your whereabouts by Sampson's credit card. While Quentin was alive, the bank reported only to him. After his death, they came to me. That's how we knew you were in England. We heard about the car bombing and searched the hospitals. We've been behind you ever since." Brohaugh laughed. "It was simple."

So much for Sampson's untraceable cards. "You weren't responsible for the bombing?" Jared asked, swallowing hard. If Brohaugh represented the group that had shot at them in France, then obviously they didn't care if Cassi and Jared lived or died, just as long as they took Sampson.

"No. That was another party."

"Who?"

"You don't need to know."

Jared snorted. "I do if they're after us."

"Look," Brohaugh gave him an impatient stare, "all I'll tell you is that they tried to get you and Sampson in England, and for some reason I can't fathom, they abducted some reporter my men were following. That's it."

"So now what?" Jared asked, not pressing the issue further. "What happens to us? We've only been doing what your brother-in-law asked us to do."

Brohaugh glanced at Sampson, who looked up at him with enlarged eyes. "Why, we will reward you for your help. I think half a million for your interrupted honeymoon will be sufficient."

Did he really mean it? Jared thought. *Or was he going to kill them once Sampson was out of sight?* "But—"

"You want more?" Brohaugh's eyes glittered dangerously.

Jared shook his head. "I was only going to ask about your relatives who have died or have disappeared. Perhaps Sampson would be safer with us."

Brohaugh laughed. "They almost got you in England—twice, if my reports are correct. What makes you think they won't find you here? Of course they will. That's why I had to come first."

"You want to take over Holbrooke's operation." Jared knew he was treading on dangerous ground.

"I am his only living relative."

"No, Sampson is his son. So where does that leave you?"

Brohaugh didn't miss the veiled accusation. "I don't care what you think," he sneered, "but I tell you that I loved my sister very much. I admit that Quentin and I had our differences, but Sampson is Maura's son, and I care for him."

Jared didn't believe him for a minute.

Brohaugh turned to his thugs. "We're wasting time. They could be here soon. You know what to do." He put his hand on Sampson's shoulder. "Let's go."

"But my stuff, and I want to say good-bye."

Brohaugh looked as though he would like to say no, but he gave a curt nod. Sampson bounded up the porch steps and came to stand before Jared and Cassi. "Uh, thanks guys. I—I—" Tears gathered in his eyes, and Cassi put her arms around him.

"Look us up back home, okay? Come to the gallery. We'll be there." Sampson nodded and pulled away. Then he stuck out his hand to Jared. He didn't say anything, but stared at him for a long moment. In his eyes, Jared saw many things.

"I know," Jared said softly. He pulled Sampson's hand forward, enfolding him in a hug. After a brief moment, they pulled awkwardly away.

When Sampson went inside to get his things, Jared walked across the porch until he stood on the top stair above Brohaugh. Slowly, he descended the three steps. One of the thugs pointed his gun at his chest. "Easy," Brohaugh told his man.

Jared was taller than Brohaugh by at least six inches, and he could easily see the receding hair on the man's head. Jared raised a finger and pointed it at Brohaugh. "If anything happens to him, I'm coming after you, despite your goons. No accident, no sudden disappearance. I'll be watching you."

Brohaugh's face darkened in anger. He swore at Jared.

"Hell?" Jared asked. "Hell? No, Brohaugh, I've already been there. Your brother-in-law helped put me there, and I crawled out. I'm not afraid of you." Jared found he meant the words. He wanted nothing more than to live his life with Cassi, but he was involved with Sampson now, too. He wouldn't let him die.

Brohaugh met Jared's stare for a full minute, his jaw clenched. The tension was broken by Sampson, coming out of the cabin with his suitcase. Without another word, Brohaugh turned his back on Jared.

The silence was abruptly shattered as a man raced from the trees. "They're here," he shouted. "Must have followed us. They got Baker!" The man's eyes went suddenly wide and he fell at Brohaugh's feet, blood spreading from a bullet hole in his back.

Jared had heard but a small sound. *A silencer. They're using silencers.*

"Get inside!" Brohaugh hardly needed to utter the command as everyone jumped for the cabin door.

One of Brohaugh's thugs and Anderson fired into the darkness from the porch, covering the others. Simultaneously, both stiffened and fell to the ground. Jared stopped to help Anderson inside, but Brohaugh pushed him through the door. "Are you a fool? He's dead. There's nothing you can do."

A deep sorrow filled Jared's soul. He knew the mob boss was right, but he couldn't bring himself to be so callous. Anderson had tried to protect them.

Inside the cabin, the front window shattered. Worthington had his gun ready and used it to knock out some of the glass so he could fire better. Brohaugh's thug was on the other side of the window, shooting with him as though they held an unspoken truce. Their shots were loud in contrast to the silenced guns of their attackers.

"Is there a back way out?" asked Brohaugh.

Jared shook his head. "A window."

"It'll be watched."

The shooting intensified, and Jared wished he had managed to get Anderson's gun before he had come inside.

"Are you going to use that?" Cassi asked, pointing at Brohaugh's gun. Her eyes challenged the man as she held out her hand, asking for his weapon. With a glance at Sampson, Brohaugh went to the door, cracked it open, and began firing with his unhurt right hand.

How much ammunition did they have? Jared had seen the ammunition brought by the FBI agents, and even now Worthington was reloading for the second time. But did the bullets fit the mobsters' guns, or had they brought their own supply? As if in response to Jared's mental question, Brohaugh's remaining thug flipped in another clip, and Jared caught sight of many more on his belt. They had come prepared to fight someone—probably the FBI agents.

While Cassi and Sampson huddled together in the corner next to the cupboard of dishes, Jared began searching for something to use as a weapon, keeping his head low. Then all at once the shooting from the trees ceased. Uncertainly, those in the cabin stopped firing at targets they couldn't see.

"Send us out the Landine couple and the child," said a deep voice from outside. "The rest of you can go free."

"No!" screamed Brohaugh through the door. "The boy is not negotiable."

There was a long silence. "Then just the Landines. You can keep the boy."

Brohaugh's eyes were calculating. Jared saw that Worthington and the thug now had their guns trained on each other.

"No, Uncle! You can't let them be killed!"

Brohaugh's smile was grim. "Look, Sampson, you are more important than they are. Sometimes sacrifices have to be made."

Sampson's face took on a look of horror. "No!"

The plea bit into Jared's heart. "Brohaugh," he said, "sending us out there will only put Sampson in more danger. I suspect that for some reason those people want Cassi and me alive, at least if they're the same ones who were after us in England. They drugged Cassi; they didn't try to shoot her. Can you say they feel the same way about you and Sampson? What's to stop them from burning this cabin after we're out? Or using some other means to get in? Face it, we're your protection. Or was it you who was responsible for getting rid of Holbrooke and his relatives?" The words were a gamble. If Brohaugh had been responsible—as Jared thought he was—Jared's argument meant little. But if by some remote chance Brohaugh hadn't killed all or some of the relatives, then the people who had were outside the cabin at that moment, ready to do the same to him and Sampson.

Brohaugh's lips twisted in an ugly frown. He shook his head at his man, who immediately fired into the clearing. A shadow there fell, and the furious shooting began again.

Jared sighed, trying to digest this new information. Had Brohaugh been innocent all along? That wasn't a thought Jared was ready to completely entertain. Perhaps Brohaugh was just worried enough about those outside to keep Cassi and Jared for protection. He could have killed Holbrooke and the others and still be afraid. Or could he?

A man burst through the back window, followed quickly by another. Two more came through the front door, pushing Brohaugh back. Jared jumped on one of the men coming through the door. He saw the man raise his gun, then hesitate when he saw Jared's face. He fumbled at his chest for something else. Jared didn't wait to see what, but slammed his foot in the man's gut, followed by rapid punches. The man was strong, but Jared was faster. This was a fight he could win. But what about the others?

From the corner of his eye, he saw Worthington whirl on the first man who had come through the back window. Both fired and slumped to the floor. The second man through the window quickly bore down on Cassi and Sampson. Desperation filled Jared's mind. He had to help them. *Please, someone help them!*

Next to him, Jared saw Brohaugh grappling with another man, saw Brohaugh weakening as he tried to use his wounded arm. Jared spared a kick at Brohaugh's opponent, hoping to free the man enough so he could help Sampson and Cassi, then turned back to his own fight. To be of any use to Cassi, he must finish this now.

He landed two swift kicks to the man's knees and three punches, one to his stomach, the other two to his head. At some point, the butt of the man's gun hit Jared's shoulder, barely missing his head. Jared grabbed the gun from him and fired. A dart shot into the man's neck.

So this is what he had been searching for.

Jared turned to see if he was in time to help Cassi, but she held Worthington's gun at the man who had come after her. He raised his hands in defeat. Close to the door, Brohaugh stood over his opponent, gun in hand. But Brohaugh's hired man lay motionless by the front window. In two strides, Brohaugh crossed to the remaining intruder, who stood with his hands in the air before Cassi, and hit him on the back of the head with his gun. The man fell and lay still. Distaste swept over Jared.

But it wasn't over yet. Three more men rushed into the cabin. Two went down quickly with Brohaugh's and Cassi's guns. The third, who had come through the back window, pointed his weapon at Sampson and shouted, "Put down your guns or I shoot him now!"

Cassi lowered her gun, but Brohaugh made a growling noise in his throat and leapt in front of his nephew. A dull thud sounded, and Brohaugh moaned in pain. Jared used that moment to hit the intruder on the head with the now-empty drug gun he had taken from his first attacker. The man crumpled, but still breathed. Jared slammed the door shut and found the lock was broken.

"Uncle, are you all right?" Sampson plucked worriedly at Brohaugh's sleeve.

"Yeah fine," Brohaugh said through gritted teeth. "Just a little scratch."

"Let me see it," Cassi said.

The mob boss waved her aside. "I'm fine. Now let's get out of here."

"Henry?" came a voice from outside. "You got 'em?"

Jared stared at the lifeless bodies around him. Which one was Henry? Pity and nausea filled him. Brohaugh opened his mouth to say something, but Jared stopped him. "Let's play along," he whispered. Louder, he said in a grunt that he hoped resembled the man he had just hit, "Yeah. All done. Bring the car."

"But—"

"Hurry!" There was silence on the other side of the door, and Jared hoped the man believed him.

"Now what?" Brohaugh said. His teeth were still clenched, and Jared wondered if he had been hurt more than he let on. Why had he done it? Why had he sacrificed his own body for Sampson? Could it be that he really did love the boy?

Jared was beginning to believe it was true.

"Quick, out the back window!" Jared ordered. "Most of their guys are probably in here, or they would have kept coming. Even if there are more outside the window, they won't shoot. They don't want us dead."

"They don't want *you* dead," Brohaugh said.

Jared grabbed his arm. "If we hurry, we'll make it. We'll shield you."

Brohaugh tried to rise, then sank to the ground and groaned in pain. "I can't."

Jared tried to lift him, but Brohaugh pushed him away. "You go. Take Sampson. I'll hold them off. Make them think you're still here." He grabbed a fallen thug's gun and pointed it toward the door.

Jared hesitated.

"Go!" Brohaugh ordered.

"We can take you with us."

Brohaugh's gun focused on Jared. "Take Sampson to safety or I'll kill you myself. Is that clear?"

Jared nodded. "Come on, Cassi. Sampson." He sprang toward the back window.

"But, Uncle!" Sampson stared unbelievingly. Jared could only imagine what the boy was thinking. Could he see the death already creeping into Brohaugh's eyes? Death from a wound that had been meant for Sampson.

Brohaugh took Sampson's hand. "Go, boy. I'll be along later. Don't worry about me. I'm just going to teach these guys a lesson. Go now. And be a man." Sampson clenched his jaw, his eyes filled with tears. He nodded at his uncle and turned to the window.

Jared peered out. He could see nothing in the dark. How many were waiting out there for him? Or had most of them come inside? Jared didn't dare to hope that the man who had called for Henry had believed Jared's lie. It was only a matter of time until the enemy regrouped.

Taking a deep breath, Jared climbed out the window. He waited for the sting of a dart or a bullet. But there was nothing. Sampson came next, followed by Cassi. Behind them, they heard Brohaugh yelling at their attackers. "Get in here, you fools, and I'll give you what you came for! He let off a cacophony of shots and a few from the front echoed in reply. Brohaugh had their attention.

Jared thought he saw something move in the trees a few yards to his right. He grabbed Cassi and Sampson and shoved them to the left. As he did so, he heard a projectile slam into the cabin. It was impossible for him to determine if it was a real bullet or a dart full of sleeping drugs. So much for thinking the enemy had been fooled.

"Run!" he said to Cassi. She grabbed Sampson's hand and took off through the trees, dodging the shadows.

Jared also ran—smack into a man. A large hand grabbed him, and Jared knew that in the man's other hand was a gun. If he didn't act, he would soon be dead—or sleeping like a baby. His foot came up and hit the hand with the gun. An answering fist slammed into Jared's stomach. This man was strong, at least as strong as the man in the hospital. Was he also full of strength-enhancing drugs?

Jared knew there was no way to win a fight with such a man. He just needed to distract him enough to . . .

Suddenly the thug fell. Jared had heard a shot but hadn't understood what it was until his opponent collapsed. Jared glanced at the back window of the cabin and saw a shadow. Brohaugh. He must have struggled to the window so he could make sure Sampson got away. Taking a shot like that had been risky because he could have so easily hit Jared, but the man had succeeded. Jared waved a hand in thanks before running after Cassi. He heard shouts coming around the sides of the cabin.

Reinforcements? From which side?

Jared felt something whiz past his head. Well, that answered his question. Redoubling his efforts, he ran at top speed, zigzagging through the trees in a random pattern, heading toward the water. Hopefully, Cassi and Sampson were already in the canoe.

Near the dock, Jared saw a man sitting on the ground, writhing in agony as he grabbed his upper left thigh. Jared smiled grimly. Cassi must have held on to Worthington's gun. He only hoped there weren't more attackers en route to the boat. "Which way did they go?" Jared demanded.

The man pointed, then gasped as he recognized Jared. "You!" He tried to leap for Jared. Dodging the grasping hands, Jared sprinted toward the water. He had expected the moonlight to reflect off the water, but clouds had moved in, leaving everything dark.

Finally, he reached the dock. His feet clumped noisily on the wood. "Cassi?" he called, eyes searching.

"Here!"

He saw them several feet off the dock, in the canoe. Sampson was at the oars, and Cassi held her gun ready. Jared was glad he had called out so she hadn't hit him by mistake. He picked up speed and jumped, hoping he had enough energy to make the canoe.

His feet landed with a loud clanging sound, and the canoe rocked as though it would overturn. "Row," Jared told Sampson, reaching for one of the oars himself. If Jared could make the jump in his weakened condition, so could another man.

His pursuers had already arrived on the dock. One prepared to make a leap, but Cassi let off a shot into their midst. Her gun was answered by others, and several darts clinked into the sides of the metal canoe and into the water, their sound distinct from regular bullets. But already Jared seemed to be pulling out of the darts' shorter range. Cassi kept the men from following by shooting until she had no more bullets left.

"Sampson!" Cassi gasped. Jared saw that the boy lay motionless in his place at the front of the canoe. She pushed past Jared, rocking the small craft dangerously, and knelt by the boy. She ran her hands over his body and came up with something Jared couldn't see. "A dart."

"Is he still breathing?"

"Yes."

"Then he should be all right."

Cassi laid the boy gently in the bottom of the canoe and took up his oar.

The men on the dock were fading, and Jared now blessed the fact that the clouds obscured the moon. Any watchers wouldn't know where they were going. But Jared knew it wouldn't be long before the men found a way to follow and track them. He and Cassi had to hurry to the far shore, where perhaps they could hide and get Sampson the attention he needed.

Jared almost didn't see the hand on the side of the boat until it was too late. With a shout of warning to Cassi, Jared raised his oar and hit the hand. There was a muffled curse, but the hand reappeared, joined by another. Jared raised the oar again, this time aiming for the man's head. He heard the crack of impact. The canoe rocked and he tipped over the side.

The cool water made Jared gasp. "Cassi?" he shouted.

"Right here." She was in the water too, struggling to reach Sampson, who floated face upwards, saved by his life jacket.

A hand closed on Jared's arm. Jared pushed it off, but the hand kept coming. It pulled him under the water. He tore away from the grasping hand and swam to where he had last seen Cassi. When he hit the surface, he could see that she was still clinging to the boat a short way off. Jared's attacker was nowhere to be seen. Had he given up? Or had he drowned? Guilt assaulted Jared and he wanted to vomit. *Why, why, why?* he kept asking. But there was no answer.

"Jared?" Cassi's voice sounded frightened.

"I'm here."

"Is he . . .?"

"He's gone."

She threw something at him. A life jacket from the boat. Jared treaded water while he put it on. Immediately it was easier to stay afloat, and he let himself rest for a few moments.

Sampson began thrashing in his sleep, as though trying to wake. "We need to get him in the boat," Cassi said. "Help me turn it over."

After four unsuccessful attempts, they gave up trying to right the canoe. Both were too tired to manage much effort. "We've lost the oars anyway," Cassi told him. "Even if we could climb inside, we'd be stuck. We'll have to swim."

Jared had learned that in the case of capsizing, one should always stay with the boat. But the breeze that had begun earlier was blowing them back in the direction of the cabin—not a good idea. The other shore was far away, but reachable if they let the boat go and took turns towing Sampson. "Let's swim for it," he said to Cassi.

She thought a moment and then let go of the boat. "Maybe they'll find the canoe and think we drowned."

"We can always hope."

Jared pulled Sampson first, hoping the cold water wouldn't cause any further damage to him. At least the night was warm, despite the breeze. Sampson occasionally thrashed his arms and legs, and once he yelled out something Jared didn't understand. He prayed for strength.

They would have been lost without the life jackets. At times they had to rest on their backs, floating and staring up at the dark sky, where only a smattering of stars shone through the clouds. In the peace and near stillness of the water, Jared could almost believe none of it had happened. But a look at Sampson's inert form made it all too real.

His muscles ached by the time they arrived at the far shore. He and Cassi wearily carried Sampson up on the bank and laid him in the knee-high grass. They were too tired to do more than take off their life jackets and soggy sweaters and huddle on either side of the boy for warmth.

"We have to get out of here," Cassi said. "They'll be looking for us. Even if they find the boat and think we've drowned, that won't keep them for long. They knew we had life jackets and would expect to find some trace of us." She smoothed the blond hair on Sampson's head that now hung in short, wavy mounds. "I'm worried about him. That man in the cabin tried to kill him, and would have if Brohaugh hadn't stepped in the way. Whoever these men are, they want us alive. But they don't seem to care much about Sampson."

"They could be the ones who killed Holbrooke."

She nodded, eyes luminous in the dim light. Her dark hair curled in hundreds of tiny ringlets. "I think you're right. Brohaugh was not a good man, but he loved Sampson." Cassi began to weep softly, and Jared wanted to cry himself. His insides felt shaky, his body exhausted. He held her as tightly as he could with Sampson between them, noting that she spoke of Brohaugh in the past tense, as though she too had seen the death in his eyes.

"The darts were meant for us," she said, gulping back her tears. "Maybe there's too much drug in it for Sampson. He's not that big. It could kill him."

"Let's try to get him to wake up." He heaved his aching body to his feet.

Cassi seemed to understand what he meant. They had both seen the movies where someone had taken an overdose of sleeping pills, and their friends made them walk and take cold showers until help arrived. Well, Sampson had taken the equivalent of many cold showers, and he had been somewhat aware during the swim. But since they had brought him to shore, he had been utterly still.

On either side of the boy, they hauled him to his feet and began to walk. "Wake up, Sampson." Cassi rubbed his cheek.

Jared slapped his back. "Sampson, come on, boy."

There was no response. Not even an eyelid flickered. "Come back to us, Sampson," Cassi pleaded. "We can't let them win!"

Nothing.

They kept trying until Cassi slumped to the ground. "I can't do it anymore. It's not working."

Jared knew they had to find help—now.

"Let's make a bed of this grass and some leaves, enough to keep you and Sampson a little warmer. Then I'll go find someone to help."

He saw that she wanted to protest the separation, but knew it was the only way. Sampson was just a boy, but in their weakened condition they couldn't carry him for long—their attempt to wake him had proven that. And who knew how long they would have to walk? They didn't even know in which direction to begin.

"Okay," she said. "But let's make it between those trees." She pointed to the side of the small clearing. "That way we can hide if anyone comes."

They worked quickly and quietly, forcing already overtaxed muscles to comply. Then they carried Sampson to the grass bed. "I'll rub his arms and legs," Cassi said. "That will help keep his circulation going."

Jared took her in his arms, kissing her deeply. Her touch sent warmth through him as the exertion of making the bed of grass hadn't. "I love you so much." He knew his voice was rough with emotion.

"Just come back to me, Jared."

"I will." What they had between them was good and right. A once-in-a-lifetime kind of love. They needed each other. They kissed again, neither seeming to want the moment to end. At last, Jared pulled gently away and walked into the night, feeling her eyes upon him.

CHAPTER 11

No news was supposed to be good news, but Fred felt uneasy. He wished he knew for sure that Jared and Cassi were safe. The FBI agents with them were required to check in once daily with their Legat office in London, using the personal satellite telephone Worthington carried in a pocket. Only if something happened would he make an extra call.

What really bothered him was Brooke's continued disappearance. He had selfishly put Justin back on that case and worked on it as much as possible himself. With all the resources of the FBI, they would find out who the real Brooke was.

Justin came into the room, looking jubilant. "I've found her parents. We've called just about every Erickson in the phone book, but we've found her."

"Are you sure they're the right ones?" Fred felt stupid asking the question. Of course Justin was sure. He didn't make such mistakes.

"They live in Indiana," Justin said. "Apparently, Brooke, their daughter, moved to Utah a year ago. They knew she worked at a newspaper. In fact, they think she's still there."

"You have a positive ID?"

"Yes, I sent them the drawing of Brooke that our artist made up. It's our Brooke, all right. But her parents are as puzzled as we are at her disappearance. They have no idea what she's doing in San Diego. Or where's she's staying."

"Someone in this city has to know," Fred said. Ideas began to churn in his mind. "What if we check out all of the job applications sent to the San Diego Union-Tribune? Let's just see how close our

Brooke came to working there. Maybe we'll find a piece of truth in her lies."

"There is good news," Justin said. "According to her parents, she's not married."

Fred grimaced. "What about the hospitals?"

"Only one Jane Doe. Estimated age around fifty."

"Not Brooke." Fred sighed inwardly. He regretted ever letting her become involved at all. Maybe it was his fault she was missing.

But she lied, he told himself. Could there be an explanation? He didn't think so.

"Why the ring?" he said aloud.

"To keep the creeps away."

Fred shook his head. "Maybe she's involved with one of our suspects. Maybe with Brohaugh."

"Her and Brohaugh? I don't think so. But if you're determined to go along those lines, Donelli's nephew would be a better candidate, don't you think?"

Fred had to admit that the man had charisma and dark good looks that women seemed to find attractive. "Let's find some reason to search Donelli's. Something, anything. If Brooke's there, whether willingly or not, we'll find some trace."

"I'll get right on it. But there is also another avenue we might try."

"What do you mean?"

"Well, I was thinking of the plants that were authorized six months ago. Didn't we put one in Donelli's organization?"

Fred and his superiors had tried to place someone in every suspect organization that the budget would allow. Donelli's name had been on the list, but Fred hadn't heard anything come of it. "You might be right."

"I'll check it out on my way to get the search warrant."

* * * * *

Brooke looked at herself in the mirror. Behind her several paces hovered the hairdresser, waiting for approval. The doctor was also in the background, an ever-constant annoying presence. Like a buzzing fly.

She brought a hand to her hair. Now she looked more as she remembered, like the face in the video. Her pale blonde locks were sleek and smooth, curled slightly under at the ends. Though shorter than on the video, the overall image was perfect. Her face wore a considerable layer of expensive makeup that made her cheekbones more prominent and her lips slightly thinner. The lips were now painted a bright red like her long nails. Daggers. She smiled. That was what Jared had called them.

The biggest change was her eyes. She hadn't remembered wearing contacts before, but the bright green color was right, not the pale blue the green contacts hid. Those had been too innocent. But green—the color of money, the color of power and passion—was meant for her.

Brooke put on another coat of lipstick. Then, not of her own volition, she opened the empty vanity drawer. Her hand shook for a moment as though writing with a pen on the wood inside. A silly show of weakness, she must not let the doctor see. Without capping the lipstick, she dropped it in the drawer and slammed it shut.

The voice inside her protested. *You may need it later.* It was the first thing the inner voice had said that she agreed with.

Brooke removed the lipstick, capped it firmly and said, "I want this with the clothes I picked out." She chose other items from the hairdresser's assortment—base, blush, shadow, eyeliner, several more lipsticks, fingernail polish and remover—and set them in a neat pile on the desk. "And these."

She arose and turned from the mirror, smoothing the tight-fitting green evening gown over her shapely figure. Not fat, but fuller in certain places than she remembered seeing in the video. "It is sufficient," she told the hairdresser. "You may go." Obediently, the matronly woman picked up the remainder of her equipment and left. *I will use her again,* thought Brooke. *She's not much to look at, but she knows her work and her place.*

Brooke crossed the room toward the doctor, swaying rhythmically in her high heels. The carpet in this room made it more difficult to walk, but it was only a matter of technique. "I am ready."

"Almost." The doctor's sharp, seemingly colorless eyes watched her carefully. Too carefully. It was annoying. If he pushed her too far . . .

"We will leave in a little while," he said. "Then we will continue to work on the plane. We have a few more days."

"But I am ready now." Brooke kept her voice even and smooth, convincing. "I don't need any more work."

"But it is too soon. You have been ill."

Brooke glared at him. "I'm sick of hearing about how ill I've been! I feel fine. I look fine." She stepped closer, until their faces were an inch apart. "Don't I look fine? Tell me!"

The doctor backed away, paling. "You look beautiful." She knew he meant the words. "But there is that other voice," he continued. "Has it disappeared completely?"

Brooke knew he was right. What was that voice deep in her head that protested nearly everything she did?

The doctor nodded. "See? You aren't quite ready. And you need sleep. You haven't slept in over thirty hours, since I arrived. It's only the drugs I have given you that have sustained you this long. You need rest."

"I'm not tired." But as she said it, exhaustion fell over Brooke. The odd voice inside her head clamored even louder. *Run,* it said. *Find Fred!*

Who was Fred?

The doctor approached her again with a needle. Brooke stepped backward. "It will just help you sleep." His voice was soothing, reasonable. "On the plane we will work again. You are almost ready." Still she hesitated. Then he said, "This will silence the voice."

Brooke let him inject the substance into her veins. How many times had he done this? Too many, she knew. Her arms were riddled with the tracks. In her mind, she recalled a faint memory of protesting the first few injections. That had been yesterday. But what bothered her more was that she remembered nothing beyond that faint protest, except for the memories the doctor recalled for her. She knew his words were true because she'd seen herself on the video talking about them, but why couldn't she remember? Perhaps she really had been ill.

Jared.

That name had been foremost in the doctor's recounting of her lost memories, and also in the video. Jared was a man who had scorned her cruelly instead of falling under her spell. Her relationship with him was the only time she had not been in control. Oh, how she craved control!

Where was Jared now? With that other woman? The doctor said they were married. An overwhelming anger built in Brooke's chest. *I will crush them both!*

To her horror, the voice inside began to pray. Pray? Her? Laranda? *No, I don't believe. That's for Jared and other fools.* The sooner that idiotic voice was silenced, the better for her.

The drug began to take effect, and Brooke felt the doctor leading her to a bed she didn't remember being in the room. Once lying down, she was vaguely aware of the sensation of movement.

"Take her to the plane," someone said.

The voice inside kicked and struggled to get out of the corner where the drug had restrained it. For an instant, Brooke was one with the voice, and a terrible fear consumed her. Nothing was under her control. She had to get away! Then the impression faded as the world around her went black.

* * * * *

"Here's the warrant." Justin slapped it down on Fred's desk.

"What about our mole? What's he saying?"

"Well, that's just it. He hasn't contacted anyone in the department for a month. We don't know if that means he's dead or been caught, or that he simply hasn't been able to call in. So it's not something we can depend on."

Just Fred's luck.

What's more, he knew the charge of smuggling drugs inside wine bottles was probably true, but they didn't have enough evidence to make it stick in any court. At least it had been enough to give him a search warrant for Donelli's properties. He planned to send his most trusted men to the various business establishments and residences, but would reserve the main house for himself and Justin.

"The Union-Tribune also called on those job applications," Justin informed him. "They found one for Brooke. I have the address she listed. I thought we could stop there on our way to Donelli's."

"Well, at least she tried to work for them." Fred still hated that she had lied to him.

At the small, dingy apartment building where Brooke was renting, it didn't take long for them to convince the manager to give them access. Inside, the studio apartment was impossibly tiny, but neat for all its shabbiness. The closet was full of clothes and the bed made. There was plenty of food in the refrigerator.

"Doesn't look like she planned to go anywhere." Justin pointed to several suitcases on the top shelf in the closet.

"No, it doesn't."

There was nothing more to see, no secrets they could unravel here. Not even a computer to check out. "We're wasting time." Fred turned to the door, more sure than ever that Brooke wasn't coming back. From the contents of the room, he was beginning to believe that she hadn't left of her own free will. Of course, he could be wrong. It wouldn't be the first time. "Let's get to Donelli's."

Once at the mansion, he expected a delay, or threats at the minimum, but Donelli himself was absent, as was anyone else with any real authority. The butler read the court order and allowed them inside, obviously feeling there was nothing to hide. Even Fred was beginning to believe the search was a waste of time.

He had hoped at least to see Giorgio, to question him about Brooke. Were the two romantically involved? The idea made him very uncomfortable. Why was it that Fred was always attracted to the wrong woman? First the faithfully married Renae; then Darla, the former secretary who had betrayed him; and now Brooke, who had lied to him.

Fred and Justin began at the top of the mansion, sending the other two men to the bottom floor. Given the size of the house, they were going to be here some time. One room on the top floor aroused Fred's curiosity. The room was small for the house and bare except for a straight-backed wooden chair and a large-screen television. Above the TV, there was a spotlight that shone down on the wooden chair. Not even carpet softened the austere decor.

"An interrogation room?" Justin asked.

Fred nodded. "It certainly has the look of it."

"And the TV would be to show the victim what? Pictures of their families? Of what will happen to them if they don't participate?"

"Something like that." Fred wasn't too surprised to see a room like this on one of Donelli's properties, but the fact that it was in his main residence was odd. Still, it proved nothing—and certainly not that Brooke had been interrogated here.

He was about to leave when he spied something glinting under the stiff chair. Bending, he picked it up gingerly on the edges. "Could be Brooke's."

Justin pulled out a plastic sack and placed it carefully inside. "Is it the same type of ring she wore? I never noticed."

"It's the same."

"Maybe it'll have a partial print that we can match with ones in her apartment. It's not big enough for much."

That Fred already knew.

They went to the next rooms without finding anything out of the ordinary. Fred's frustration mounted, but he forced himself to be calm and thorough. When he walked into a lady's dressing room, all his instincts gave him warning. But there was nothing in the closets or on the vanity table. The full-length mirrors lining the walls were clean and free of noticeable fingerprints. The plush carpet revealed nothing.

"Hey, look at this."

Fred went to the vanity where Justin was searching inside a drawer. It was empty except for some odd markings. "Is that lipstick?"

He bent for a closer look. "It's writing. Very messy. It says . . ." Fred met Justin's eyes. "Help Broo—" Nothing more.

"Could be Brooke."

Fred pulled out the drawer, ignoring the stinging in his wounded right arm. Maybe he should still be wearing the sling. "I think our handwriting experts will want to see this. We do have those handwriting samples from her parents, don't we?"

"Yeah." Justin headed from the room.

The rest of the house revealed nothing, but when they called on Fred's cell phone to talk to the men who had searched Donelli's businesses, they learned that Donelli's private jet had left the airport an hour before.

"What's the ultimate destination?" Fred asked. His stomach tightened at the reply.

"Where?" Justin asked, seeing his face. "Oh, no. Don't tell me."

Fred nodded grimly. "Portugal. But there's still time to intercept them before they leave the country. I need to know if Brooke is on that plane."

CHAPTER 12

Cassi rubbed Sampson's arms and legs, and was rewarded by warmth coming into the sleeping boy's limbs. When her fingers couldn't rub anymore, she lay down beside him, hoping to keep him warm with her body. The night wasn't cold, but a gentle breeze made her wet clothes feel cool against her skin. At least down in the soft bed of grasses, she was somewhat protected.

Her eyes closed in exhaustion. She didn't notice the stinging sensation in them until it stopped. How long had it been since she'd slept a full night? Of course there had been that drug-induced sleep that had left her brain foggy for so long. No, that wasn't rest.

In her mind, she replayed the terrors of the evening: bodies falling in the cabin; the sound of Worthington's and the mobsters' guns, mixing in with the muffled sounds coming from the silenced weapons of the attackers; the mad dash to the canoe and the man springing up in front of her. She had still been holding Worthington's gun, and instinctively she fired. He had gone down, grabbing his leg in pain. The heavy burden of guilt that came with shooting another human being assailed her, but what else could she do to protect herself and Sampson?

Cassi's eyes flew open. No sense in further reliving the horror, the terrible fear that Jared wasn't going to be following them. No, if she wasn't going to sleep, there were other things she could be doing.

Coming to her feet, Cassi began to search for branches that she could use to further hide their location. A light sweat broke out on her body as she worked, despite the cool breeze. The heat was welcome. When she was satisfied that her position was well-protected, she returned to Sampson and rubbed his legs again. He looked so helpless, lying with his head propped up on one of the life jackets, his body partly covered in grass.

Sampson's father was dead, his uncle was dead, and he had nearly been killed himself. Tears slipped out of Cassi's eyes. This little boy was alone in the world, and no one cared. Except for her and Jared.

Where was Jared? Without a watch, she had no way of knowing how much time had passed. Had he found help? Or had he been captured? If he was able, Cassi knew he would return, but would it be too late for Sampson? Even now his breathing was faint and shallow. Cassi stretched out next to him and laid a gentle arm across his chest. She felt the slow rise and fall as he slept. The motion was comforting, and she kept her arm there. If the movement stopped, she would be ready to give him CPR.

She closed her eyes and prayed for Sampson, for Jared, and for relief from the visions of horror that kept coming to her mind. Finally the images faded, and Cassi dozed—but always she was conscious of the rise and fall of Sampson's small chest.

A sound made her jerk to full alert. Voices and footsteps. Could it be Jared coming back to take them to safety? Cassi wanted to run from her hiding place to meet him. A whisper to her spirit urged caution. Cassi recognized the warning and lay very still, her heart pounding.

"Any sign of them?" a voice said in English.

"Not so much as a hair. This is practically useless until daylight. We'll have to wait and find them then."

"No! We must find them tonight. The boss will soon be here, and you know who will get the blame for losing them."

"Don't you think I know that? But we got Brohaugh; that's a bonus."

"But we lost the others. This failure will still get us transferred back to the loading docks."

"What's done is done. We'll find them. And when I do, they're going to learn a lesson. The both of them." The speaker gave a wicked laugh. "We are supposed to bring them in alive, but they said nothing about a few bruises."

Cassi knew these men were talking about her and Jared. No matter what, she couldn't let them find her. But suddenly her breathing seemed loud in the darkness. She clenched her hands and forced herself to breathe slowly.

Sampson gave a tiny groan and moved his head from side to side. Cassi put her face next to his and patted his cheek. *Not now, Sampson. Not now!* The boy began to calm under her touch. But was it too late?

"Did you hear that?" said one of the men.

"No. What was it?"

"Just a sound."

"Maybe it was one of our guys."

"Yeah, probably. But look at this. Why's all this grass short here? And look, there's some wet on it. Maybe they came this way after all."

"What, and stopped to pick some grass to eat? Right. It was just some animal. I don't see any signs of a canoe. Let's move on."

Cassi was relieved until she realized they would be walking next to the clump of trees where she and Sampson hid. Would the branches she arranged be enough to keep the men from finding them?

In her fear, she had stopping stroking Sampson's cheek. Now the boy began to move his head again, jerking it from side to side. *Please, Sampson. Be still.* She smoothed his cheek and prayed.

* * * * *

Jared knew he had been colder and more tired at some time in his life than at that moment, but he couldn't recall the day. He stumbled along almost blindly, wishing his sore body could move fast enough to work up a sweat. His head pounded, and each new bruise on his body ached worse than the rest. Thoughts of Cassi made him push onward. There had to be a cottage or cabin somewhere nearby. And perhaps they would have a car to take them into town. Jared checked his pockets and found his wallet missing—it was probably back at the cabin. What could they do without money? Would anyone at all help them?

He remembered Sampson and how unmoving he had been on his grass bed. The boy was in grave danger. Someone had to take pity on them. But how would he communicate his need?

Jared walked on, forcing one foot in front of the other. The exhaustion he felt overwhelmed the coldness until he moved in a daze. He tried to take careful note of landmarks so he could find his way back to Cassi. He put them in a chant in his mind—gnarled tree, boulder, four trees, berry bush, two trees grown together, little pond, and so on. Each time he added a landmark, he recited all the rest. It was something to take his mind off the weariness.

Then he saw the cabin. At first he wasn't sure it was anything more than a wish, but it didn't disappear as he approached. There was still a light in the window, and Jared saw a rusty red car parked in front.

Taking a deep breath, he hurried on. The cabin had no porch, but did have three wooden steps leading to the door. Jared stumbled up them and knocked. After a few minutes, a dark-haired man with leathery skin opened the door. He wore a gray plaid robe, and around his neck hung a thick silver chain with a large cross pendant.

"I'm sorry, but I need help," Jared said. "Please can you help?" He felt the man's sharp eyes take in his appearance, and hoped his bruised and battered face didn't cause the man to slam the door in his face.

"Eu não percebo. Você não fala Português?" The man's thick mustache moved when he spoke.

"I don't understand." Jared shook his head in frustration. "Look, I'm from America. Do you understand? America. And we had an accident on the water. See?" He touched his wet clothes.

"Americano?"

Finally, a word they both recognized. Jared nodded vigorously. "Yes, yes. Please, will you help?"

The man turned and yelled into the cabin. "Marisa, vem cá! Há alguêm aqui que fala Inglês. Parece um Americano."

Jared didn't know what the man said, but shortly a young girl about Sampson's age came running. She had long dark brown hair that reached past her waist, and soft brown eyes that reminded Jared of Cassi. "Americano?" she said in obvious excitement.

"Sim, sim." The man waved a hand at Jared. "Vês se o entendes. Ele está muito animado com qualquer coisa. Talvez precisa de ajuda."

The girl looked at Jared and spoke with a decided British accent. "My father say maybe you need help?"

"Yes! We had a boating accident."

"You fell in water?"

"Yes. My wife and a boy—he needs help. Can you take us into town? To a doctor?"

The girl turned back to her father and spoke in rapid Portuguese. He turned and went inside. "Come in," the girl said. "My father will move his clothes."

Jared stepped inside the cabin, enjoying the warmth that gradually seeped into his bones. The cabin was very similar to the one across the dam, except that this one had electricity and even a television. He suspected they lived here all year round. Handmade crocheted items were visible throughout the room, giving a strong sense of home. He also saw many pictures, and his eyes were drawn to one of the man and his daughter standing in front of the cabin with a laughing, dark-haired woman. The girl saw him staring and pointed at the picture. "My mother," she said. "She is . . ." Her school English failed her. "She is gone."

"She's dead?"

The girl nodded. Jared knew she missed her mother, but he also sensed that her father had taken very good care of his little girl. For the first time in his life, Jared wished he had the gift of tongues, that he could share the gospel with this family who was so willing to help a stranger in the night.

"You speak pretty good English," Jared said.

She smiled and tugged at one of the thin hoops of gold in her ear. "My teacher say I no speak very good, but I will learn."

Jared gave a wry smile. "Your English is much better than my Portuguese."

When the father returned from the bedroom, dressed in brown work pants and a button-down shirt, Jared turned to lead them outside. But the man shoved a dry shirt into his hands and motioned for Jared to change. Then he spoke again to his daughter, who disappeared into the bedroom. The man turned his back and Jared changed his shirt quickly, glad that the man couldn't see how Jared left on his undergarments. He couldn't begin to explain their importance now.

The girl returned with several blankets, and gratitude swelled in Jared's heart. For all they knew he could be a cutthroat, but they were still willing to help. "Thank you," he said, holding his hand against his heart. The girl turned to her father, translating.

The man shrugged and gave Jared a slight smile. "Claro que vamos ajudar. É o que o Senhor gostaria que nós fizessemos. Vem." He turned and strode out of the cabin.

"My father say the Lord wants us to help. Come."

Jared had heard of the hospitality of the Portuguese people. Now he saw that it was more than a rumor. This man likely had few shirts, but had willingly given one to Jared without requesting any kind of payment. They were a humble and prepared people. He felt they would be open to hearing the gospel.

Jared led his new friends into the woods. He feared he might have lost his sense of direction, but the landmark chant he had made up served him well. Even so, it seemed to take much longer to reach the place where he had left Cassi, though he knew it was actually less time. Would Sampson still be alive when they arrived?

At last he reached the place where they had pulled themselves from the water. Cassi was nowhere to be seen. Was it the right place? The cut grass said it was, but Jared felt uneasy. Where were the trees where he and Cassi had made Sampson's bed? Everything appeared changed.

"Look!" The girl picked up something on the grass and handed it to Jared. "Yours?"

Jared stared at the stub of an airline ticket from England to Portugal. It wasn't his. *The men from the cabin!* Jared felt sick. "Cassi?" he asked tentatively.

What if she had been taken?

* * * * *

As Cassi stroked Sampson's cheek, he calmed. But she knew it was too late. The men had heard and were coming toward her hiding place. Had she been alone, she would have run, but she couldn't leave Sampson to them.

Then she heard a male voice. "Found them yet?"

"No. There's something weird about the grass over there, though. And we thought we heard a noise."

"Sheep," the newcomer said. "We've run into quite a few of them. Come on, you've wasted enough time here. Let's continue the search."

Cassi couldn't believe her luck as she heard them move off into the trees. She said a heartfelt prayer of thanks and added a plea that the men wouldn't run into Jared. Sampson was calm now, as long as she stroked his cheek, but he felt hot to her touch. She sat up carefully, wondering what to do. Should she try to find Jared? More footsteps brought Cassi's thoughts to a quick stop.

"Cassi?"

Jared!

Cassi hesitated a few seconds to make sure he had not been captured by the thugs and was being used as bait to lure her into the open. She stood cautiously and saw that Jared was accompanied by a short, heavyset man and a young girl with long hair. "I'm here," she called.

Even from this distance, she heard Jared's sigh of relief. He ran to where she hid and began pulling back the dead branches and driftwood she had used to obscure Sampson's bed. "No wonder I didn't recognize it," he said. "Good thinking." He cleared the rest of the brush, then pulled her into his arms.

"They were just here," Cassi told him. "The men from the cabin. We have to be careful."

"I've brought some help." Jared motioned to the people behind him, and the girl brought her blankets.

"Thank you." Cassi wrapped Sampson in one of the blankets.

"You are welcome," said the girl. She stared at Sampson steadily. "Why is it that he sleeps?"

"He's sick."

"What is he called?"

"Sampson."

"Samp-son?"

"Yes. And I'm Cassi. Who are you?"

"Marisa Santos. And this is my father, José. We take you to our house."

Jared started to lift Sampson, but José nudged past him and picked up the boy, cradling him gently in his bulky arms. Jared wrapped the remaining blanket around Cassi, but she insisted on sharing it with him. On the way through the dark trees, they quietly exchanged stories. Around them the night sounds were normal, but Cassi couldn't shake the feeling that unseen eyes followed them.

CHAPTER 13

FBI agents telephoned Fred when they caught up with Donelli's plane in New York. Unfortunately, they had nothing on which to hold the plane, nor did they find anyone matching Brooke's description. All passports, papers, and flight plans were in order.

"Weren't there any women on board at all?" asked Fred. The handwriting expert had given his opinion that the scribbled message in the drawer could have been written by Brooke Erickson, although absolute identification was impossible due to the nature of the instrument she had used to make the letters and the brevity of the message. The ring had held equally useless smudged partial prints that had not identified Brooke. Still, the two together made him sure of her involvement.

"There was one woman," said the New York agent. "But her hair was different and her eyes were green. She didn't look much like that picture you sent, and she certainly wasn't there under duress. She and one of the guys were actually quite cozy."

"Giorgio."

"Yeah, that was his name."

"She didn't try to send any hidden messages?"

"None that I could see. I tell you, she's not the person you're looking for."

"What was the name on her passport?"

"Let's see. It's here somewhere."

Fred heard the shuffle of papers and stifled his irritation. He rubbed the bandage on his arm.

"Found it. The name's Laranda Garrettson."

Fred pulled his hand away from the bandage as though burned. "Garrettson?" he barked. "Are you sure?"

"Yes. Does that mean anything to you?"

"Laranda Garrettson is supposed to be dead." Fred let the sentence hang in the air. "Stop that plane."

"Too late. It's gone."

"I want a photo or drawing of this woman immediately. And have someone waiting for that plane in Portugal. At the least, the woman is an imposter. At worst, she's a wanted criminal who faked her own death."

Fred had barely hung up the phone when another call came through, this one from London. "One of our agents called from Portugal," he was told. "The cabin was attacked. The Landines and the boy aren't there. Brohaugh is there, but he's dead. That's all we know."

He broke the connection, feeling stunned. With Brohaugh dead and Donelli in a plane over the Atlantic, who was responsible for the attack on Jared and Cassi? The fact that Donelli was headed to Portugal was not in his favor. Obviously, the mob boss knew more than he had let on. But where did the woman calling herself Laranda fit into all this? And where was Brooke?

Fred thought for a long moment and then called Justin into his office. "I'm turning this investigation over to you."

"What?" Justin blinked several times in amazement.

"You heard me. It's about time I take a vacation like those up the line have been ordering me to do for the past five years. I'm entitled. And you're more than able to take care of this case."

A sudden understanding smile played on Justin's lips. "I take it you'll be flying to your destination?"

"You got it."

"You'll keep in touch?"

"Of course. But that means I'll need one of those global satellite telephones."

"I'll take care of it." Justin typed something into the new mini hand computer he now carried in his pocket, the information kept private by a series of key words. Never again would someone steal his notes. "So I guess I know where you're headed."

Fred smiled grimly. "I've always wanted to visit Portugal. Now, what kind of permits do I need to take my gun? Or maybe that new contraption you're carrying in your pocket can tell me where to buy one once I get there."

* * * * *

In the Santos cabin, Cassi felt warm and comfortable. But Sampson's color was worse and his breathing more difficult. "Look, we really should get him to a doctor," she said to Marisa.

"No doctor here. In Alvito you will find one. But not until the morning."

Cassi glanced at Jared in frustration. It was now in the early hours of Saturday morning. A few more hours, and it might be too late.

"I think we should try to wake him again," Jared said. "To get his circulation going. And after he wakes, liquids should help get that drug out of his system faster."

Marisa and José watched with interest as they tried unsuccessfully to wake Sampson. Finally Marisa asked, "Why no let him sleep?"

Cassi hesitated a moment. "Some bad men gave him a drug. It made him sleep. We are afraid he won't ever wake up."

Marisa translated for her father, who nodded in understanding and said something in reply. For the first time, Cassi noticed what a beautiful-sounding language Portuguese was—like a fluid melody.

"My father say he have something to help," Marisa said.

José went to a corner of the cabin and took a black bottle with a thin neck from a shelf. He handed it to Cassi with a soup spoon and motioned for her to give it to Sampson.

Cassi stared at it. She realized that the thick bottle was brown, not black, but the liquid inside was so dark that it made the bottle black except for the half-inch at the top where no liquid reached. "Jared, I don't know about this."

"What is it?" Jared asked Marisa.

"My father make it. It is called anti—" She broke off and went to the shelf where a few schoolbooks were stacked. There, she looked in a small Portuguese-English dictionary. "Plague. Do you say that way?" She showed Jared the word.

"Yes, plague."

"It is anti-plague formula. It cures almost any illness."

"This drug was injected into him," Cassi said.

Marisa spoke again to her father, who was adding wood to the fire. "He say it will help."

Cassi shook the bottle. Could it really help? Or would she be endangering Sampson even more? She met Jared's eyes. "Could you give him a blessing?"

"Yes. I don't have any olive oil, but they should have some. From what Worthington was saying, the Portuguese use it in just about every dish they make."

Jared talked to Marisa, who shook her head. "We use the rest of oil two days past. Tomorrow we go into town to buy more."

"What about any kind of oil?" Jared asked.

"We no have more."

Cassi stared at Jared in dismay. "We can pray together. And you can give him at least some sort of blessing. You know, like a father's blessing."

They prayed together aloud, and Jared blessed Sampson with a special blessing, but Cassi could hear the worry in his voice. This was treading new ground for both of them. If only they had olive oil and could give him a proper blessing for the healing of the sick.

"We just have to have faith," she said.

José nodded his approval. "He say it good for you to pray to God," Marisa said. "But now you also give medicine. It is good to use herbs of the earth that God has gave us."

Cassi continued to hesitate, but Sampson looked more frail every second. She slowly uncapped the anti-plague formula and sniffed. The smell made her eyes water and her stomach want to retch. She handed it to Jared. "What do you think?"

He poured a tiny bit on his finger and tasted it. "Ugh!" he said with a grimace. "That's the most terrible stuff I've ever tasted!" He glanced at Sampson. "But I don't know that we have any other choice. He doesn't look good."

Cassi knew José's homemade remedy might well harm Sampson, but there was nothing else they could do. They were miles from help, and she was almost certain they wouldn't get him to a doctor in time.

"How much do I give him?"

"Two of the spoons," said Marisa after conferring with her father.

"I'll hold him." Jared sat on the floor where Sampson lay on a blanket. He lifted the boy's head. "Pour it slowly," he warned.

"Yeah, I don't want to drown him." Cassi measured the foul-smelling liquid and lowered it to Sampson's lips. She let a thin stream flow into his mouth. He immediately choked, then swallowed convulsively. His head jerked to the side, checked only by Jared's hand. In the same manner, Cassi gave him the rest of the dose. His eyelids fluttered as though in silent protest.

"Well, that's it," Cassi said. "Now what?"

"We wait." Marisa stood near Cassi's shoulder. She had a dented metal bucket in her hands, and Cassi wondered what she planned to do with it.

For an hour they kept vigil over Sampson. There was no change in his condition. Then all at once, his body twisted and writhed. Marisa knelt beside him and held the bucket near, just in time for Sampson to begin to vomit repeatedly. Jared held the boy's head, while Cassi tried to keep his twisting body from overturning the bucket. She was unsure if Sampson was fully aware, but his eyes had opened a few times. Was this a good sign?

At last Sampson lay still, his head on Jared's knee. His eyes opened weakly. "Am I dying?" he asked. "I must be dying. I feel awful."

Tears filled Cassi eyes. "No. At least I don't think so."

Sampson heaved again twice more, then lay back and shut his eyes. His breathing was steady and strong.

"That was some medicine," Jared said.

Cassi looked at José, who sat in a large chair with his arms folded across his large chest. He smiled and said something in Portuguese. "My father say," began Marisa, "that the medicine always works. You get so sick you want to die, but then you get better."

Sampson was asleep again, but his color was good and his breathing continued regularly. Cassi felt sure that José's medicine had helped save his life. Cassi picked up the bottle of black herbs. "We should get the recipe. I'll bet we'd make a million or two."

Jared smiled. "I don't think Americans would get past the taste. Besides, we already have a million or two."

Cassi kept forgetting that Linden had left her the gallery, not to mention the newly-bought mansion where he had been shot. They were selling the mansion because of the unpleasant memories, but the gallery that carried Linden's name they would keep for as long as they lived. Ironically, Cassi had once dreamed of owning her own gallery and also the security money could give her, but now she would much rather have her friend alive. She gripped Jared's hand hard. He and Sampson were most important to her now. She couldn't lose them.

They sat by Sampson's makeshift bed until the early morning light streamed through the curtained window. Cassi judged it to be near five in the morning. Marisa and José came out of the bedroom where they had slept briefly, and Marisa began to make breakfast. José picked up a bucket by the door and left the cabin, presumably for water. Soon, a delicious smell filled the air.

Sampson's eyes opened and he groaned. "What happened?" he said. "I had a dream that someone was twisting my insides."

"How do you feel now?"

"Pretty hungry." Then his eyes grew haunted. "But what happened last night?"

They told him briefly. "I guess it's lucky I was wearing a life jacket," he said. The pain that had been almost constant in his eyes since his father's death was back in full devastating force.

"We're hoping to get these people to take us into town," Cassi said. "Hopefully soon, since I'm afraid someone will be watching for us. But I don't know how willing they're going to be. They've already done so much, and we don't have any money to pay them. My purse is back at the cabin, and Jared's lost his wallet."

Sampson felt for his back pocket. It took him a moment to work it out of his still damp jeans, but he held up his wallet, wet but intact. "We've got plenty of cash and my credit cards."

Cassi nearly laughed. "I forgot all about your wallet. Why didn't I think about it?"

"I assumed it was lost like mine," Jared said. "After all we've been through. Now maybe we can offer something to our host, then find a hotel or something to hide out in until the police arrive."

Marisa came from the stove, where she watched the food far more adeptly than any American eleven-year-old Cassi had known. In fact, better than Cassi—and she was twenty-nine.

"Finally you wake," Marisa said, tossing her long dark hair behind her with a shake of her head.

Sampson stared. "Who are you?"

"I'm Marisa. It is nice to know you. I like America. Tell me about it." Her dark eyes flashed in anticipation.

Cassi and Jared withdrew slightly and watched the young people interact. Sampson, for all his education and wealth, was at a considerable disadvantage to the gregarious Marisa. For the moment, at least, he seemed to forget his pain.

"I think he likes her," Jared said.

"She's a beautiful girl."

"Just like another dark-haired beauty I know."

Cassi grimaced and brought a hand to her hair. A few weeks ago her hair had been down to her waist, but she had cut it as part of a disguise when she had been running from Big Tommy's thugs. She missed the hair now, and knew Jared was fascinated by the tight, natural curls. But it would grow back. Already it had grown an inch.

Jared's face came closer to Cassi's, as though he wanted a kiss, but an odd sound coming from Sampson drew their attention. "What? You know how to speak Portuguese?" Cassi asked.

He looked up at her from the blanket where he sat on the floor with Marisa. "No, not really. But I speak Spanish, and a lot of Portuguese words are the same, except with a different accent and some of those French nasal sounds thrown in. The sentences are said the same way—kind of backwards from English. It's easy."

"I give him my book old," Marisa said.

"I gave him my old book," Sampson corrected. Then he said something in Portuguese and Marisa corrected him. They laughed.

"I better check food." Marisa rose gracefully to her feet just as her father rushed into the cabin. He spoke in rapid Portuguese, and the color drained from Marisa's face. "Quick," she said to them urgently. "Men are coming. My father say they look for you. You must hide."

They followed Marisa into the bedroom, where she removed a carpet from the bare wood floor. Under it was a trap door. "Hurry," she said. "My father will try to make them leave."

Jared descended the rickety ladder first, followed by Cassi and an unsteady Sampson. Before Sampson had reached the rock floor, utter darkness fell over them.

"Where are we?" Sampson asked in a whisper.

Cassi felt for his shoulder. "From what I saw, it looked like a cellar."

"Under the house?"

"What better way to have it handy and protect it?" Cassi said. "My parents have some neighbors in Utah who made a cellar under their shed out in their backyard by their garden. In a pinch, I bet they could hide in theirs, too."

"Yeah, but Mormons are weird," Sampson said.

"Who said they were Mormon?" Cassi didn't hide the amusement from her voice.

Jared sniffed the stale air. "I bet they have dried meats and pota-toes and stuff. They probably have a garden out back and raise a lot of their own food. And this is the way they preserve it."

Sampson moved away from Cassi's hand as though to search around the small cellar. "It might be better if we don't move around too much," Jared told him. "If they search the cabin, they may hear us."

"I just think we ought to move out of the way of the trap door," Sampson said. "That way if they look here, they won't see us right off. There's room for all of us over here behind the ladder, if we squeeze."

"Seven years bad luck," Cassi muttered. "It's a good thing we Mormons aren't superstitious."

Sampson snorted. "Like our luck could get any worse."

She wanted to remind him that they were still alive, but with all he had lost, she doubted he would see that as a blessing. Maybe if they got out of this mess, she could make him understand that there could be happiness after such loss.

They huddled together under the ladder. Some strands of light did make their way inside the cellar, and gradually their eyes became accustomed to the dimness. Cassi could make out vague shapes of vegetables and dried meat. Above them, everything was still. Then they heard footsteps, too heavy for Marisa's and too many for José's. They froze, waiting for discovery. Sampson's hand found hers, and Cassi blinked back the tears the gesture brought to her eyes.

For a long time they waited, terrible visions of what could be happening to José and Marisa playing through Cassi's mind. Would they end up like Anderson and Worthington, who had only been doing their jobs? She prayed, grateful for the release it gave her. In her mind, she began humming *The Lord Is My Shepherd.* The song gave her comfort.

A noise above cut off her mental song. The trap door was pulled back. Next to her, Cassi could feel Jared's muscles tense as he prepared to defend them. "They are gone," came Marisa's melodic voice.

Each let out a sigh of relief. Sampson scrambled up the ladder first. "What happened?"

"They saw my father come so quickly inside. They thought you were here. My father let them look around. They did not find you, and they left."

She led them out of the bedroom. In the main part of the cabin, Jared walked up to José and held out his hand. "Tell your father he has saved our lives twice. We are grateful."

Marisa translated. "My father say he does the Lord's will. But now he must go to work. He and his partner have many sheep. He must take care of them. Please eat, and he will take you into town before he work."

"I'm afraid those men may be waiting there for us," Jared said. "Do you have a police station?"

She shook her head.

"Do you know of someone who rents cars?"

Again she shook her head. "Not many here have a car. We are very lucky. But there is a store."

"Isn't there a bigger town nearby?" asked Jared. "We need to find a police station and a hotel."

Marisa thought for a moment, then conversed with her father. "My father say if we hurry, you go into Alvito with his friend. His friend will take his vegetables to market, but he leave very early. We must go now." She scooped thick slabs of the meat she had been cooking and put them inside large chunks of bread. She distributed the food to each person. "We eat in the car."

"So they have a police station?"

"Oh, no. But they have the national guard. The places here are too small for a police station, except Évora and we do not go there today. But the guard will know what to do."

Cassi and Jared kept a close eye on the terrain as José drove along a narrow dirt road. They couldn't risk running into the men, not when they had come so far. José drove with abandon, and from the way Marisa clutched the back of the seat, Cassi suspected that he normally drove at a more sedate pace.

"This is good meat," Sampson said, chewing heartily.

Marisa smiled. "It is sheep."

"We call it mutton," Jared said.

Sampson made a face. "I never liked mutton before, but this is good." He took another bite.

"Our sheep feed on the best grasses," Marisa informed them. "I cooked this meat two days ago with the last olive oil and salt. Today I cook it more. It is very soft."

"It's excellent." Cassi looked at Jared. "Maybe you ought to get the full recipe."

Sampson laughed. "Yeah, Mrs. Landine," he said in falsetto. "Maybe you should get the recipe."

Undaunted, Jared turned to Marisa. "I love to cook. Please tell me exactly how you do it."

Marisa explained about onions and salt and cooking temperatures that meant nothing to Cassi. She sat back and enjoyed the meat and bread, feeling more relaxed with each minute that passed. Once they arrived at the national guard, she planned to wait there until Fred sent someone for them. More than anything, she wanted to go back to the United States. Maybe there Fred could protect them properly.

Then there was Sampson. What would happen to him? What relative would claim him now? As Cassi thought about it, she felt uneasy. She knew she was already attached to Sampson. There was something about him, something great, and she wanted to be a part of it.

When they arrived at the small farm, José's friend, Rui, already had his ancient brown truck loaded up and ready to go. Cassi had never seen the sides of a truck built up so high with a lattice of wood, nor so many home-grown vegetables. As they approached the truck, the clean, earthy smell filled her with a sense of peace. José's friend was a short, wiry man with skin darkened and wrinkled by hard work in the sun. He was apparently a man who loved the land, and whom the land loved and gave her bounty.

José quickly explained the circumstances, and Rui immediately consented to take them with him. "You will sit in the front with him and his daughter," Marisa told Cassi. "Jared and Sampson will ride on the back with his son."

Cassi and Jared thanked the man profusely, and bid a heartfelt farewell to José and Marisa. The girl shoved her old textbook in Sampson's hand, her eyes large and friendly. "You study and come back soon. We will speak Portuguese. And we go fish."

"Okay," Sampson said. "I will. Thanks." He pulled out his wallet, counted out five one hundred dollar bills, and gave them to Marisa. "For you and your dad. It's just a little something to remember me by." Marisa tried to refuse, but Sampson glowered at her. "I want you to have it. It is nothing to me."

Finally, José allowed his daughter to take the money. Cassi knew that neither had any idea of the worth of the bills, and they would find out only when they made the trip into a larger town to a bank that could exchange them. She also knew that to Sampson the amount was negligible, but to José and Marisa, it could very likely be more than they made in an entire month.

Jose's farmer friend motioned toward his truck. "Vamos."

Cassi soon found that when Marisa said "on" the back of the truck, she meant it literally. Jared, Sampson, and the farmer's teenage son stood on the back bumper and held onto the wooden slats that made up the sides of the truck. Cassi was worried about Sampson holding on after his recent brush with death, but the boy refused to trade places with her. "I never rode on a bumper before," he said. "And no way am I sitting inside with a girl when I can stay out here."

"I'll keep an eye on him," Jared told her. He also looked worried, but he added in a quieter voice, "Look at him."

Cassi saw that Sampson was smiling and laughing with the farmer's son, as though he hadn't recently lost his father and seen his uncle shot. Like Jared, she wanted to allow him the escape from reality. "Have fun then," she said.

As before, she kept a strict watch in front and to the sides of the dirt road. There was no one about except a motorcycle or two, also loaded up with marketable goods. The dirt road joined with a paved one and the pace picked up. Cassi looked out the window repeatedly to catch sight of Sampson. Once, he caught her gaze and waved.

In the first tiny town they passed, the farmer and his son drove to a small store and unloaded a few heavy boxes of vegetables. While they worked, Cassi stared about anxiously. There was no protection for them here should their pursuers find them. All she had were some squash and tomatoes—not of much use against guns or sleeping drugs.

The farmer's son finished unloading and jumped up inside the back of the truck, where there was now enough space for Jared and Sampson to squeeze in beside him. Cassi was relieved, especially when the farmer pulled out onto the paved road and began to travel faster.

Occasionally, they saw other traffic—motorcycles, old cars, bicycles, and a few newer cars that made Cassi's heart beat rapidly. But if the men were following them, they were staying out of sight. The farmer's teenage daughter smiled shyly at Cassi, revealing white teeth against her darkly tanned skin. She didn't speak except occasionally in response to her father. Obviously the girl didn't have Marisa's command of English, nor her outgoing personality. Cassi was comfortable enough with the silence. So much was going on inside her head that to carry on a conversation would have been a chore.

She judged that they had been in the truck for a total of forty or fifty minutes when they arrived at the bigger town of Alvito. Rows of quaint buildings with red terra-cotta rooftops flanked narrow cobbled streets. Signs in several windows proclaimed that they accepted Visa and MasterCard.

"Ah, civilization," Cassi breathed. Well, almost.

The farmer pulled to a stop and pointed out a building. A sign above the door read *Guarda Nacional.*

"Thank you," Cassi said. Then she tried it in Portuguese she had learned from Marisa. "Obrigada."

They smiled and nodded.

Jared and Sampson jumped out of the truck to stand on the cobblestone sidewalk with her. They watched the farmer and his children go on to the busy marketplace that they could just glimpse down the road. The farmer's son waved to them from his place among the vegetables.

"Well, let's go in," Cassi said. But inside there was only one old man in view behind the desk. He shook his head when they tried to speak to him. He pointed at the clock and said something in hoarse Portuguese.

"He doesn't know English," Sampson said.

"Can you talk to him?" Cassi asked.

"No. I can understand a lot of what he says, though. I think someone knows English, but he's not coming in until later. It's not even seven yet."

"Okay, we'll come back," Cassi said. They walked out the door and paused in front of the building. "But where to now? Maybe we should wait here." At least it seemed unlikely that their pursuers would look for them at the national guard.

"We could go to the marketplace!" Sampson said eagerly. "Paulo said there was lots to see."

Cassi bit her lip. "Paulo?"

"The farmer's son."

"Do you think we should?" She couldn't shake the feeling that the men chasing them would soon arrive. Where else could they look but in the nearby towns? And this one certainly wasn't large enough to offer much anonymity.

"We could try to find a car to rent," Jared said, "and go on to the next town, but there's no way we will know if it'll be this big. We don't even know where we are. The map is back at the cabin."

"We could go to a hotel and call Fred," Cassi suggested. "He'll know what to do."

"Marisa said the old castle here has been made into a hotel of sorts." Sampson's eyes were bright. "We could stay there."

Jared's brow wrinkled in thought. "They might be waiting for us. That's the first place I'd look. I'd have people placed at all the hotels and public phones. It would be better to wait here, but after what happened in the cabin, I'm not so sure our being at a national guard post this small would stop them. They might just shoot everyone. The other idea would be to hide out someplace with a lot of people. And around here, that appears to be the marketplace."

"Yeah!" Sampson cheered. "Let's go!"

Cassi didn't have the heart to wipe the eagerness from his face.

"Okay. Maybe we can buy some of the native clothes to blend in better."

"Do you mean a disguise?" Jared asked with a grin. No doubt he remembered the old man and woman disguise they had once used when trying to hide from Big Tommy's thugs en route to New York, and also the French maid disguise Cassi had used only weeks before in front of Laranda Garrettson.

Cassi shrugged. "Why not? It's getting to be a family tradition. I can just see our kids now, running around in little Portuguese disguises."

"We have to *make* the kids first," Jared said. "If you remember, this was supposed to be our honeymoon."

Cassi put her arms around his neck and kissed him. "I seem to remember that very faintly, oh-husband-mine." Jared laughed and kissed her back.

"Gross!" Sampson said, making a sour face. "Can't you guys ever give it up?"

"You're just jealous you didn't kiss Marisa when you left. I saw her try. You know, it's customary here for friends to kiss on both cheeks in greeting or parting."

Sampson's face turned red. "You weren't kissing on the cheek."

"All right, stop it, you two," Cassi said, moving away from Jared's embrace. "Let's go to the marketplace. But if you see one person who looks American, or anyone suspicious, tell us immediately. And try not to talk too loudly, so people won't suspect we're not Portuguese. Of course, since both of you have blond hair, that might be hard to hide. You need hats. That should be the first thing we buy."

They walked down the sidewalk, neatly cobbled like the street. At another time, Cassi would have marveled at the patterns and the work that had obviously gone into each rock, but now she was too busy looking for shadows.

They passed a stone bench several stores down from the national guard building, where grizzled, toothless old men with white or iron-gray hair talked and grinned at the passersby. One man on the end wasn't quite as old and somehow looked familiar to Cassi. She stared, but couldn't place the memory. His brown hat—an oversized beret—was pulled low on his head, and his eyes were shut, but Cassi had the feeling he watched them behind dark eyelashes. Where had she seen him before?

"Jared, do you know him?" she asked softly.

Jared stared a minute. "No, I can't remember seeing him before. But it is odd that a man of his age isn't up working—even on a Saturday. Let's hurry. I think the sooner we get our disguises, the better." Sampson was only too eager to walk faster. Cassi tried not to look back, but when she did, the man she had seen on the bench rose and slowly walked in the opposite direction.

Where had she met him before? The thought wouldn't leave. Could it only be her imagination? Perhaps. She fought the desire to run back to the national guard building. Jared was right. With only one man in front and possibly only a few more in the back, they would be easy targets for men who had bested two FBI agents and Brohaugh and his thugs.

There had to be a way out of this mess. But how?

CHAPTER 14

For several hours Jared, Cassi, and Sampson wandered in the open marketplace. They quickly discovered that while many of the stores in town might accept Visa, no one did in the marketplace. But the farmer who had brought them to town arranged for them to exchange some of Sampson's American bills. Jared had no idea if the exchange was fair, but was grateful for the help and the ability to buy their disguises—hats and shirts for him and Sampson, a flowing black skirt for Cassi.

Jared almost stopped looking behind him. Sampson's enthusiasm was refreshing and welcome, and the market full of Portuguese culture. He found himself laughing. Occasionally, he met Cassi's eyes. Oh, how he wished he could be here with her under other circumstances!

Who was after them? *Laranda is dead,* he told himself repeatedly. *I saw her ashes.* The thought didn't reassure him.

After a few hours, they returned to the national guard building and were interviewed by a man who spoke terrible English. But at least he understood enough to realize the seriousness of the situation. Hours passed as he talked to his superiors, who in turn talked on the phone to their superiors, who made phone calls to the American Embassy in Lisbon, which in turn contacted the FBI.

Each time the door to the room opened, Jared stiffened and prepared to protect Cassi and Sampson by any means possible. He wished he had a gun. Two of the three dark-haired men in the room with them appeared seasoned and strong, but how much action had they seen in this small town? Could their experience protect them?

The third man—the translator—looked as frail and sedate as his English was poor. The only thing remarkable about him was the thick gold necklace he wore around his neck.

Finally, a phone call came through and the guard handed it to Jared. "Hello?"

"Jared, this is Special Agent Justin Rotua in San Diego. I hear you haven't been having a great deal of luck in Portugal."

"What an understatement! So are you sending someone?"

"Yes, the best. Fred is already on his way. He should be with you sometime tomorrow morning. Meanwhile, I've arranged for you to stay at a bed and breakfast there with some escorts from the national guard."

"Are you sure they're up to this?"

"They've promised me their best men."

Jared wondered what that could mean in such an outback where there must rarely be any disturbances.

"They'll be prepared at least," Justin said. "And Fred will be there soon with some more backup. He'll stop to check out the cabin first. You just sit tight."

"Not much choice," Jared said.

"Are they still trying to drug you?"

"Yes, but I can't think why."

"Neither can we. It doesn't make sense. But for some reason you are valuable to them."

Jared knew that was the only reason they were still alive.

"Look, here's the number on Fred's new phone. If something develops, let him know." Jared wrote down the number and hung up. He quickly recounted the conversation to Cassi and Sampson.

"Well, I guess there's nothing to do but wait." Cassi eyed the Portuguese men. "I wonder who our escorts will be." Then more quietly she added, "I hope they don't get hurt."

The two seasoned-looking men were assigned to be their escorts. Immediately they took Jared, Cassi, and Sampson to a nearby house where they were given two rooms, each of which held two single beds. "I guess I'm bedding down with Sampson again," Jared said.

Cassi shook her head vigorously. "I'm not staying by myself. When it's time to sleep, we can stay in the same room. All together."

"That way when the shooting starts, we can help each other," Sampson added. His words were light, but there was fear in his eyes.

"I think we're safe for the time being," Jared felt compelled to say.

Lunch time had long since passed while they had been at the guard station, but the matronly landlady prepared them an afternoon lemon tea with small cakes, biscuits, crackers, and rolls with ham and cheese. Then they rested in their rooms until dinner. Jared was jumpy and felt his sore muscles aching from the constant pressure. The stitches on his forehead itched.

Over their evening meal, the landlady stared openly at his bruised face. She had curious brown eyes and short black hair streaked with gray. Her dress was brown and stretched tightly over her ample body, which was large without being fat. She wore gold earrings, a necklace, and several bracelets and rings. Occasionally she directed a comment at the two national guardsmen who stood by the kitchen door, alert and ready. She also patted Cassi's hand in sympathy several times and spoke to her, though Cassi couldn't understand her words.

Jared endured the dinner, waiting for what he knew was coming and praying that he was wrong, that Fred would arrive in time.

Nothing happened. It was too good to be true.

They went early to their beds, trusting the guards to watch the doors to the house. Without being asked, Sampson settled on the floor, leaving the beds to them. They lay down in their clothes, as they had once again left their luggage behind. Soon Sampson's soft snores echoed in the small room, but Jared heard Cassi moving and knew that like him, she couldn't sleep. He arose and went silently to her bed. Without a word, she welcomed him with open arms.

The nearness of her was overwhelming—her scent, her softness. Jared's arms tightened around her as their lips met. He thought fleetingly of the room next door and the privacy it offered, but neither he nor Cassi wanted to leave Sampson alone in case they were needed. Jared let out a long breath and held onto her more tightly. "I love you more than anything," he murmured. Her answering kiss showed that she felt the same. Jared knew that in spite of all their problems, he was a lucky man.

Nestled together, they finally dozed. The nightmares Jared had suffered since being held by Laranda returned that night in force, but he was aware of Cassi's arms around him and the terror was bearable. One day, he would leave the dreams behind.

* * * * *

Sampson awoke early Sunday morning, feeling much better than the previous day. He stretched and noticed that his strength was back to normal, with no traces of the drug in the way he moved. His stomach growled. There was certainly nothing wrong with that part of him.

Grinning, he looked around the room and saw Cassi and Jared sleeping together in one of the single beds. Their arms were entwined, their heads close together. For a moment, Sampson felt the old jealousy that had bothered him with his father's girlfriends. After his mother died, his father had dated, and Sampson hated it. His father had tried to explain, but only since Cassi had visited his house that night had Sampson understood. He thought he could love Cassi. She was so beautiful. He had even agreed with his father's decision to send him to her in France, before he realized that she and Jared were married. At first he had hated Jared, but had since changed his mind. Jared had turned out to be an okay guy, and Sampson wanted both of them to be happy.

Rising silently to his feet, Sampson went to the tall, narrow glass door which opened onto a tiny balcony, large enough for only one person. He didn't go outside, but watched the activity below. There were considerably fewer people in the street than at market time the day before, and the people he did see were dressed differently. He still saw the prominent snatches of black that marked many of the widows, but now there were happier colors and nicer dresses on the women. The men wore dress pants or suits. Where were they going? He had to know.

Sampson was consumed with curiosity and hunger. He glanced back at Cassi and Jared, sleeping soundly, and then grabbed his hat and quietly unlatched the glass door to the balcony. Outside, he looked around for a moment and then scrambled over the railing, down a drain pipe that shook with his weight, then onto a stunted tree, and from that he dropped to the ground. He looked around, sure no one had seen him.

"I'm not afraid," he told himself. "They won't find us here." His uncle TC had probably chased them down and would soon come for him. There wouldn't be much time to investigate this small town, so he'd better do it now. Besides, no one would look twice at a Portuguese boy alone. With his hair hidden inside his hat and his new shirt, he shouldn't look much different from the many other brown-eyed boys here. His skin was paler, but that shouldn't matter.

He started down the cobblestone sidewalk, stooping to examine the rocks. When he got home, he would have cobblestones put in the driveway like at the family estate in France where he had spent so much time with his mother. His father would have liked that.

An aching sadness filled Sampson's heart, and he almost cried. *I must be a man,* he thought. *I will get my revenge!*

Of course, first he would have to grow up a little and learn the business. He shot a glance back at the building where he had left Cassi and Jared. *I'll miss them.* But that wasn't until later. They still had to find his uncle.

Sampson moved quickly down the sidewalk. On the next street, he saw a large, tall building with a cross in front and immediately recognized it as a church. "Of course," he said aloud. "They're going to church." He had been to mass many times with his mother before she died. But that was a long time ago. Maybe too long. Sampson went up the stairs to the door and peered in. Tiles covered the walls, beautifully depicting scenes from the Bible. Some showed saints and told stories Sampson didn't recognize, though he did understand that they were very old. His mother would have enjoyed seeing them.

In the back of the church opposite the doors, he could see a large statue of Jesus with his arms outstretched on a cross. Strangely, he felt an uneasiness instead of the comfort that had always accompanied him before in such a place. The pictures in the old *Book of Mormon* he had seen in France seemed to hover in his mind. Those had been satisfying, and hadn't given him this odd feeling.

Sampson left the church and sat outside on a stone bench. Shortly he heard singing, and unlike the statue of Jesus, the melody made him feel better. He wished he could understand the words. He hated not understanding. His father had said that his thirst to know was why he was so good with languages. He began to hum along. Pigeons landed at his feet and lurched around as though expecting to be given food. Sampson's own stomach growled. He scanned the area, but couldn't see any small stores open. *That's right,* he thought. *This is Europe, where most things close on Sunday.*

His father had tried to explain it to him. He said that in Europe, most of the businesses were owned by families who took Sunday off to be with their families. "In America," he had said, "we have the large corporations that simply hire some person to be there instead. That's all. As the big corporations take over in Europe, you will see that it will be the same as in America."

But Sampson's mother had disagreed. "Many Europeans have a great faith in God," she said. "They know the Sabbath isn't for working."

"Then why don't most of them go to church?" Sampson's father had taunted. "They are baptized, married, and buried by the church. That's about it."

"For them it's enough," she replied. "Their faith in God is strong. It's not their fault the preachers have nothing new to give them each Sunday. Better they live their religion in their hearts and actions than not at all."

At this point Sampson's father would let the argument drop, but Sampson had always wondered who was right. Maybe a little of both. He knew that his mother had been a woman of great faith, and she had not attended church each week, but only on special occasions. Had it not fulfilled her quest for knowledge? Sampson wished he had the answers. But where to find them? Inside the church behind him there were none.

A man sat beside him. With his hat pulled low over his eyes, he seemed very familiar. "You recognize me, huh?" the man said. "From outside the national guard building. Or perhaps from England."

Sampson started, realizing the man spoke perfect American English. Before he could leap to his feet, the man's strong hand closed around his wrist. His blue eyes flashed a warning. "Not so fast, boy. I've been waiting for my chance. This time we will get the Landines—using you as bait." He stood, dragging Sampson with him. He walked over to the edge of the sidewalk and raised an arm. A white limousine pulled away from the curb down the street and drove up to where they stood. The car was incongruous in this quaint setting. Where had it come from? The door opened and Sampson struggled for freedom. The man slapped his face, hard, and thrust him inside. Sampson reeled.

"Easy, boy," came a soft, sultry voice. "We're not going to hurt you. Good work, Taggart."

Sampson whirled his head toward the familiar voice. Could his ears be deceiving him? But the woman who had poisoned his dogs had been killed! His father had seen it happen.

Looking like a figure from the past, she wore a snug, funeral-black suit and a matching hat with a lace veil that partially obscured her face. But there was no mistaking the green eyes and the sleek blonde hair. "Laranda?" he choked.

"Yes, it's me, Sampson. How nice to see you again."

Of all the women his father had dated, Sampson had most hated Laranda. After knowing she had killed his dogs, he had been happy she had died herself.

Yet here she was.

Across from them on the other seat in the limousine, next to the man who had captured him, were two men with large handguns. One with olive skin and black hair and eyes stared at Laranda with mixed amusement and adoration.

"Did you kill my father?" Sampson demanded of Laranda, fear almost paralyzing his tongue.

"Now, now. That's no way to treat an old friend."

Sampson couldn't reply.

"That's better. You just sit right there. It won't be long now until Jared and Cassi join us." She smiled at him seductively. "It's all too fitting that this reunion take place at a church. Jared was always so religious."

A nervous-looking man on Laranda's other side watched her anxiously. "How are you feeling?" he asked.

"Would you shut up?" she said, her voice full of venom. "I've listened to you for more than long enough. I'm fine. I can do this." She looked at the olive-skinned man opposite her. "Giorgio, if you can't control our concerned doctor, I'll kill him myself."

"He'll behave himself, Laranda. And we might yet need him."

Sampson gulped. "Are you Giorgio Donelli?" He prayed it wasn't true. He knew there was no love between the Donelli family and his father.

"Yes. That's me." The man's teeth looked white in his dark face. Sampson felt all hope drain from him. He was as good as dead.

* * * * *

Fred tried to tell himself that he was going to Portugal to find Jared and Cassi, but inside he wondered if Brooke wasn't a big part of why he was going. He wanted to hear from her own lips why she had lied. Then there was the odd message in the drawer. Had it really been from her?

The FBI artist's drawing of the woman in the New York airport didn't resemble Brooke much, but neither did it look exactly like Laranda. Snatches of video from a security camera in the airport showed a woman who walked with a silky grace and a strange seductiveness. She had the same exceptional figure he vividly remembered as belonging to Brooke, but moved like someone else. It was almost as though Brooke was masquerading as Laranda. But why?

These were the questions that haunted him as he flew to New York and then waited four hours to catch his plane to Portugal.

His phone rang and he quickly pulled it out. "Justin?"

"Yeah, we found Jared. Or rather he found us."

"Where is he? Are they safe?"

"The Landines and the boy are fine. They're in a little town in the Alentejo. I'll send the exact address to your phone after we get off. But apparently, what happened at the cabin was pretty bad. They're scared, and I think they have good reason to be. They verified Worthington's report that Brohaugh is dead or dying. I tried calling London for more information, but they said Worthington's not back yet. They mentioned that he had been wounded. They're sending someone in after him."

"You mean he called in the attack on his cell phone?"

"Yeah. Just after it happened."

"He's probably with the local police."

"National guard," Justin corrected. "They're pretty much out in the boonies. No police station. But I've talked with the Embassy, and they didn't know anything about an FBI agent. I did call Jared directly. I told him to sit tight until you get there."

"Will they be able to protect him?"

"I hope so. But it's possible whoever attacked them at the cabin doesn't know where they are yet. Just hurry up and get there."

Fred looked at his watch in frustration. "My plane's late, but I'll be there early in the morning."

"That's what I told Jared. And I've informed the boys in London in case they get there sooner."

"Did you give Jared my number?"

"Yeah. He'll call if he needs something—providing he can find a phone handy."

"What about Donelli's plane?"

"We couldn't get someone there in time. Too much red tape."

Fred had suspected as much. The FBI Legat office nearest to Portugal was either Madrid or Paris, and it always took some time to coordinate matters with local authorities. "Well, keep me posted."

"Wait. I did find out more about Brooke."

"What?" Fred's response was curt.

"She has actually worked for the Union-Tribune. She wrote about ten freelance articles that were published under a pseudonym. Some of them she sent in from Salt Lake, but at least the last two were done while she lived here. My guess is that she was trying to get on the paper full time."

"And hoped the Big Tommy story would get her there."

"It makes sense to me. So I guess she didn't really lie about the paper."

"Well, no. But there's still your notebook."

Justin was quiet for a moment. "Everybody makes mistakes. Even Mormons. Don't be too hard on her. I think she's one of the victims here."

"Maybe you're right." Fred had hoped so all along. Wasn't that why he was here? To save her? *Please don't let me be too late.* He paused. "Thanks, Justin. You've done good work."

"Talk to you later."

Fred punched the cutoff button on his phone and began to pace within a few steps of his flight bag, his only luggage. Inside, he carried state-of-the-art tracking and listening devices he hoped wouldn't be necessary, but had brought along just in case. It was his nature to be thorough and prepared.

At last, he was on the plane and settled down for the nearly seven-hour flight. By the time he had landed in Lisbon early Sunday morning, local time, he was feeling more rested. He hadn't been home to his own bed for more than a few hours the entire week, and these hours for rest were a luxury.

Maybe I should quit, he thought. *Settle down and have a few kids.* No woman wanted to be married to a man she rarely saw and who couldn't be a father to her children. He had seen how much that had meant to Renae Benson and her five children. Maybe he should follow the good example of the Mormons he had met.

And where did Brooke fit into all this? She was a Mormon, and based on his experience with the other Mormons he had met—Jared; Cassi; Robert, Cassi's brother; Carl, the art expert whose light shone in his eyes despite his ruined body—he had trusted her.

Enough! he told himself.

He was met by someone from the American Embassy and immediately given a car and a driver. "I'm Alberto Sanchez," said the short, dark-haired native. His English was excellent. He put Fred's flight bag into the car and then drove rapidly, without apparent concern for the local speed limit. For once, Fred blessed the concept of diplomatic immunity.

Hours passed as Fred worried in silence about the case. Their pace slowed only slightly as they left the smooth roads of the freeway for the smaller rough road that would lead to the cabin and then on to the bed and breakfast where Jared and Cassi would probably still be sleeping. He thought about bypassing the cabin altogether, but the fact that Worthington was missing tugged at him. The map, brought from San Diego and carefully marked, showed him that the cabin wasn't much out of the way. Five minutes perhaps.

The paved road turned into dirt with ample washboards. Alberto scarcely slowed. Fred expected to see police or the national guard or some other sign of life at the cabin, but impossible as it seemed, the entire area was deserted. "Justin said they had no police this far out, but this is odd," Fred mumbled.

"What?" asked Alberto.

"You'd better stay in the car."

The man did as he was told. Fred pulled out the weapon Justin had arranged for him and carefully approached the cabin from the side in case someone was looking out the front window. Birds sang in the trees surrounding the cabin, and the smell of the trees and loam evoked a sense of earthy peace.

Fred didn't relax his guard. He knew something terrible had happened here, though the extent of the damage was still hidden from him. His instincts were never wrong. Closer to the porch, he spied two lifeless bodies he had previously thought to be a mound of clothing. One man had no identification; the other was Special Agent Anderson of the FBI. Fred felt a rush of sorrow for the man's loss, but there was nothing he could do now except see that the agent was shipped home to his family.

Leaving the bodies, he pushed at the open door with his foot. With no resistence it swung halfway open, then stopped as though something was behind it. "FBI!" Fred shouted.

No reply. Nothing in the cabin moved.

Fred sprang through the door, pointing his gun in front of him, ready to fire if confronted. But the bodies he saw littering the cabin floor didn't move. He moved farther inside and saw one of the corpses barring the door from opening wider. He glanced at the face, recognizing it. TC Brohaugh. The man had apparently taken at least one fatal wound to the chest. There was no pulse.

All at once the smell of blood and decay assaulted Fred's senses, and he had to stifle the urge to be sick. The sound of buzzing flies was louder than his own pounding heart. Breathing deliberately through his mouth, Fred forced himself farther into the cabin, his gun still at the ready.

Before checking the other bodies for signs of life, Fred went to the small bedroom in the cabin. It was vacant, but he saw several unopened suitcases. If he didn't already know, this alone would tell him it was no ordinary robbery. He spied a purse—*Cassi's,* he thought—dumped it out and searched it. A few items of makeup, a travel book, keys, a checkbook, cash, credit cards, and even her passport were all intact.

Fred went back into the room and began checking the bodies, searching for the other FBI agent. He saw a likely man, lying face down by a tall, freestanding cupboard. Fred knelt quickly, feeling for the man's pulse. He found it, very faint, but discernable. He gently turned the brown-haired man over. A cellular phone, similar to the one Fred carried, lay under the man's body, spotted with blood. *Worthington,* he thought. Sure enough, the identification in his wallet verified Fred's suspicion.

Rage burned in his heart. Over thirty hours since the shooting, and Worthington was still here waiting for rescue. But no one had come. He searched the cupboard, grateful to find a pair of dusty scissors. With a little more searching, he found a battered chest filled with clean-looking sheets. Letting his training take over, he deftly cut the sheets and made bandages to tie over Worthington's wounds. In all but the largest one on Worthington's thigh, the blood had congealed somewhat, but Fred didn't want to risk any coming open again when he moved the man out to the car. By the look of his clothes and the discolored floor around him, he might have already lost too much blood.

As he double-bandaged Worthington's thigh, the man's eyes fluttered open. They were blue. "It took you long enough," he said, his voice scarcely more than a whisper.

"Well, I had to come all the way from San Diego." Fred purposely kept his own voice light.

"Water. Could you get me some water?"

"Yeah." Fred grabbed a cup from the cupboard and headed outside to the pump he had noted earlier. As he filled the cup, breathing in air untainted by death, he glanced at the trees for signs of hidden mobsters.

Nothing.

That is, nothing except a few more dark mounds that might just be bodies.

He waved an arm at Alberto. Slight as the man was, it would be easier for Worthington if there were two of them to move him. Alberto came cautiously. "There's a wounded man in there. We've got to get him to the car and to a doctor. There has to be someone available in one of the nearby towns. We'd better hurry. We might be too late already." Truth was, Fred felt anxious not only to get help for Worthington, but to find Jared and Cassi. Men who left messes like this behind weren't likely to respect the local authorities, who certainly weren't prepared for such a murderous attack. Every second Fred delayed, they were in greater danger. Even so, he was happy he had stopped at the cabin. Worthington could not have survived much longer without help.

Fred led the way inside the cabin. At Worthington's side, he knelt and held the man's head while he gulped the water. "Thanks," he gasped.

"We're going to move you to the car now," Fred said. "I wish it wasn't going to hurt." Too bad he didn't carry a painkiller.

Fred looked up at Alberto, who had paused by the doorway. The man had a look of frozen terror on his face as he stared at the wreck of the cabin. He put his hand to his mouth as though gagging and ran out of the cabin. Fred heard heaving outside.

"Sorry, Worthington. It looks like I'm going to have to do this myself. At least as far as the door." Fred struggled to lift the man, feeling his muscles strain at the weight. He had been called burly by some and he was in good shape, but Worthington, though thin, was a tall man who weighed a great deal.

Fred staggered along slowly, but made it to the door. Alberto had his head under a stream of water coming from the pump. "You think you can help me from here?" Fred asked, passing the corpses on the porch.

Alberto nodded, his face almost as pale as Worthington's. "I'm sorry," he muttered as he grabbed Worthington's legs. "I'm not used to seeing that."

"That's okay. It's something you never get used to." But Fred had gotten used to it—at least to some degree. It was his job.

They balanced Worthington's body between them. The agent moaned and lost consciousness. *It's just as well,* thought Fred. *He's in a lot of pain.*

They carried him to the car and settled him in the backseat. Alberto used his own cell phone to call someone to the cabin. Fred wondered how much longer before they would arrive. Jared had obviously told them about the shooting, but no one in authority had visited it yet. Perhaps Jared's story had lost something in the translation. It was also possible the Portuguese authorities hadn't yet learned the location of the cabin.

In minutes, they were flying over the bumps in the dirt road once more. Fred worried about the rough ride for Worthington, but he dared not ask Alberto to slow. He was relieved when they reached a paved road.

A shrill ringing cut through Fred's thoughts. He grabbed his phone out of his pocket. Only two people had this number. Of course it would be important. "Fred here."

"Fred, thank heaven! It's Jared."

"Are you okay?"

"Sampson's gone. Someone delivered a note just now. It says they have him. They want to trade us for him."

CHAPTER
15

Jared knew the moment he awoke that something wasn't right. But for a moment, it was hard to pinpoint the problem. Cassi's arms were wrapped around him, and he felt an overwhelming tenderness inside. She was his wife. Not just for now, but for all eternity. How could a man be so lucky?

Then the events of the past week deluged his mind. Immediately, he noticed Sampson's empty bed. Fighting the sinking feeling within, he shook Cassi gently. Despite his carefulness, she awoke with a start. He wondered if she, too, had been having nightmares.

"Sampson's gone," he said.

At once she was out of bed. "His hat's missing." She met his gaze. "He wouldn't be so stupid as to leave. Doesn't he realize how serious this is?"

"Maybe he's downstairs eating."

"That's right. He's always hungry." As she spoke, Cassi straightened her clothes. Jared followed suit, wishing briefly that he had a toothbrush and time to use it.

They hurried down the narrow stairs to the small kitchen. The landlady looked up at them in surprise. "Sampson?" Cassi asked, putting her hand at the level of Sampson's head. "Where is he?"

Because of the language barrier, it took a while for them to make her understand. Then her eyes opened. "O rapaz!" she exclaimed.

They followed her as she ran to the front door, where one of the men from the national guard sat on an uncomfortable chair, his weapon resting on his knee. Jared assumed the other man was at the back door.

The landlady spoke rapidly, and the two began to search the house. Jared and Cassi helped, their fear mounting. "When I get hold of him, I'm going to strangle him!" Cassi said. At another time, Jared would have laughed. How many times had his mother said the same words about him and his brother?

Sampson was nowhere in the house. One of the national guardsmen used the phone, presumably to call in the disappearance. As he did, the doorbell rang. The guardsman peered out the window next to the door before opening it. A little girl with the typical dark hair and eyes held a note in her hands. The guardsman glanced at it briefly and began to question her. She shrugged, babbled something in Portuguese, and skipped down the stairs.

The guard handed Jared the note. Startled, he saw that it was written in English:

We have the boy. If you want to make an exchange, we will trade him for both of you. Meet me inside the church in an hour. I won't wait. The next message you receive won't be as pleasant.

"They have him!" Cassi said. "What are we going to do?"

Jared didn't know. He had seen what little value life held for these people. He had no way of knowing if Sampson was even still alive.

"I'm willing to make the trade," she said. "I mean, they want us for some reason. I don't think they'll kill us."

"I don't want you in danger."

Her eyebrows scrunched together in determination. "Well, I'm not letting you go alone. We're in this together. Besides, the note says for both of us to go." She looked at him earnestly. "And Jared, we have to do it. He's a special kid and we're responsible for him. We would never forgive ourselves if he ended up dead in some alley."

She was right. "Let's call Fred. He's supposed to be here soon; maybe he'll have some ideas." He took out the number and went into the sitting room where the lady kept her phone. Without asking permission, he began to dial. The landlady nodded, hope written on her face. *She's been watching too many American movies on her TV,* Jared thought. *She's expecting us to save everything.*

The phone rang and someone answered quickly. "Fred here."

"Fred, thank heaven! It's Jared."

"Are you okay?"

"Sampson's gone. Someone delivered a note just now. It says they have him. They want to trade us for him."

"Don't you dare do it, Jared! Sit tight. I'm almost there."

"We *have* to do it," Jared said. "He's just a little boy. He has no one."

"He has you! But not if you go in half-cocked. All you'll do is get yourselves killed."

"Then what'll we do? Cassi and I are both willing to make the exchange, but we were hoping you could come up with some way of making sure they let him go and then somehow get us back."

"Okay." Fred's voice was calmer now. "That's more like it. First off, we know from all that has happened that they don't want to kill you, so we have to assume you will be safe until you give them what they want."

"But we don't *know* what they want."

"I know. Neither do we. We don't even know who they are, though the process of elimination points strongly to a man named Nicolas Donelli."

"You mean now that Brohaugh is dead."

"Yeah, something like that, though there are some other people involved for sure."

"If I didn't know better, I'd say it was Laranda." Jared felt stupid as he spoke, but to his surprise, Fred didn't refute him.

"She might have more to do with this than we suspect."

Jared felt as though he had fallen off a mountain. "You can't be serious. She's dead. I saw her ashes."

"I know, but there's a lot I can't explain. Someone bearing a passport with the name Laranda Garrettson flew to Portugal Friday night in a private plane owned by the Donelli family. I don't know what the connection is yet, but when you make the exchange for Sampson, be on the lookout for something very strange."

"What if they don't let him go? What if they keep him to make us do whatever it is they want?"

"We'll make sure they don't," Fred said. "Besides, they'll have both of you to play off each other for that."

"But you'll protect us."

"I'll do what I can. But you know as well as I do, Jared, how these boys play hardball."

"Yeah, I know." Jared's mouth tasted bitter.

"Are sure you want to do this?"

"No. And I certainly don't want to risk Cassi. But we have no choice. He's only eleven, Fred. His father is dead, his uncle, his mom. I feel responsible. I hate it, but I feel responsible. And he's a good kid, Fred. A genius. You should see him."

There was a moment of pause before Fred spoke. "Okay, look. Here's what we'll do. You go to the church alone. Talk to whoever is there and tell them Cassi will join you after they turn over Sampson."

"What if they refuse?"

"They might, but you just hold firm."

"Okay, so how do we make sure Sampson gets away?"

"We'll have Cassi standing across from the church with a few of the Portuguese national guards. The people after you may not fear them, but they are well-trained. And I believe that in broad daylight, with so many people around, our opponents will think twice about opening fire."

"So I tell them to send Sampson to the national guard, and Cassi will walk to us."

"Something like that. They'll insist, of course, that the exchange happens at the same time."

"But what if they know I'll do something like this?" Jared had learned enough about organized crime to know that they planned for every contingency.

"To be honest, Jared, I don't believe they'll let Sampson get all the way to the guards. I think as soon as they are sure they have Cassi, they'll have someone in position to recapture him, national guards or no. I believe they want him dead, just like his father and uncle and all the rest of the family. There's more than money at stake here. I just don't know what."

Jared felt despair engulf him. "Then how—?"

"That's where I come in. I'll be parked near the church, and as soon as I see the exchange happening, I'll drive up and get Sampson. I'll get to him long before he gets across the street."

"But what if they try the same thing?"

"I'll handle it, Jared. Trust me."

"I do, Fred. But let's say it all works and you have Sampson safe. What then?"

"After the exchange, I'll be following you. I've brought a tracer and a few bugs I'd like to place on you and Cassi. I'll have to stay within range to pick up on the signals, but you two can give me clues to your destination through the transmissions."

"So how soon can you be here?" Jared asked. "We only have about fifty minutes left of the hour they gave us."

"Just a minute, I'll ask." There was a brief silence before Fred came back on the phone. "My driver says we'll probably be there in twenty-five minutes. That'll give us enough time."

"You're coming here? I'd better give you the address."

"No. I'm sure your location is being watched, and they'll know if we meet. For right now it's better that we keep our contact a surprise—at least until I have reinforcements. After we're done talking, put one of your guards on the phone and he can arrange for someone to meet us at the national guard station. My driver will pass the stuff to him and he can carry it back to you. It'll take longer, but it will seem more natural."

"It'll look like these guardsmen have called for help after receiving the note."

"Hopefully. And as soon as I drop off the stuff, I'll go wait in my car outside the church."

Jared took a deep breath. "Okay, I got it. But let's run it through once more, just to be sure." He rehearsed everything, making sure of the details. Next to him, Cassi looked nervous, but still determined.

"We'll see you then, Fred," Jared said.

"Real soon. I'll do everything I can to get you free."

"I know you will, Fred. Oh, but there's one more thing. Sampson's not going to know you. We need a code word for you to help get him into your car."

"I was just going to grab him, but that might be easier. What'll it be?—providing they let you talk to him first."

"I didn't think of that. But I'll try to talk to him. What about the Book of Mormon?"

Fred laughed without mirth. "First the Mormon temple, and now the Book of Mormon. Well, at least it's one the average person wouldn't guess."

"So I suppose you still haven't started the one I gave you."

"Jared, if we get out of this I'll read it. I promise."

Jared knew that was Fred's way of saying how impossible this venture seemed. "I'll hold you to that." He passed the phone to one of the guards and turned to Cassi. "That's it, then. We just have to wait."

She held his hand tightly. He knew she was as afraid as he was. "We've seen miracles," she said. "We can pray for another."

Jared was amazed to feel a smile on his face. She was so wonderful, so full of faith. So unlike the crass, money-hungry Laranda. "Let's go upstairs," he said. "It'll be more quiet there."

* * * * *

A third national guardsman came to their door shortly before Jared needed to leave for the church. He and Cassi paced in front of the door while the landlady and the other guardsmen watched them with bright, nervous eyes. Jared took a deep breath, recognizing the man who had spoken in poor English the day before. Without a word, he handed Jared a briefcase. He fingered his thick gold necklace while Jared opened the case.

Inside, Jared saw the listening and tracking devices that Fred had promised. Everything was labeled and an explanation attached. One of the sound transmitters was a pair of gold earrings in the shape of sunflowers. A matching barrette was a signal booster. The second transmitter was cleverly disguised as a man's silver-colored necklace, with a large book charm as long as Jared's middle finger. He could just make out the words *Holy Bible*. The tracking device was built into a woman's compact, complete with a purse and other womanly items to make it appear authentic.

"I feel like we're in a James Bond rerun," Cassi said, holding a lipstick tube. "I wonder if this is really lipstick or poison."

Jared's laughter died on his lips. "Look at this," he said. What he held was a man's bulky ring. The directions said it hid a tiny needle and a sleeping potion. "This evens the odds just a little."

Cassi fingered the woman's compact and tracking device. "I wonder how it transmits. Well, I guess it doesn't matter as long as it works. Fred certainly came prepared."

"He's a good man. If anyone can help us, he can." Jared picked up the necklace and put it around his neck. "Now I really look native."

Cassi gave him a tight smile. She looked in a mirror on the wall as she put on the sunflower earrings and matching barrette. The barrette held back a few strands of hair from her face, accentuating her fine cheekbones.

"It's time to go," Jared said. "I'll leave first, and you follow in about two minutes with the guardsmen." He looked at the guy with the gold necklace for approval.

"Yes," the man said. "Be careful."

"Thanks."

Jared pulled her into his arms. "I love you, Cassi. No matter what happens today, remember that."

"I love you, too." They kissed once, long and hard, before Jared turned away and walked out the door.

Jared searched the street as he strode quickly to the church near the center of town. People around him were dressed in their Sunday best and walked without hurry. The delicious smell of olive oil and cooking meat filled the air as many women had already begun to prepare their Sunday feasts before leaving for morning mass. Jared's stomach rumbled, and he remembered he had forgotten to eat.

Unseen eyes followed him, but he couldn't be sure if he was being watched by hostile eyes or curious native ones. He approached the church cautiously, making sure no one jumped him from behind. He saw absolutely nothing out of the ordinary, not even a vehicle that did not belong. Was Fred already in place? Was he using an Embassy vehicle, or had he borrowed something less conspicuous?

The note had said to meet the kidnaper inside the church. Jared didn't believe in the Catholic religion, but he felt much respect for those who did, and having such a meeting inside the church violated his deepest sense of honor and faith. Who would do such a thing?

He walked in, feeling curious eyes upon him from the native population. No one approached his position. He chose an aisle seat on a bench in the third row from the back, ever watchful and alert.

For five minutes he sat alone. Then a woman slid past and sat gracefully on the bench beside him, her expensive perfume filling Jared's nose. He had smelled that fragrance before. He looked sharply at the woman. She was dressed in a form-fitting black suit with a matching hat and veil which fell almost to her jawbone. Jared could see that her hair was blonde, much too blonde for any native Portuguese. Large diamond earrings glinted through the veil, and a matching necklace shone on her neck. On her hands she wore black lace gloves that left the tips of her fingers bare. The long red nails recalled memories he would prefer to forget.

"Where is Sampson?" he asked.

The lady's veiled face turned toward him slowly. He saw the red-painted lips smiling. Green eyes pierced him to his very core, despite the veil. Jared felt sick. "Hello, Jared," she said. "It's nice to be with you again. I've missed you."

The voice was also familiar, but Jared wouldn't let himself believe. Laranda was dead. Dead! This person before him was an imposter, and he would expose her. But first he had to free Sampson. "Look, I don't know who you are," he said, "but the note said us for the boy. Where is he?"

"This church is quite extraordinary, don't you think? Look at that magnificent tile work. All hand-painted, of course. The guidebook says it's from the seventeenth century. So quaint, so original, so expensive. It's a pity we can't take it with us."

"You would try."

The woman laughed, and a chill crept up Jared's spine. Whoever she was, she sounded exactly like Laranda.

"For the third time, where is Sampson?"

Her red smile didn't fade. "I said I'd trade for both you and Cassi. Where is she?"

"You expect me to trust you? You show me the boy and let me talk to him to make sure he's all right, and then we'll do the exchange."

The woman's hand shot out and grabbed Jared's in a tight squeeze. "I'm the one who's calling the shots, Jared, my love. You are along for the ride."

"No, I'm here because you need me. And Cassi isn't joining us until the boy goes free. That's final. So make up your mind."

"Tell her to come, Jared, and we'll all talk about this rationally."

"Rationally?" Jared snorted, shaking off her hand. "The last time we tried to talk rationally, you almost killed us both!"

The woman's laugh was deep and amused. "So now you remember me, do you?"

Jared realized his mistake. Laranda was dead, but whoever it was impersonating her gave such a real performance that he had forgotten for a moment she was only an actor.

"If you really are Laranda," he said, "you'd take off that veil. Let me see your face."

"You can see enough of it. You know who I am. And you wouldn't ask a lady in mourning to take off her veil, would you? You know that Big Tommy is dead."

"I know Laranda was the last person on earth to mourn anyone."

"Oh, but that is where you are wrong," said the silky voice. "I mourned you, Jared. When you married last Monday in San Diego, I mourned you." There was a pause before the voice continued, sounding abruptly strained. "Of course, I don't believe in religion."

"Don't you?" Jared pushed. The real Laranda might not believe in religion, but did the imposter? "Then why are we here?"

"This is not a religious place," the woman said. "These people know nothing of real truth." The voice was firm, the strained tones completely vanished. So much for any advantage.

"Where is the boy?"

"Why won't you call me by my name, Jared?"

"Because you are not Laranda."

"Aren't I? Don't you believe your ears and your eyes? I'm here, and I'm not leaving until I get what I want."

"And what is that?" Jared's voice was sharp. The problem was, she did look and act like Laranda. But his heart rebelled at the recognition.

"I want *you*, of course. As I always have. And Cassi, because she means so much to you."

"Then where is Sampson?"

"And you would trade him for her?" She laughed again. "You don't know the meaning of real love."

Anger swept into Jared's heart and mind. "You're the one who knows nothing about love or sacrifice. Sampson is a little boy who has no fault in this whole mess, and he is going to walk free or I leave now." He began to rise.

"Stop," she commanded.

Jared saw the glint of a pistol in her hand. "Go ahead, shoot me in this church. You don't believe in God anyway. Do it." He saw her hand waver. "But you can't, can you? Because you need me alive. So where is the boy?"

"Sit down." The voice was calm, but the anger behind it was like a slap to Jared's face. He sat again on the bench. "Now, look over there by the entrance."

Jared looked and saw Sampson with an olive-skinned man. He looked young and scared.

"You may go to him and talk to him for one minute. Then we make the trade. But first you must tell me where Cassi is."

"She's across the street with three guards. When she sees Sampson coming toward them, she'll leave and join us in front of the church."

"Very well. But it must be a simultaneous exchange." The woman stood and walked briskly to the entrance of the church. Jared's stomach clenched again as he followed her. She even walked the way Laranda had walked. Could it really be her? Then who had he seen cremated?

No, his mind said. *That's what she wants you to believe.*

Sampson's eyes lit up as he saw Jared. He rushed into his arms. "Jared, it's Donelli's nephew," he said quietly and urgently. "And Laranda. They're going to kill me. I know it!"

Jared glanced over at the olive-skinned man who had been with Sampson. Darkly handsome, he did look the part of a mobster's family, but there was also a marked uneasiness in his face. The imposter Laranda might not be bothered by conducting business in a church, but Jared guessed that Donelli's nephew was very disturbed by it. He noticed, however, that the restlessness seemed to fade as Laranda came to stand by his side. *One more conquest for the witch.* Jared pushed the thought aside.

"Sampson, they're not going to kill you. Look, we have a plan. First you have to walk across the street toward three Portuguese national guardsmen. Cassi will walk toward you, but you mustn't talk to her or get too close, because the Donellis are going to try to get you back."

"So I go to the guards?"

"No. You pretend you're going there, but a car is going to stop for you. Don't let it too near you until they give you a password. Then get in as fast as you can."

"What about Cassi?"

"She'll be with me. Don't worry. The man in the car will know how to find us."

Sampson's brown eyes grew large. "Jared, you and Cassi won't die, will you?"

Jared looked firmly into Sampson's eyes. "No. Don't even think that. We're going to do everything we can to come back to you. I promise. And you remember how important a promise is, don't you?" The boy nodded, and Jared prayed as hard as he had ever prayed in his whole life that he wouldn't let this child down. So many had already deserted him.

"The password is that book you were reading in the car in France," Jared said hurriedly as he saw the woman and Donelli approaching their position. "Do you remember the title? I won't say it aloud, just in case they have planted a bug on you." If they had put a listening device on Sampson, it might complicate matters, but he didn't think they'd back away from the opportunity to capture Cassi, regardless.

"I remember it."

"Good. Now be brave. You can do it."

Sampson gulped and nodded. He cringed as Donelli stared at them, but Jared kept his hand on the boy's shoulder to reassure him. "Let's go," Donelli ordered.

"Yeah, it's better we don't mock God, don't you think?" Jared said.

Donelli's face darkened, but he didn't reply. Jared suspected he had been thinking along the same lines. "So you're Donelli's nephew," Jared continued. "What's your name?"

"Donelli, to you," snapped the woman. "Now enough of this. We have things to do."

Jared shrugged and led them from the church. Outside, Sampson began his brisk walk to the street. Jared saw Donelli speaking into a cell phone. *Here goes the counterattack,* Jared thought.

Across the street, Cassi also began walking. She lifted an encouraging hand to Sampson as they passed within ten feet of each other.

Sampson was nearly across the cobblestone road when a small blue car drove up beside him. A man with dark hair opened the door. Sampson began to back away, then ran as the man lunged at him. He ran not toward the guards, but around the car and down the street. The man jumped in the car as it turned and followed the boy. Further down the street, another car door opened, a white, mid-sized vehicle, and someone inside shouted something Jared couldn't hear. Sampson altered his angle and dived into the car. A shot rang out. People ducked and screamed. The white car drove onto the sidewalk to pass a few cars that had paused to watch, then disappeared around a bend. The blue car followed, its engine roaring.

Cassi had turned to watch the commotion, and Jared saw two Portuguese men rise off the stone benches in front of the church and grab her arms. Who were they? The men shoved her into a tan car as the national guardsmen ran across the street after her. Jared was grateful for their attempt at rescue, but the tan car sped down the street and was lost to his sight.

Jared felt a strong hand close over his own elbow. Donelli. On the other side, the woman hooked her arm through his. "Not one tricky move," she said icily. She led him beside the church and down a narrow street where a limousine awaited. A man in the front seat opened the door for them.

"See if they got the boy," the woman said to Donelli.

Donelli pulled out his phone, and Jared waited to hear the news. He thought Sampson had gotten away, but had he? And where was Cassi? Who had taken her?

CHAPTER 16

The little blue car was no match for the power of the white car the Embassy had given Fred. Its power and Alberto's fear made their getaway almost certain. Even so, Fred breathed a sigh of relief when he no longer saw the blue car behind them. Alberto also relaxed. Fred had to give the man credit. He was doing his best in a terrible situation. Far beyond the duty of his calling.

"You did well, Alberto."

"Thanks, Fred."

Somewhere along the way, while discovering corpses, delivering Worthington to a doctor, and surviving a car chase with armed men, they had started relating to each other on a first-name basis. If the man had been an American, Fred would have asked if he was interested in working for the FBI. Then again, they always needed contacts in Europe as well, and the guy already worked for the American Embassy . . .

The beeping of the tracking equipment Fred had set up in the front seat diverted his thoughts. "They're on the move," Alberto said.

"Follow them. At a safe distance. But remember what I told you about getting too far back. We must not lose them. Until our reinforcements arrive, we are all the hope they have. The receiver will beep a warning if we begin to drop too far back."

He put first one pair of earphones on and then the other to see if either Cassi or Jared was giving directions, but he heard nothing of interest. Not at all like the earlier conversation between the woman and Jared. Was it really Brooke? He wished he could be certain.

"Who are you?" asked Sampson.

Fred had nearly forgotten the boy. "I'm Fred Schulte."

"I mean who *are* you? Who do you work for?"

"I'm with the FBI, and I'm Jared and Cassi's friend."

"Well, I gathered that much, with the Book of Mormon stuff and all." Sampson studied Fred for a long minute. "FBI, huh?"

"Yeah."

"So are they going to be okay?"

"We're going to do everything we can. They're both set up with listening devices and with a tracking device. We're waiting for backup."

Sampson nodded gravely. "How can I help?"

"You can start by telling me everything you saw and heard."

"Nothing, really." Sampson said. "But Giorgio Donelli was there, and so was Laranda."

"Laranda? Are sure it was her?"

"Yeah, it was her all right. Look, can I help you with those?" Sampson pointed to the earphones, each of which was connected to a receiver. "I can listen to one of them."

"Okay," Fred said. "Sure. But write down on this pad anything you hear. And let me know if any of them say anything about their destination or something else important."

"I will." Sampson put on the earphones that linked to Cassi.

Fred dialed Justin and told him what had happened. "At least Worthington's alive," he said. "And with a positive identification on Donelli's nephew, we know the family is behind all this."

"You want me to arrest him?"

"Well, first see if Donelli himself has returned to the States. I have a suspicion he hasn't. I think whatever is going on will happen here in Portugal, or he wouldn't have come himself."

"And what about Jared and Cassi choosing a cabin in Portugal?" Justin asked. "Was that coincidence?"

Fred sighed. "You know, I think for once it really was. I'm almost positive that Cassi's friend in England didn't betray her. Look what happened to his wife."

"Perhaps God really does work in mysterious ways."

"Maybe. Is there any news from England? About Cassi's friend. How is the wife?"

"Still unconscious, last I heard."

"Well, check again when you get a chance. For once, I'd like to have good news for Cassi and Jared."

"First you have to catch up to them."

"Right. Let me know when my backup will arrive. Give them this number so I can tell them where to meet me."

"Any sign of Brooke?"

"Not yet. But I'll find her."

* * * * *

Cassi had been close enough to see that Sampson had dived into Fred's car, but had seen nothing after that. Where was Jared? He had been in front of the church, but after the shot and all the screaming, she hadn't seen him anymore. She hoped they would be reunited soon. Or had someone else jumped into the fray?

She studied the two men on the seat beside her. They both had dark hair and moustaches and looked Portuguese. Had they been hired locally? She thought of all the men who had lost their lives at the cabin. Maybe the enemy hadn't yet received American reinforcements. Then again, maybe these men weren't even part of the same group. The thought worried her.

"Where are you taking me?" she asked.

The men looked at her with their intense dark eyes and said something in Portuguese. "Dang it! Don't you even know what I'm saying?"

The driver in the front seat turned around. "I do," he said in perfect English, turning blue eyes briefly in her direction. "And don't worry. We won't hurt you." There was an unspoken "yet" in his voice that made Cassi's flesh crawl.

"Hey, you're the guy outside the national guard building!" she said, recognizing both him and his brown beret.

He smiled, but this time didn't take his eyes from the road. "I've been following you a long time," he said. "Since England, when I failed to get you at the car bombing."

"You were responsible for that!" Cassi found herself trembling with rage.

His shoulders lifted in a gentle shrug. "I only follow orders, but I take pride in my work. I'm paid to do a good job. Unfortunately, your husband packs a pretty hard punch."

"You were the man he knocked out on the sidewalk."

"Yeah, beautiful, that was me."

"But you should still be in police custody."

"What, me? An innocent bystander? You and your husband are lucky my lawyer didn't sue you for attacking me." Taggart gave her a maddening smirk. "They had nothing on me."

Cassi sat back in her seat, clenching her teeth. He was nothing more than an irritating lackey. She would save her anger for whoever was really in charge. At least she knew that whoever he worked for had tried to abduct Jared in England as well as herself. Odds were that whoever had taken Jared worked for the same person, and they would eventually end up together.

One of the Portuguese hirelings touched her leg and squeezed. She slapped him. "Please tell your apes here to keep their hands off," she said coolly.

The driver turned and raised a gun, saying something in Portuguese. The men beside her moved away, but still cast her side-long glances. Cassi shivered.

They drove for hours, and Cassi was beginning to feel faint with hunger. Her thoughts raced. If only she knew what was going on, it might ease her distress. Maybe the driver would let something drop.

"So who is your employer?"

He chuckled. "You'll have to wait, beautiful. I'm not paid to tell you anything."

"At least tell me where we're going." Cassi hoped to get some information to Fred.

"To a place. Keep quiet and you'll soon see."

"I'm hungry."

He flashed her an amused smile. "Yeah, and I bet you have to go to the bathroom, too."

"So, what if I do?"

"You'll have to wait. It won't be long now."

Cassi sighed and sat back, praying the tracking device was working. How long would it be until Fred rescued them?

More time passed—hours, Cassi thought—but she had no way of knowing exactly how much. A large city sprang up around them. They drove across a long bridge that spanned a river; Cassi was sure she had seen it on their way from the airport.

"So we're going to the airport."

Again came that irritating smile. "Nope."

"Well, then, we're going to Lisbon. I recognize it."

"Good for you."

Cassi was confident she had given Fred some information. They weren't going to the airport, and they had driven to Lisbon. What now?

She kept her eyes open for street signs, reading them aloud when she could pronounce them and spelling them when she couldn't. The Portuguese men were amused at her attempts and helpfully pronounced the street names for her.

Eventually they stopped, and the driver exited the car. The other men followed, pulling Cassi after them. The driver hooked his arm through Cassi's. "Let's go, beautiful." Cassi tried to step away but felt the barrel of a gun pressed to her side. Was it real or full of sleeping potion? Either way, she didn't want to find out. She craned her neck to see a street sign, but there were none.

"Not one word, beautiful," the driver warned. "And I mean it."

Before she had a chance to see the name of the building, he whisked her inside what appeared to be a hotel. "Where are—"

The pistol jabbed painfully into her side. "Shut up."

He took her up an elevator, the two Portuguese coming with them. They stopped before a door and knocked. "Here she is," he said when the door opened. Leaving the Portuguese outside, he forced Cassi forward, then abruptly left her alone in the middle of the room. She saw Jared, sitting in a chair in front of an olive-skinned man with dark hair. Relief washed through her.

"Thanks, Taggart," said a silky voice.

Cassi's gaze ripped from Jared and stared at the woman in black. "Laranda?"

The woman laughed. "Yes, it's me. See, Jared? Your lovely wife recognizes me. Why don't you?"

"She's not Laranda," Jared said.

The woman came closer to Cassi. "But I am. See?"

She looked and sounded like Laranda, but Cassi trusted Jared. "Then take off your veil."

The other woman laughed. "Maybe you two really do deserve each other. Luckily, I won't need either of you for very long."

Cassi met Jared's gaze uneasily.

"Search them," said the olive-skinned man to Taggart. "It's time we got to the house."

Cassi's driver stood and went toward Jared. From his pocket, he pulled out an unfamiliar rectangular device about as large as her video camera's battery. What was it? She knew that in a minute he would either discover the bugs or not. Cassi thought of her own listening transmitter in her earring, and more importantly the tracking device. *Great, now what?*

Searching desperately, Cassi's eyes fell on a small black purse on the table across from where Jared sat. *Must be that woman's.* Cassi let herself slip into a chair next to the purse. Her own large purse, filled with the makeup Fred had provided, felt heavy on her shoulder. The woman who looked like Laranda glanced at her briefly, but kept her focus on Jared, as did Taggart and the olive-skinned man.

Carefully, Cassi slipped her hand inside her purse and found the compact with the tracking transmitter. She palmed it awkwardly and slowly lifted it to the table, inching her hand closer to the small black purse, her heart beating rapidly. She looked up to see if anyone had noticed her movements and met Jared's eyes. He nodded almost imperceptibly and then began to struggle against Taggart's hand and the small rectangular box, which ran the length of his body, searching for something out of the ordinary.

The olive-skinned man held Jared down, and the Laranda imposter leaned forward anxiously. In that moment, Cassi gently opened the flap on the small purse and slid the compact inside a zippered pocket. Hopefully, the other woman wouldn't realize it was there before it was too late. And maybe if she did find it, she would use it unsuspectingly, thinking she must have purchased it at an earlier time and had forgotten. Cassi knew there were a lot of ifs involved, but seeing Taggart's thoroughness, it was the only chance they had.

The black box in Taggart's hand began vibrating. "Ahh," Taggart said. "Look what we have here." He pulled the silver necklace from Jared's neck. "State of the art, this one."

"A bug?" asked the Laranda woman.

"Yes. I hope you didn't give much away on your journey, because someone has been listening in. I've disabled it now." He tossed the necklace to the olive-skinned man. "There, Donelli. If you want to feed some false information to them, let me know."

Donelli. For some reason, the name was familiar to Cassi. She was sure she had heard it connected with organized crime. Donelli examined the necklace, then put it in his pocket.

"Unless she has one, too." The Laranda imposter turned on Cassi. "Then they'll know we found it."

Taggart approached Cassi with a smile. "I should have checked her before."

"It is of no concern," the woman said. "This is a big city. And that's why we came here first. At best, those who listen will be led here. But we will be long gone."

Taggart nodded and put his hands on Cassi. He was very thorough, and Cassi barely managed to endure his touch, wanting to slap his hands away. Finally he came to her hair. "Here it is," he said, extracting the thick hair clip and earrings. He also handed them to Donelli.

"What about her purse?" asked the woman.

Taggart dumped Cassi's purse and ran the black box over the contents, as well as the fabric itself. "Nothing here," he said.

"Well, well, well," the woman said with a satisfied smile. "I guess it's time to get to the house." She smiled at Donelli. "Your uncle will be waiting, Giorgio, and we have a big day tomorrow."

"Maybe we should use a signal scrambler just in case they have more hidden on them," Giorgio said.

"No need." Taggart held up his bug detector. "This would have found them all. It's very thorough. They're clean."

Giorgio and the woman appeared satisfied. This time they took Cassi and Jared together in a white limousine. It wasn't exactly low profile, but the car seemed to fit the woman in charge. But was she really in charge? And who was she? Cassi held Jared's hand and wondered.

They were taken to a two-story house on the outskirts of Lisbon, cut off from the street and other houses by a tall, wrought-iron fence. The house was stately, encircled by lush gardens and cobbled walks. Inside, Cassi saw wood furniture and beautifully woven throw rugs on the pale blue ceramic tile. Though not inexpensive, nothing looked of gallery quality, and Cassi decided the house wasn't owned by the mob family; perhaps it was rented. But why? The reasons still escaped her.

The Laranda woman herself and Giorgio Donelli escorted them to a room with bars over the windows. She flashed Cassi and Jared a smile behind her black lace veil. "Don't get too cozy," she said. "There are hidden cameras."

"Why?" demanded Jared.

"Because I don't *want* you to get cozy. Jared, dear, when will you learn? You were supposed to be mine. I won't let you be happy with anyone else."

"You're not Laranda!" Cassi said. "I don't know who you are, but Laranda is dead. Dead!"

The woman suddenly put her hand to her head as though dizzy. Giorgio Donelli steadied her. "Shut up," he growled at Cassi. He added more softly to the woman, "Come, Laranda, let's go see the doctor."

She shook him off. "I don't need that imbecile. I just need to get the information at the bank, and then we can give these two their reward. I get to do that myself!" She tossed her head like a horse trying to free itself from its bridle. Her breath came quickly now, in short gasps. "Remember, I get revenge! You'll rue the day you denied me, Jared!"

"I never denied you!" Jared insisted. "I don't even know who you are! You are *not* Laranda."

Donelli let go of the woman's arm and hit Jared in the mouth. He reeled with the unexpected blow, raising his hands belatedly in defense. Donelli waved a gun. "Not today, pretty boy." He again put his hand on the woman, and this time she let him lead her from the room.

Cassi went to Jared. "Are you all right?"

"Yeah." He touched his split lip. "I would have ducked, but I wasn't expecting it."

"You should have. That guy is totally in love with her."

"Laranda always had a slew of male followers."

Cassi took a tissue from a box on the nightstand next to one of the two single beds and began to clean Jared's lip. "She's not Laranda."

"I know. But who is she?"

"And why does she want us? It doesn't make sense, Jared."

He put his arms around her. "I know." In a quiet voice he added, "We just have to hope Fred will find us."

* * * * *

"They've found the bugs," Fred told Justin. "But the tracking transmitter is still working. I hope it's leading us to the right place."

"The others will join you by nightfall."

"Good."

"What are your plans?"

"For now, we'll just watch and wait. I want to learn what's going on. We have to make sure Jared and Cassi are really there. And then I'd like to wait for a good chance to take them. I don't want to risk their lives any more than necessary."

"Sounds good. Let me know what I can do from here. Oh, and Fred, I've been in contact with Cassi's friend in England. The wife's out of her coma. Looks like she's going to make it."

"That's good news." Fred was surprised at the warmth he felt toward people he had never met. "Cassi and Jared will be relieved." *If I get the chance to tell them.*

He hung up the phone and looked at Sampson. "That lady in England is going to be all right."

The boy's eyes suddenly began to water. "I'm glad. I really liked her. She's a great cook."

"Are you hungry?"

"Yeah."

"When they stop moving, we'll grab a bite to eat."

"Okay," said the boy. He looked pensive. Without warning, he shifted the conversation. "Did you know my dad?"

"I met him a few times."

Sampson's eyes didn't leave his face. "Did you like him?"

"I don't know that you want to hear the answer."

"I do."

"Well, he was responsible for the death of a very good friend of mine, Linden Johansen."

The boy showed no surprise. "He was our neighbor. I met him once. Old guy, white hair."

"Yeah. He was great. I really miss him."

"I miss my dad, too."

"I'm sure you do."

"I wish he hadn't hurt anyone, though. Maybe then he wouldn't be dead."

"I'm sorry, Sampson, really I am."

"Are you a Mormon?"

"No. But I know a few. They're nice people."

"Do they keep their word?"

Fred thought of Brooke. "The ones I have known well always have. I don't know about the others."

"I wish my dad had been a Mormon," Sampson said. "Maybe he would still be alive."

"Maybe." Fred's heart went out to the child who missed his father so desperately. How alone he must feel! Much like Fred in his own apartment at night, with no wife or children to warm his soul.

"But Jared and Cassi are Mormons," he added. "And they like kids. Maybe you can live with them."

"I don't know," said Sampson. "I might never see them again."

Fred grimaced. Unfortunately, the words were all too true.

* * * * *

Brooke let Giorgio lead her to her bedroom. The doctor was there waiting. "What happened?" he asked anxiously.

"They insisted she wasn't Laranda, and she started acting funny."

"I see." The doctor looked at Brooke. "I'm going to give her a little something for that headache."

"I don't have a—" But she did have a headache. Why did it hurt so badly?

She sat down at the dressing table and removed her hat. Her face was pale and moist with perspiration. She opened her purse and fumbled through the contents that she vaguely remembered choosing in America. In a zippered pocket, she found a compact and patted the powder on her face. Then she searched for the right shade of red lipstick. She forced herself to breathe deeply, trying not to worry. But why did Jared and Cassi say she wasn't Laranda? And why, for that short time, had she suddenly stopped hating Jared? Why had she stopped wanting to have his arms around her? Her stomach twisted and she started to heave.

"Lie down and it'll pass." The doctor helped her to the bed. She felt a needle slide into her arm, and in a minute, she did feel better.

"What went wrong?" Giorgio asked.

The doctor shook his head. "You tell me. I was the one who said I needed more time with her."

Brooke spoke, making her voice calm. "I'm fine now. You may go, doctor."

He withdrew, but he didn't leave the room. Giorgio sat beside her on the bed, caressing her arm. For some reason, his touch felt violating and she pushed him away.

"But you said—"

"I'm tired." She recalled all too vividly how earlier she had led him on. Now the thought made her sick. What was happening to her?

It's just that inner part that you need to get rid of, she thought. *The accident must have been very bad.*

Giorgio kissed her brow, and Brooke could barely stop herself from hitting him. He crossed to where the doctor waited by the door. "Fix her," he said.

"I'll have to increase the drugs."

"Do it."

"I'll wait and see how she is in an hour. Another session with her could work better."

"You do what I say."

But the doctor stood firm. "Look, I'm the one responsible for her care, and your uncle employed me. If you have some problem, I suggest you take it up with him."

"I will." Giorgio stormed from the room.

Brooke felt a peace fall over her when he was gone. She was safe. Safe. At least for now. Her eyes closed, and the room faded from her view.

* * * * *

"You must calm your hormones, Giorgio," Nicolas told his nephew. "What is important is our plan. Tomorrow the bank, and then the fortune. What happens to any of them after that means nothing to me."

"Fine," Giorgio said. "But I don't want her hurt."

"No, you just want to keep her drugged." Nicolas let the irony show in his voice. "Come on, let your more reasonable side take over. That woman is not Laranda, and we can only make her act like it for a time. What then?"

Giorgio took a deep breath. "I know that. It's just that when I'm with her I—" he broke off, as though not willing to show his uncle more weakness.

Nicolas knew then that the girl couldn't be allowed to live. Somehow he would arrange for her to die by Giorgio's own hand. That was the only way he knew to cure this type of infatuation. Love was a trap. It was a shame he hadn't taught the boy that lesson earlier. But better late than never. Afterwards, Giorgio would be a proper heir—and both of them many times richer than they were today.

CHAPTER
17

They left the house at nine the next morning. Jared had been given a pair of blue dress pants, a white shirt, and a khaki blazer. Cassi wore a long flowered skirt and a white blouse. "It seems we have to be dressed appropriately for where we're going," Jared said.

Cassi grimaced. "At least it's not black."

Jared knew what she meant. In this circle, black was associated with death and funerals. "Well, it's only a matter of time now. We'll be free soon." He didn't mention Fred, but knew she would take the hint. Fred had to find them.

As they were led from the house and into a white van they hadn't seen before, Jared strained his neck to see if he could see signs of Fred and his backup. Nothing. *They have to be there,* he thought. Of course, the Laranda imposter could have found the tracking transmitter Cassi had hidden in her purse. Maybe he and Cassi were on their own.

Once again Giorgio, Taggart, and the two Portuguese were their companions. Taggart was at the wheel in the van. The woman posing as Laranda sat in the other front seat. She still wore a hat and veil, though it was teal now to match her new suit. Giorgio sat next to Cassi and Jared, and the two Portuguese were in the rear seat. Jared noticed that everyone but the woman carried a weapon. That was unlike the Laranda he knew. Of course, it could be hidden in her small black purse.

"What are you doing?" Cassi asked suddenly, her voice showing terror.

Jared looked to see Giorgio strapping something on Cassi's wrist. "What is that?" he demanded.

"Just a little insurance," Giorgio said, checking the lock on the strap. "Now, let me tell you what's going to happen. You two will go inside the bank with Taggart. He'll help you contact the person you need to see. You will go inside and open the safe deposit box assigned to you with this key." He handed Jared a key. "You get what is there and you come out. It's simple."

"Then why that?" Jared pointed to Cassi's wrist.

"If you make any trouble, Cassi won't make it back to the van unless you carry her." Giorgio smiled without mirth. "The drug inside can be activated remotely. And it's not a sleeping drug. Only we can give her the antidote in time."

The woman in the front seat held up a vial containing a clear liquid. "She always was your weakness, Jared. This guarantees that you will come back like a good boy."

Jared's stomach twisted. This was exactly something Laranda would do. "But your man will be with us."

"What is one against two inside a bank?" asked Giorgio. "Besides, I suspect he won't be allowed inside the vault with you."

"Put it on me, then," Jared said.

The woman laughed. "Yeah, right, Jared. I don't think so."

They drove to the bank in silence. Jared wondered what could be so important in the safe deposit box that people were ready to kill for it. Drugs? Art treasures? No, there wouldn't be enough room inside the box. But perhaps diamonds or money? Well, they would soon know.

After four turns around the block, Taggart found a parking place opposite the bank. He jumped out of the van and came around for Cassi and Jared. "Remember, not one false move," said Giorgio.

Taggart grinned and pushed his beret down to conceal his forehead. Jared couldn't tell where the brown fabric ended and the man's hair began. Cassi's hand slipped into his. "I don't like him," she whispered. Jared didn't like the man either. It was too bad the police in London had let him go.

"Hurry," Taggart ordered. He motioned for Cassi and Jared to precede him to the bank. The Portuguese thugs followed, but waited at the doors outside.

Once in the bank, they had to stand in line for a teller, and with the small crowd, Jared could see that he and Cassi might have had a chance to escape. But not with the drug poised over Cassi's wrist. Jared thought about the sleeping drug he carried in the ring around his finger. Taggart hadn't found that, at least. He wished he could use it on the man now.

Their turn arrived and Taggart spoke to the clerk, who nodded and disappeared. "They need to make sure you are who you say you are."

"But we don't have any ID," Jared said. "We left our things back at the cabin."

Again Taggart flashed that annoying grin. "Don't worry. I'm prepared." Out of his pocket, he brought two passports.

"Those aren't ours," Jared said, noting the date inside.

"We had them made for you."

Another man came out and led them to a small office. There was a file on the desk. He spoke to Taggart. "Give him your passports," Taggart said. Cassi and Jared obliged.

But this went far beyond any check Jared had ever seen. The man pulled out photographs of them, along with fingerprints. There were also photographs of the clothes they were wearing, and even hair samples. The man carefully read the rows of notes inside the file. Then he insisted on taking fresh fingerprints and scanning them into his computer for comparison.

Jared and Cassi exchanged amazed glances. "She's not Laranda," Cassi said. "But I'm beginning to believe Laranda is somehow behind it. This is not your typical bank check. I don't think banks have this kind of software, do they? She must have paid for it."

Jared felt the same way. As impossible as it might sound, this had Laranda written all over it. "Maybe this was her backup plan in case she didn't kill us the first time."

Taggart watched their interchange with amusement, but didn't comment. "It seems our banker friend here is finally satisfied that you are who you say you are. He's going to let you in now."

The banker stood and led them from the room.

"You're right about the software," Taggart said, almost too casually. "Laranda did pay for it."

"Laranda is dead," Jared insisted.

"Perhaps. It makes no difference. But what is in that box does."

"What do you care?" Cassi said. "You're only a hireling."

Taggart smiled. "We are working on the same side. I'm with the FBI."

"You!" Cassi gasped.

Taggart nodded. "Don't let on, now. I just thought you'd both feel better going along with all this until we get to the end if you knew I was here to protect you."

"So that's how the police let you go so easily in England," Jared said.

"Not at all. Donelli's lawyer got me free. Until a few minutes ago, the FBI didn't even know I was here."

"So can't you free us?" Cassi asked.

"Not yet. You do want to know who's behind this and why, don't you?"

"Of course we do," Jared said. "But that doesn't mean we won't try to get free the minute we can."

"Soon," Taggart said.

They had reached a glass door lined by metal bars. The banker let Cassi and Jared inside, but Taggart was forced to wait on the other side of the glass. "I don't trust him," Cassi whispered to Jared.

"But he's with us." Taggart's revelation had made Jared feel more relaxed.

Cassi frowned. "I still don't like him. I just get this feeling. Oh, maybe it's because he found the bugs. Why would he do that if he's on our side?"

"What if he hadn't, and they were discovered later?" Jared countered.

"Yes, well, let's keep an eye on him."

The banker gave them the box and left the room. Jared opened it with the key Taggart had pressed in his hand at the vault door. Inside was a single sheet of folded paper.

> *The treasure is in Algueirão. But to open the door, both Jared and Cassi must be present and go in with me. Once inside, there will be more information. Hope you enjoy the show. Laranda.*

There was an address written across the bottom. Jared shook his head. "This is her writing. I'd know it anywhere."

"Could it be that she was worried we'd get away?" Cassi asked. "After all, it's very odd this bank being here in Portugal, where she also stashed the real paintings from which her little genius was forging those fakes. I mean, she had plans for everything else."

"So maybe this was her last-ditch effort at revenge." Jared sighed. "That makes a strange sort of sense. Well, we'd better get this out to the car so they can take that off you." He pointed at the strap on her wrist.

"But Jared, don't you see? I've just realized that this means Laranda really *is* dead, or at least not here. If that woman out there was Laranda, she'd know what was on this paper. We wouldn't need to come in here at all."

Cassi was right, and Jared felt relief. He had known the woman wasn't Laranda, but the likeness was uncanny. He smiled. "Maybe this will break through her shell. Funny thing is, I think she really believes she's Laranda."

"And Giorgio half believes it himself." Cassi refolded the paper.

"What do you suppose that bit about going in with Laranda meant?" Jared asked. "It makes it sound as though she'll be there."

"It's spooky. You're sure you saw her cremated?"

"I'm sure."

"Then maybe it's just another show like the one with this woman."

"I don't like it, Cassi. She tried to kill us once. I think she's trying again."

"Maybe we should talk to Taggart." Her grimace showed she didn't like the idea.

They waited to be let outside the glass doors, where Taggart awaited them curiously. "Well?"

Cassi handed him the note with more than a little reluctance. Taggart read it before passing it to Jared. "Do you make anything of it?" Jared asked.

"Not yet," he said. "But I do know some fancy highbrow lawyer brought Donelli a package from Laranda Garrettson. Maybe there is something inside to explain it all. I'll do some snooping."

"What do you suppose is in Laranda's treasure?" Cassi asked.

"Paintings and other fine art," Taggart said without hesitation. "Stolen or bought on the underground. One is rumored to be a

Vincent Van Gogh worth forty million dollars. And there is apparently much more involved. Garrettson was a master at swindling and stealing. She did it her whole life."

Jared whistled. "No wonder Donelli is so interested."

"Yeah. With these kinds of funds, he'll be at the top. Make no mistake. Especially with Holbrooke out of the way." Before they arrived at the outer door, Taggert paused. "By the way, the FBI was in here. I talked to their man and told him to hold off a bit. With that thing on Cassi, there's nothing much we can do now anyway. I'll get another message to them when the coast is clear. Now that we know where the art is stashed, there isn't such a big hurry. This is going to be the biggest sting the world has ever known. We might as well get it right."

They walked calmly out to the van. Jared immediately handed the note to the woman, but Donelli intercepted it. He read it as quickly as Taggart had before placing it in the woman's outstretched hand.

"Isn't that your handwriting, Laranda?" Jared asked with a mocking voice.

She hesitated. "Of course it is." Her hand went briefly to her head as she turned and faced the front, ignoring him.

"I wonder why you put it in the bank." Jared pushed as hard as he dared. "Don't you remember the address? Why did we need to go in and get it?"

She turned toward him again. "Shut up, Jared. I have my reasons."

Giorgio waved his gun. "That's enough. You heard the lady. You are nothing. Just do as you're told."

Jared felt it wise to keep quiet, but he would bring it up again as soon as he could. Why did the real Laranda want this woman with them? Who was she?

"We did what you want, now take this thing off." Cassi held up her wrist to Giorgio, and Jared watched with relief as he removed the strap. For a moment, he had forgotten the drug and Cassi's danger. *Stupid,* he told himself. If something had happened to Cassi, it would have been his fault. He wished for the millionth time that he had never met Laranda Garrettson. Of course that might mean he would never have met Cassi, either. Jared let out a long sigh.

Taggart started away from the curb, and Jared saw several other cars also pull into traffic. Was Fred or another FBI agent in one of those cars? Or could Taggart be trusted at all?

* * * * *

Nicolas Donelli called a meeting with Giorgio and Taggart in his makeshift den in the rented house. "Okay, so now we know where the paintings are."

"So what do we need *them* for?" Giorgio asked, referring to the Landines.

Nicolas stifled his anger, reminding himself that Giorgio was still young. "This entire thing has been engineered by Laranda Garrettson," he explained. "What if we had gotten rid of the Landines earlier? We would never have learned the whereabouts of this treasure. And I doubt we'll be able to get in safely without the Landines. I wouldn't put it past Garrettson to destroy all the art if we don't do exactly as she has planned."

"So what do we do now?" Taggart asked.

Nicolas studied the man who had risen so quickly in his organization. He was obedient as well as intelligent—something you didn't often find in an underling. It had been Taggart's idea to set the car bomb in England, a stunt that had almost worked. "Giorgio, Taggart, you will go in with the girl and the Landines. There, Garrettson's whole plan will be revealed to you. You will follow the directions given inside to the letter. I want absolutely no variation whatsoever. Do you understand?" The others nodded.

"When do we go in?" Giorgio asked.

"Tomorrow afternoon." Nicolas reached into a box sitting on the wooden desk whose flaws bothered him more than he would admit. Why hadn't the owner bought quality furniture? They certainly charged enough for rent. His hand came out of the box with a gas mask. "Inside the building is a vault. Garrettson did say in her notes that you must use these when you are allowed to go into the vault." He paused for effect. "And then we clean out, load up the van, and go."

"What happens to the Landines?" asked a silky voice from the doorway.

Nicolas started. "How did you get here?"

Brooke walked farther into the room. "You have the nerve to ask? I am in charge here, and don't you forget it."

Fury fell over Nicolas in waves, but he forced a smile. "Of course, my dear. As for the Landines, I'm sure that *you* will take care of them."

"I don't think she should go," Giorgio said.

"I am going, make no mistake," Brooke replied. She held up a pistol. "I've been waiting a long time to see Jared get what he deserves."

"She's supposed to go inside," Nicolas said with a pleasantness he didn't feel. "I'm sure she'll be all right." Of course, he didn't know or care what would happen to Brooke—as long as the art treasures were intact. Garrettson's note said for the Landines to go inside with "me"—and that meant Brooke.

"Only you three will go in with the Landines. The boys will be outside with the van. I'll be waiting for you with the others on the plane. Don't be late."

Giorgio nodded and Brooke smiled. She really was beautiful. But too much of a danger to his nephew.

"If you two will excuse me," Nicolas said, "I have to talk to Taggart about other matters."

Giorgio took Brooke's arm and they left, looking for all the world like two young people in love. Nicolas watched them with barely hidden disgust. The moment the door was closed, he turned to Taggart. "They are too close. She has to be taken care of once the treasure is secure."

"I'll see to it."

"No." Nicolas raised his hand. "I want Giorgio to be responsible." He paced the room. "I had the doctor put a couple of phrases into her brain during her programming. One will make her attack Giorgio."

"Attack him?"

"Yes. Of course, I want you to make sure she doesn't hurt him, but that he feels threatened enough to kill her. Perhaps make sure her gun is unloaded. How you work it doesn't matter. I trust you can do it." Nicolas wrote on a paper. "Here's the code in case you need it."

Taggart looked at it before putting it in his pocket. "About the FBI."

Nicolas looked up. "They're here?"

"Yes. I talked to one of their London agents at the bank. I don't know how they found us, but they have. I didn't give them any information, but I hinted a lot. They'll hold off until they get my word. And by then it will be too late."

Nicolas smiled. "How fortunate they picked you to infiltrate my organization—especially when you were already on my payroll."

Taggart gave him an answering grin. "I volunteered for the job, you know. I even get extra pay."

Nicolas put his hand on Taggart's shoulder. "This deal is going to make you rich beyond your wildest dreams."

"I don't know. I can dream pretty big."

Nicolas laughed and slapped his back. "You'll see. Just one of those paintings is worth forty million dollars. And I bet there is a lot more worth the effort. Rumor has it that Garrettson played Big Tommy and many others for fools and sucked away their assets. Now they'll be ours." He moved around the cheap desk and sat in the chair.

Taggart faced him from the other side, placing both hands on the desk. "What I don't get is why we need that reporter at all. Why the elaborate hoax about whether or not Garrettson is still alive?"

"Ah, the question I've been expecting, but no one has asked until now." Nicolas himself had asked the question from the first. And now Taggart, but not Giorgio. Too bad Taggart hadn't been born his nephew. He had the natural instincts of a mob boss. But at least he would be around to keep Giorgio in line. A good right-hand man could make up for the faults in the boy until he learned.

"I was curious about that myself, but in the papers Garrettson left me, she was very specific. She told me that to vary one bit would mean failure. I believe her. Take that envelope she prepared for Holbrooke. I wanted to make sure she wasn't crossing me, but had I opened it I would have suffered his fate. And at the bank today. As hard as it was to capture them, we needed both the Landines alive to find the stash. So I'm playing along. If she wants to pretend to be in the midst of this, so be it. I'm sure the reason will present itself. But

I've no doubt that without her we won't get our money. And meanwhile, the FBI is confused about whether or not she is really dead. By now they know a woman is using her passport, and when it's over, our reporter friend will be left to blame. That's another reason it's so important that she doesn't make it. As the saying goes, dead people tell no tales. We'll get off without so much as a hand slap, and that alone is enough for me to go along with the ruse. It's very amusing, don't you think? And the real Garrettson would be content."

Taggart nodded his agreement. "Just leave everything to me."

"Oh, and one more thing," Nicolas said. "I think perhaps it's a good idea if we also arrange a little show for your FBI friends—one that gets them a little confused tomorrow. They can't have many men here to begin with."

Taggart's slow grin covered his face. "Divide and conquer? What do you have in mind?"

CHAPTER 18

Monday passed without word from their captors. Cassi and Jared were brought food by a shy Portuguese maid who appeared to speak no English. They were let out in the garden for an hour in the evening, under guard. Cassi was hoping to see Taggart, to ask him about the FBI, but he didn't appear. They did see the woman posing as Laranda in a window on the upper floor. She looked out on them briefly before turning away. Cassi wondered what she was thinking. Did she hate them as completely as the real Laranda had? Maybe it made no difference. If Laranda was behind the whole thing, as Taggart had implied, the outcome would be the same. Cassi shivered, though the air in the garden was warm.

"Fred's close," Jared said, putting his arm around her.

"I know. I hope Sampson's holding up okay. This has to be hard on him."

The night came, and still they were told nothing. They didn't dare discuss their situation or hopes for fear of being overheard, though they couldn't find a trace of a camera or bugs in the room. Either they were hidden well, or the Laranda imposter had been lying. Cassi and Jared slept in the same bed, cuddled together under the blankets. No one disturbed them.

In the morning, the house bustled with activity. Sounds came from all over, unfamiliar sounds they hadn't heard before. They waited. At noon they were served a light lunch, and then Taggart appeared. "We'll be leaving now. Just play along. I'm going too, so don't worry."

Cassi felt better, despite her continued distrust of the man. After all, he was doing his job, which included more than seeing that she and Jared were safe. Once they were finished, Donelli would be put behind bars for a long time.

"I guess it doesn't matter what we wear this time," Jared said, looking down at his wrinkled blue pants from the day before. Cassi also still wore the long flowered skirt and blouse she had been given.

"No. Not important," Taggart said.

He led them to the white van in the small garage. Cassi didn't have a chance to spot any cars parked outside the house, though she doubted Fred would be conspicuous about his surveillance. But he would be there, especially now that he was in contact with Taggart. Even now their escape could be planned.

Once again the Laranda imposter and Giorgio were present in the van, but the two Portuguese men had been replaced by three American guards. *Too important to risk to outsiders,* Cassi thought. Or maybe their backup had arrived to replace the men killed in the cabin. Her heart pounded in her ears. *It'll be over soon.*

"Get down until I say," Giorgio said.

Bent over in her seat, Cassi pondered the command. She wondered if it meant they suspected the house was being watched and didn't want prying eyes to see them leave. How had they found out about the FBI?

They drove for nearly an hour before they arrived at their destination. Cassi watched as they passed picturesque houses and rolling hills. Such a peaceful, beautiful country, but once again Laranda had violated it. The very trees and bushes seemed to scream betrayal.

At last they arrived in Algueirão and searched out the address of what appeared to be a large apartment building. Taggart parked the white van across the street. Giorgio, dressed in a black jacket, made a show of putting his gun in the pocket. "Easy now," he warned. He helped the woman out of the van. Cassi noticed that she didn't have her purse with her. Had she left it in the van? Or back at the house because it hadn't matched her sleek red suit? Cassi tried to see past the red fishnet veil that now obscured the woman's features, but saw nothing new. She hoped Fred had been able to follow them.

Taggart donned a bulky backpack before joining them on the street. The three other guards leaned against the van, watching them. One lit a cigarette, as though they knew they would be waiting for some time.

The group crossed the street and paused in front of the building. "Look," Jared said to Cassi, pointing to a plaque by the door. "It's a Mormon church." From the outside, it appeared that half of the building's bottom floor was being used to hold meetings. The practice was common where there was not enough membership for a large constructed chapel, but the fact that Laranda had known about the meeting place was unsettling.

"I don't like this," Cassi whispered.

Taggart and Giorgio didn't stop in front of that door, but went to another nearby. "Here it is," Taggart said. "What now? Do we ring the bell?"

Giorgio lifted his hand and rang. For a long while nothing happened, and he shifted his feet nervously. Cassi felt eyes on her and turned to look at the woman. She wasn't watching Cassi, but had her gaze fixed on Jared. Cassi wished she could see her full expression.

Abruptly, a short man opened the door. His tiny jet-black eyes darted from one to the other, saying nothing. He started to shut the door again but paused when he spotted the woman behind Giorgio. "Ah, it is you." He ducked his head in deference. "I did all that you say. I no let anyone inside."

He waited, but the woman said nothing. "Is it you?"

Giorgio snorted impatiently. "We need to get inside."

The little man shook his head. Before Taggart or Giorgio could react, he pulled out a pistol and pointed it at Giorgio. "I make sure it is her, and then I turn off the trap. You come in first and boom, everything all gone."

"I think he's serious," Taggart said. "Laranda, why don't you take off your hat and show him it's you? We don't want your treasure going up in flames, do we?"

Laranda pushed past Giorgio. "Relax," she said in a silky voice. "Of course it's me."

The dark little man in front of them lowered the gun slightly. "Let me see. Excuse me, my lady, but that is your order, not mine."

She removed her hat and veil. Cassi looked at the woman, startled to see that it was Laranda, or perhaps her twin sister. She looked toward Jared to see the same dismay on his face. "No," he whispered. "It can't be. The cheekbones. They're not quite right. But someone has gone to an awful lot of trouble to make it appear to be her."

Cassi couldn't be sure if there was doubt in his voice.

The little man ducked his head again and opened the door to let them in. "I will do the codes." He laid his gun carelessly on a short table in the middle of the small room and went to a large pad of numbers and letters near a door on the opposite side. Rapidly, he punched in a very long code, keeping an eye on the small screen above it.

Cassi examined the room in which they stood. It held a bed, a television, a couch, a tiny refrigerator, and a place to cook. Basically everything a person needed to live. How long had this odd little man stayed here, watching over Laranda's treasures?

He finished at the keyboard and turned to the Laranda imposter. "Senhora Garrettson, I go now to my family. My father's debt is paid, yes?"

She nodded, but Giorgio stopped him. "You aren't going anywhere."

"But the lady promised. It was our deal. I watch and let only her inside."

"Let him go," said the woman.

"No."

"I am in charge. Let him go." The voice was sharp like a dagger. "I promised."

"And do you always fulfill your promises?" Giorgio's voice taunted. "I haven't seen any of it." Cassi sensed his frustration. Apparently, things were not going well in their relationship.

"Well, I'm not taking orders from you anymore," he continued. "We do what *I* want, when *I* say." Without warning, Giorgio spun and slammed his fist into the tiny man. He gasped once before his eyes rolled up in his head and his body collapsed on the floor. Cassi couldn't tell if he still breathed, and with murder clear in Giorgio's face, she didn't dare kneel to see.

The woman stared at Giorgio, hatred fuming in her eyes. Giorgio ignored her and strode to the door by the pad of keys. It opened easily under his touch. The others followed more slowly. Cassi felt an urge to run out of the building since Giorgio wasn't looking at them, but thoughts of the guards outside made her change her mind.

"Taggart, where is my gun? Someone seems to have taken it. Give it to me now."

A chill ran down Cassi's spine at the coldness in the woman's voice. To her surprise, Taggart took the little man's gun from the table, checked the ammunition, and handed it to the woman. She swept regally through the door behind Giorgio. Cassi, Jared, and Taggart followed.

The room was a large expanse of wine-colored carpet and white walls, a few wooden panels, nothing more. From its size, the room likely took up nearly half of the building's bottom floor. With chairs and a pulpit, it would make a good place to hold sacrament meeting for a full-sized ward. Though the light was dim, Cassi could see a metal door at the far end of the room, and a machine that looked like the generator she had at the art gallery in San Diego. Laranda had certainly taken no chances with her treasure.

Taggart shut the door behind them. Immediately, the dim lights blinked out and music began: a congregation singing *Till We Meet Again*. Something was different about the song, and Cassi realized it was sung in Portuguese. Had Laranda recorded it from next door?

The music faded, and a picture appeared at intervals along all four white walls: Laranda's face. Cassi studied it and looked surreptitiously at the woman beside them. Now she could see numerous subtle differences. The real Laranda was incredibly beautiful, but she was at least five years older than the imposter, perhaps even ten. Laranda's face also held an unmistakable cruel streak that was absent in the other woman's. Whoever the imposter was, she hadn't lived a lifetime enjoying other people's suffering as Laranda had. She was also a beautiful woman, but someone had manipulated her features to resemble Laranda.

"Hello, Jared. So we meet again." The voice came out of hidden speakers, sounding as though it was all around them. "Your being here means everything didn't go according to my original plan, but I will still have the last laugh." The image threw back its head and laughed, long and loud. Cassi fought the urge to put her hands over her ears.

"No doubt you have others with you who are here to make sure you follow my instructions. Now listen carefully, everyone. The vault is at the back of this room. It has been programmed to open using Jared and Cassi's right thumbprints. If anything else is used or tried, the contents will be destroyed immediately and a poison gas will be ejected into this room. Sorry"—the satin voice didn't sound sorry—"but it's a failsafe I felt necessary. Simply follow my directions for the minimum casualties. Jared and Cassi will go into the vault with my double. They will shut it, again using their thumbprints, and I will talk a little bit with them alone. Then the rest of you can come and get your treasure. It's as simple as that."

Cassi looked away from the mesmerizing figure on the wall and saw that Taggart had taken a gas mask from his backpack and held it ready against Laranda's threat of poison. She hoped he had more inside for the rest of them.

"I hope all this is crystal clear," the image of Laranda continued. She gave a sultry laugh. "If not, you may not live very long." The pictures on the wall flickered and vanished, and they were plunged into total darkness. Cassi felt for Jared's hand. Now would be the time for Taggart to act. They needed to be ready.

The light gradually increased until they could see again, if dimly. "Well, you heard her," said Giorgio. He pointed his gun at Cassi and Jared.

"I'm to go, too." The woman took a step forward.

"No," Giorgio said sharply.

"But I'm Laranda," she said. "I must go in, so I can talk with them one last time."

Taggart cleared his throat. "Look, Garrettson said her double has to go in, and your uncle said to follow the commands exactly."

"Yeah, and we know where she'll end up," Giorgio sneered, pointing at the gas masks.

"You do not."

"Shut up. You work for me." Giorgio's voice was ugly.

Taggart smiled. "I work for Nicolas. Frankly, we're both tired of you acting like a besotted schoolboy. And Laranda here is sick of you trying to use her. Aren't you? Isn't *Giorgio trying to take advantage of you?*" Taggart said the words slowly and deliberately.

Cassi didn't know what to expect. The woman posing as Laranda stiffened, then she lifted her gun toward Giorgio. "You're trying to take advantage of me. I won't have it."

Giorgio stared at her. "You led me on. Anything I expect is because you promised. Do you deny that? But they are only empty promises. And I've figured out why. You are only half the woman she is." He pointed to the walls, and everyone knew he referred to the real Laranda Garrettson—everyone, it seemed, except the woman holding the gun.

"You used me." Her voice was odd and twisted.

"Put the gun down," Giorgio said, bringing up his own weapon.

"No." The woman made a small movement with her wrist, and Giorgio fired. The loud click of an empty chamber filled the room.

The woman laughed. "It seems you have no bullets." She fired, and the shot sounded loud in Cassi's ears.

Giorgio grabbed his leg. "Are you crazy?" he demanded. "Taggart, stop her!"

The woman shot him again, this time in the arm. "You won't hurt me again. I *am* Laranda Garrettson, and I won't be taken advantage of." She fired a third time, but her hand jerked away at the last moment and the bullet ricocheted off the wall.

"Oh, come on. Can't you do it right?" In two steps Taggart was near the woman, and he relieved her of the gun. "It's like this." He aimed the weapon at the amazed Giorgio.

"But, you—"

Taggart fired, and Giorgio fell to the ground and lay still. The woman's legs gave out suddenly, and she would have fallen if Taggart had not supported her.

"Was that necessary?" Jared demanded. "You didn't have to kill him."

"He would have killed you."

Cassi eyed the man with mistrust. "We could have tied him up."

"So he could come after you again? Boy, you two never learn. If you had taken care of Garrettson in the first place, you wouldn't be here now."

"At least it's over," Cassi said. "Do you have a phone? Let's call Fred."

"It's not over yet," Taggart answered. As if in slow motion, he pointed his gun at Cassi.

Jared's face turned livid, and Cassi put a hand on his arm to restrain him. "What do you mean?" Jared asked, his voice threatening.

"I want to see what's in the vault."

"That can wait until the FBI arrives."

Taggart chuckled. His blue eyes glinted in the dim light, reminding Cassi of Jared's, but where Jared's were clear, Taggart's held a touch of madness. "Do you know what's in that vault?" he asked. "Have you any idea of the money and power involved? I'm not letting that go."

"You won't be able to use any of it," Jared reminded him. "You haven't the connections."

"I have Donelli," Taggart said.

"You just killed his nephew."

"He doesn't know that. The gun that killed him doesn't hold my fingerprints." For the first time Cassi noticed that Taggart wore tight, skin-colored gloves. "Alas," Taggart continued. "How was I to know that his own little creation would find a gun on site and use it on her boyfriend?"

At that the woman next to him stirred. "I am Laranda," she said. Her head twitched.

"Get to the vault," Taggart commanded.

"No." Jared stood firm. "This ends here."

"Does it?" Taggart grabbed the woman next to him by the neck. "Would you like her to join Giorgio? She really is just an innocent bystander, you know."

"I'm Laranda!" the woman insisted. "Let go of me!"

Taggart did, shoving her at Jared. "One more word and I'll shoot someone. Don't test my patience. I've been waiting a long time for this treasure."

Cassi and Jared's eyes met. *He's serious,* Cassi wanted to say, but she saw that Jared already knew.

"Open the vault." Taggart's eyes glinted dangerously.

They walked to the vault, and Cassi and Jared put their right thumbs on the small blinking screen embedded in the shiny metal door. There was a low hum, and a message flashed on the screen. *Open door.* Jared grasped the steering wheel handle with both hands and pulled. The door swung open with apparent ease. They hesitated.

Cassi knew that walking inside was as sure as walking into death, but Taggart wasn't giving them any options. They could either die immediately by his gun, or take their chances with Laranda's vicious plan. Neither promised a happy outcome. The only thing left to do was to pray that somehow Fred would get to them in time.

"Get inside," Taggart ordered.

The Laranda imposter walked inside, swaying as though she really believed she had everything under control. Cassi remembered that she had wanted to go in the vault since she had heard the real Laranda order her inside. What was she thinking? Was she really a pawn? Or a good actress?

From the entrance, Cassi could see numerous shapes on wide shelves inside the vault. But the items were draped with off-white cloths.

"I won't ask again." Taggart pointed his gun at Jared's heart.

Cassi walked inside, pulling Jared with her. Out of the corner of her eye, she saw Taggart push the heavy door shut.

CHAPTER 19

Fred watched the white van leave the house, debating what he should do. Because the van had been parked in the garage, he hadn't been sure that Cassi and Jared were inside. But the blip on his monitor told him that his tracking device was on the move again.

"Let's go!" said an insistent voice beside him. It was Sampson—with all the patience of an eleven-year-old. "They're getting away!"

He looked at Sampson and wished the boy had accepted the continued hospitality of Alberto's wife. They had gone home with the Embassy man for the night, leaving the stakeout to their reinforcements, but had been back on duty at five this morning.

Sampson had refused to stay behind. "I'll just run away if you leave me here," he had said. Fred believed him. What's more, the boy had credit cards and money to back his every desire. And right now his desire was to rescue Cassi and Jared. Better to keep him in control than to have him blunder into the house and be killed. Fred had no doubt that Donelli wouldn't hesitate to take the opportunity.

"Okay, you stay, but play it my way."

"Sure," Sampson had said. Fred couldn't tell if the boy would keep his promise.

Now Sampson's eager face watched him. "Hurry, let's move it."

In the driver's seat, Alberto glanced at him, thick eyebrows raised in question. "Do we go?"

Fred debated. He didn't know for sure that Cassi and Jared were in the vehicle, despite the tracking device. The mobsters could be using it against him. It might be more prudent to send one of the other cars after it.

"Come on, Fred!"

Fred wished he had thought to have the man who talked to Taggart in the bank ask about the transmitter. That way he would know for sure.

He punched a number into his phone. "I'll trail the van. You guys keep watching the house. I'll let you know if I need backup."

"All right!" Sampson sat back in his seat and fastened his belt. "Hit it, Alberto!"

Fred was glad to have Alberto to drive them. While he had driven in New York and downtown San Diego, here the rules were different, and he certainly didn't have time to be picked up by local police. Alberto hadn't known much about tailing people, but with a little instruction, he did an adequate job. Besides, with the tracking device they could travel miles back, out of sight.

The van led them on a long drive to a smaller city with a few large buildings, but not nearly so tall as in Lisbon. "We are near Sintra," Alberto said.

"What's that?" Sampson asked.

"A place with a big palace. It's beautiful. You should go there before you leave."

"I've seen a lot of palaces," Sampson said. "My mom and I . . ." The boy trailed off and began to stare intently at the tracking receiver.

Fred was reminded of how his own father had died of a heart attack when Fred was in his early twenties. His mother had died soon after of breast cancer. But he had learned to go on. So would Sampson.

Stifling a sigh, Fred looked at the city around him. There were new buildings and old, all with cobblestone sidewalks and asphalt roads. New meeting the old. He had a sudden desire to see the palace Alberto talked about, to stroll along shady paths and quiet roads. Maybe he did need a vacation. But what would it be like with no one to share the beauties he would discover?

Brooke.

Where was she now? What was her involvement in this mess?

"They're up ahead," Alberto said. He parked against the curb, awaiting instructions.

"I see Cassi!" Sampson shouted.

Fred saw another woman there, too. He couldn't be sure, but he thought it was Brooke. At least she was the same size and had the same golden-blonde hair. Fred also spied Giorgio Donelli and Taggart, the FBI plant, whom he recognized from photographs taken the day before by the cameras in the bank. "You know, this might be a good time to take them. Taggart's with us, and that only leaves Donelli's nephew and those three guards."

"Plus the man inside," Alberto pointed out. "And that other lady."

"Yeah." Fred didn't want to count Brooke with the enemy, but for the time being, he had to. "Obviously, they didn't think they'd be followed." He dialed a number on his phone. "I need backup," he said. "We've spotted Cassi and Jared."

"They're there?" came an amazed voice. "But we just saw some people who look an awful lot like them leave in a car."

"Then it's a trick or this is. Have two units follow them and the other two stay at the house. You come here."

There was a silence on the other end. "Donelli's leaving now. In another car. He has suitcases."

Fred didn't like the sound of that. "Stay with him. He's probably going to the airport. Look, as soon as he's gone, send a team into the house. After they check it out, send them here."

"Will do." The phone fell silent.

"What happened?" Sampson asked. "You look mad."

"They're playing games," Fred said, "trying to divide our men." He explained the situation briefly. "Now, are you sure that was Cassi you saw, and not just someone who looks like her?"

"Yes, I'm sure," Sampson said. But Fred heard a slight hesitation.

"Well, I did see Brooke," Fred added.

"Brooke?"

"The woman who looks like Laranda."

Sampson sighed. "I hope they're okay."

"We don't even know for sure that they're here."

"I just feel it," Sampson said. "It was them."

Fred sometimes had those feelings too. But right now, thoughts of Brooke overpowered his normal instincts. There had been something between them, he was sure. But had she only used him? Fred shook his head to clear it.

Suddenly four shots rang out, not rapid, but with deliberate pauses in between. Sampson bounced on his seat. "Was that a gun?"

"Sounded like it. But it could be a car backfiring."

"What if they need us?"

"Wait a little." Fred wanted to see if the shots brought any reaction from the deserted street or from the three- and four-story apartment buildings. And surely there was a small store or two nearby that would contain people who would notice the sound. But there was no reaction at all. Either no one had heard the shots or they hadn't attached any importance to them.

The door across the street from the van opened and Taggart walked out. "Strange. He didn't tell us anything was going on." Fred's instincts abruptly began working overtime. As a good agent, Taggart wouldn't be misled but would have managed to be assigned where the real action was taking place. But why hadn't he phoned in to the FBI as promised? With Nicolas Donelli heading for the airport, Fred doubted there was much time to spare. But perhaps Taggart had his own timetable—one that didn't include the FBI. He wouldn't be the first man to have gone bad.

Taggart talked to the guards and then returned to the building. Fred made an abrupt decision. "Wait here," he said. "I'm going to have a talk with those guards."

"But there's three of them!" Sampson protested.

Fred didn't feel there was much choice. "It'll be an even bigger surprise." He checked the silencer on his gun, his face grim. He didn't like killing, hadn't had to do much of it since his promotion, but sometimes it became necessary. His mind and body filled with the tingling he recognized from his pre-FBI days as a policeman on the street. Abruptly, he remembered the first time he had shot his gun as a rooky cop. His guilt had run heavy and deep, despite the fact that he had saved his partner from dying at the hands of a drug dealer. But that had been a long time ago, before he joined the FBI. He was more hardened by now, though far from immune. Tonight, if he lived, sleep would be difficult to find.

He strolled up the street casually, noting that the guards' attention was on the building across the street. So far, so good. There were no passersby to get in the way, only the occasional car. He would take out the man on the far side first, and let off another shot at the nearest before ducking behind a car to take out the last. His hand was steady and sure.

One of the guards glanced at him, but what did he see? Just a brown-haired man with a moustache, among a city made up of people with brown hair. They weren't close enough to see the American shape of his face or the gun hidden at his side.

But Fred had miscalculated. With a grunt to his companion, the guard ducked behind the van, letting off a shot. *He's using a silencer,* Fred thought, even as he hit the cobblestones. The shot hurled into the building behind him. There were more shots and Fred answered them, trying in vain to make headway. One against three, minus the surprise. No longer very good odds. His upper right arm began to ache where he had taken the bullet at Big Tommy's.

Squealing tires caught Fred's attention. He recognized Alberto's car and knew the man was trying to either distract his opponents or get help. Poor, scared Alberto, who couldn't stand the sight of a cabin full of dead men without losing his breakfast. Yet inside his heart, he was a hero.

As the car passed, the door jerked open and something landed in the road. Fred caught his breath. Sampson. *The little fool!* In his hands, he held the only weapon allotted to him: the tracking monitor. He threw it at the men as they turned their guns on him. The boy fell, even as the monitor found its target. Fred stood and shot repeatedly. One man joined Sampson sprawled on the street, but the others took cover. The shooting went on, a near silent struggle for dominance. Fred knew Alberto would get help. He knew also that it would come too late. He jammed another ammunition clip into his gun.

He saw one of the men dart partway into the street and drag Sampson to the van. Dare Fred hope he was still alive? Why else would they throw him inside the van? Or perhaps they recognized the child and wanted a death bonus from their boss.

Fred grimaced and eased closer. He felt a bullet graze his shoulder and ducked. Just a scratch, but it hurt. He had exposed himself too much, and would have to do it again to save Sampson. *My fault,* he thought. *I was too confident of my surprise. But they had been expecting something. Perhaps Taggart . . .*

Taggart. The thought helped Fred focus. If he had turned on them, then Fred had to make short work of these guards before Taggart showed up again. He also had to save Sampson. Likewise, the thugs couldn't stand around waiting for Fred's reinforcements. Things had to end soon—one way or the other.

The world around Fred spun suddenly. Perhaps his new wound was worse than he had thought. He fell to his knees. He couldn't shoot the men in this position, and he couldn't rise. All was lost.

* * * * *

"At least give us the masks," Jared said, stopping the vault door with his foot before it shut all the way.

Taggart grinned and shrugged off his backpack, slinging it toward him. "Now move your foot or I'll blow it off."

Jared took his foot away and the door shut tight. At once the lights began flashing, and a voice filled the vault, sounding eerie in the enclosed, airtight space. "Put your thumbs on the pad now. Hurry, or a poison gas will enter the vault."

"This is getting old fast," Jared growled. He opened Taggart's backpack and found nothing but a rope inside. Sighing, he let it fall to the marble floor of the vault.

"Five seconds," said Laranda's voice.

"Put your thumb on the plate." Cassi put her own on it as she spoke. Jared knew he had no choice. He jabbed his thumb down.

"Closure complete," announced the recorded voice. "Thank you, Jared. I'm sure you understand that you have to do exactly what I want. It's a lesson you haven't learned very well, I'm afraid."

"If she weren't dead, I'd kill her myself," Jared grated. The rage and helplessness in him mounted.

"I guess you're wondering why you're here," continued the voice. It was soft and sweet now, hinting at innocence. What a joke. Laranda had been a lot of things, but never innocent. "Take a look around, and see my treasures."

Jared was curious. Already Cassi and the Laranda imposter were lifting up sheets. Rare paintings, statues, and vases came to light. "Jared, this stuff is worth a fortune!" Cassi exclaimed. She uncovered the Van Gogh they had heard about from Taggart. That painting alone was worth forty million. "No, more like several fortunes! I wonder where she got it all?"

"Probably a lot of it from Big Tommy," Jared guessed. "That guy was big-time, not like her. Look, this painting's a Monet, if I'm not mistaken. I'd say at auction it'd go for an easy twenty, maybe even thirty million."

"More like thirty," Cassi agreed.

"It's mine. Leave it alone."

Jared looked up from the painting. "Who are you, really? Why are you here?"

"I'm Laranda." But the woman seemed less sure.

"Laranda?" asked the recorded voice. "Do you hear me?"

The woman jerked her face around the vault. "Yes."

"Do not be alarmed. I am you. You recorded this, but there has been an accident and you do not remember. But Jared must pay for his sins. Are you willing to help?"

The woman's chest heaved in her fitted jacket, and her gaze was wild. "Yes. Yes," she gasped.

"Jared," Cassi whispered. "I think she's hypnotized or drugged or something. Look at her eyes."

"In the back of the vault there is a little safe," continued the velvet recording. "Inside is something for you. You will remember the video and know what to do with it." Pause. "And Jared, only she knows the codes to the safe, so stay back."

But Jared wasn't obeying Laranda. He darted around the woman and made it to the safe before she did. "No, I'm not letting you open it. Tell me the code."

"No."

Jared stepped closer to her, saw fury build in her eyes. Her resemblance to Laranda was still striking, but this woman's face was fuller, more gentle. Hollows had been painted on her cheeks and around her nose to make her look like Laranda. She even wore green contacts. "Look," he said, his voice gentle. "You are not Laranda. You are being used. Look at me. Do you really know me? Do you want to kill me?"

Her mouth opened, but she didn't speak. The anger in her eyes faded. He took hold of her arms, felt her tremble. "Laranda was cold and mean and vicious. You're not. Please give me the code." He didn't know what the safe held, but maybe it would help them escape.

"No. Let me get the gun. I have to shoot—" Her eyes flickered to Cassi, and Jared knew what Laranda had planned—for the imposter to kill Cassi or for Jared to die saving her. Or even for him to have to harm this pitiful pawn to save them both.

"No," he said. "We're not your enemies."

"You married her!"

"I love her."

"You should love me."

"I don't even know you! Who are you?"

Her head began to jerk, and suddenly she gasped and collapsed into Jared's arms. Cassi helped him lay her gently on the floor. "The poor woman." Cassi's voice was full of sympathy.

"We've got to get out of here," Jared said. "Quick. Let's find something we can use against Taggart."

Minutes ticked by in silence as they searched the vault. They uncovered many more statues and valuable art objects, but nothing that would be of any use against a gun. Even so, they set the heaviest objects by the door. "I'd hate to ruin one of these on him," Cassi said, fingering a statue of a Madonna.

"I can't believe he's a double agent," Jared said. "And we fell into his trap so easily. I should have listened to you."

"Well, he didn't find the tracking transmitter. That's something. Maybe Fred will follow us in time."

Jared moved to the door. "Come on, put your thumb here. Let's try to get out."

But no sooner had they done so than a soft, mocking laughter began in the vault. The volume increased until their ears rang. "So, you both survived. I thought you might. How does it feel, Jared, to have had to hurt an innocent woman to save your beloved Cassi? Did you have to kill her? Or did you hit her? Break her arm? Either way, you used your strength for ill. The woman was innocent." The laughter reverberated from the walls again.

"How—" Cassi began. "Oh, I see. When we put our thumbs on the pad, it told the computer which of her recordings to run."

"Yeah, that's got to be it." Jared glanced at the unconscious woman on the floor. "But at least we didn't have to hurt her. Maybe if we—"

"Test two is coming up now, Jared," said Laranda's voice. "Are you ready? I don't think so. But here goes. This vault is in the bottom floor of a building with people living overhead, and a Mormon place of worship in the other half of the bottom floor. Now, this is what I have planned. A poisonous gas derived from the Cortinarius mushroom family has been rigged to leak throughout this whole building, except for this half of the bottom floor. Such a nasty little thing that just happens to cause acute kidney failure. By the time symptoms show up—sometimes not for a week—the kidney and other organs are too damaged for survival. There is no known cure. At best, people will die in three days; at worst, they'll linger for three weeks. Think of it, Jared—mothers, babies, fathers, big brothers, and little sisters. Some of them live here in this building, and some of them come only to pray to your Mormon God. A few will likely escape—those lucky enough not to live in the building and not faithful enough to come often to pray." There was a fervent laugh. "Such is my justice. The faithful and the innocent will die. Those of harder hearts live. It is the way of the real world. My world."

The voice stopped, and Jared met Cassi's eyes in horror. How many people lived in this building? Judging from its size, there were probably four apartments per floor, with perhaps four or five people to each family. Times that by three or four stories, and add the people in the branch or ward who attended church and other meetings during the week. Jared felt weak and horrified. All those people dying. The authorities would be called in, might even find the cause. But it would be too late.

"There is a way to stop the gas." The voice sounded sorry now, but Jared knew it was an act. "You and Cassi can stop it by pressing your thumbprints again on the plate. That will stop all those people from dying needlessly." Pause. "Unfortunately, it will also release a more quick-acting poison into this vault. You won't suffer too much.

"So what will it be? You or them? Are you willing to sacrifice your lives to save others? Or do you really believe in your religion at all? Now is the test. You have five minutes to decide.

"Oh, and if you do choose to live, do nothing. Another gas will be released in this room that will simply keep you out of commission for a few days until the rest of the building is thoroughly saturated with the mushroom gas. While you sleep, my friends will come and move this great treasure to a more useful location. They won't harm you, and I'm sure your FBI friends will be around soon enough to find and revive you. So, my friends, the decision is yours. You now have four and a half minutes."

"What are we going to do?" Cassi's eyebrows scrunched together in thought. He loved it when she did that. He wanted to see her doing that every day until they grew old.

"Either way, we're dead," he said. "Taggart's out there waiting for this to be over so he can come in and get the goods."

"He has a gas mask."

"No doubt there are more in the van. I'll bet at least one of those guards will come in and help load."

"Jared, we can't let those people die."

"I know that, Cassi. But how can I put my thumb on that plate, knowing you will die?"

"I'm not afraid of dying, if it will save them." Her voice shook, but was resolute. "We have the hope of eternity. Many of them do not."

"I know, but what about her?" Jared pointed at the woman on the floor. "According to Laranda, she's an innocent, too. If we save those people, she dies with us."

Tears sparkled in Cassi's eyes. "We must choose the greater good." The words were a whisper.

Jared admired her for the decision she seemed prepared to make, but he knew Laranda too well. "Cassi, listen to me. I doubt Laranda will spare those people even if we do choose to let them live. The last thing we hear will be the sound of the gas—and her laughter as she tells us it was all a hoax, and they're all going to die anyway. That is who she is."

Cassi's face was stricken. "Oh, Jared, you're right."

He held her. "This is all my fault."

"It's Laranda's fault, Jared. Not ours."

"We must fight her! There has to be a way out!"

"Then let's find it!" Cassi began again to throw sheets off art objects. Jared took the other side of the vault.

"Hey, look at this!" Cassi held up a thin, jeweled dagger that had probably been stolen or purchased from some important collection. Jared didn't recognize the maker, but the large jewels were likely genuine. She ran to the fingerprint plate near the door and began working at the screws. At any other time, Jared would have been appalled to see such a treasure being used as a screwdriver, but now he mentally urged her on.

He kept searching. If he could find something to help her, maybe they could destroy the computer before it let out any gas. Or at least get out in time to evacuate the building. Was that even a possibility?

"Three minutes left," said Laranda's voice.

Jared moved faster. He knew that when the time was up, he would have no choice but to put his thumb on the plate, hastening his and Cassi's death, though he doubted the sacrifice would help the people in the apartments above.

His hand closed on something solid. He pulled it out. A Japanese samurai sword.

CHAPTER 20

Sampson didn't want to open his eyes. He took a deep breath and let it out again. His stomach hurt, but not as badly as he expected for a bullet wound. Maybe he was dead.

Then he remembered the two extra battery packs for the tracking monitor. He had stuck them in the waist of his pants before jumping out of the car, thinking to also throw them at the guards. Had they actually saved his life?

Alberto will be mad that I jumped, he thought. *Fred will, too.*

Fred.

Sampson forced open his eyes, feeling a terrible urgency. He struggled to sit up, felt the bulk of the battery packs at his waist. Sure enough, one of them had been hit by a bullet, and his stomach behind that pack was sore and swollen. He almost couldn't breathe.

But at least he was alive.

He peeked out the window and saw the two men still shooting. Why did no one come for them? Had it only been minutes since Fred left the car alone? Sampson crawled to the opposite window in the van. From that vantage point, he could see Fred kneeling on the cobblestones next to a car, bright red covering his shirt. The color shocked Sampson, made him recall how his uncle had jumped in front of him and saved his life.

He had to do something. But what?

He spied a box with gas masks inside and remembered his father's death. If he'd had one of those in prison, he wouldn't have died. Sampson wondered if Cassi and Jared were going to be poisoned inside the building, and if that was why the bad men carried the masks. He couldn't take them to Cassi and Jared now. But he had to do something—anything. The answer came all at once to his mind: *move the van.*

Sampson crawled to the front of the van. There were no keys in sight, but he saw a lady's red purse in the passenger's seat. Searching it, he found no keys, only makeup. Next, he looked in the glove compartment and finally behind the visor on the driver's side. Along with rental papers, he discovered a key. Maybe it was an extra!

The van started smoothly, and Sampson felt a leap of joy as he shoved it into gear. He knew how to drive in principle, and had even convinced the butler to let him drive slowly around the estate when his father was out of town, but it had been a long time ago and this reality was far more frightening. The men outside the van noticed what he was doing and jumped for the door. Sampson locked it and punched on the gas. He fell back against the seat as the vehicle accelerated.

"Yee haw!" he screamed in a mix of triumph and terror as the van barreled down the street. He would only go so far and then turn around and come back to see if he could do something more. *Please be okay, Fred.*

* * * * *

Jared grabbed the sword's hilt and pulled it from the worn wooden scabbard. The raven-black shakudo metal was formed of oxidized copper and gold, and it felt solid in his hands. Though it wasn't his speciality, he knew that if the samurai sword was in Laranda's collection, it must be rare or in good enough condition to make it worth tens of thousands—at least.

Oh, well. He jumped to Cassi's side. She had loosened the screws enough for him to jab the blade inside and force off the rest of the plate. Inside was a mass of wires and blinking lights. He began to cut the wires at random.

A stuttering sound filled his ears, and then Laranda's voice was back. "I'm disappointed with you, Jared. Can't you make even one clean decision? But that's okay. I'll choose for you. In exactly two minutes, gas will fill this room and you will die. Shortly after, every chamber in this building will be permeated with that previously explained mushroom poison—less immediate, but just as fatal. You will all die, including the innocent little children sleeping in their cribs, and anyone who enters your church or this building in the next few days. It's your fault they're going to die, Jared. Take that to your grave and rot in it."

The laughter echoed again in the vault as Jared and Cassi desperately tried to cut more wires.

* * * * *

Fred fought dizziness, struggling to peer over the car and fire so they wouldn't suspect he was wounded and come after him. He managed to let off a few bullets, but knew they served only as a temporary fix. His training told him to back off and await reinforcements, but he couldn't leave Sampson.

The engine in the van abruptly roared to life, and he watched in amazement as the vehicle peeled out of its parking place. Bracing himself against the pain, he arose enough to shoot again at the two men. They fell instantly. Fred heard a window open overhead and caught sight of a terrified face. "Call the police!" he screamed, not knowing if they would understand English. The window slammed shut.

Fred staggered to his feet, somehow finding the strength. As he knelt by the guards to check their pulses and remove their weapons, the white van came barreling back up the street, followed closely by Alberto's car.

"Did you get help?" Fred asked Alberto.

"No, I came back for you . . . and the boy. You are hurt. Let me put on a bandage. I have a kit somewhere."

Sampson jumped out of the van. In his arms, he carried a box of gas masks. Fred looked at them and understood the significance at once. What was going on inside the building? Was he already too late to save Jared and Cassi? What about Brooke?

"That was a darn foolish thing you did," Fred said to Sampson.

"I saved you, didn't I?" Sampson's reply was cocky, but his face was haunted.

"Look, I have to go in." Fred grimaced as Alberto wrapped his right shoulder. He wasn't sure what hurt worse, the barely healing wound in his upper arm or the new one on his shoulder. At least they were on the same side. He couldn't shoot quite as well with his left hand, but fair enough. *Better than Taggart,* he thought.

"You guys go get help."

Alberto and Sampson both shook their heads. With determination on his face, Alberto picked up one of the thugs' guns. "I know how to shoot."

There wasn't time to argue. "Okay, but stay back." Fred glared at Sampson. "Especially you. Bring the masks."

To his surprise, the door to the building was unlocked. Fred peered cautiously inside. He saw nothing but the inert form of a small, dark man sprawled on a ceramic tile floor. With steady steps he entered the room, then crossed it. He sensed Alberto following him. There was another door in the far wall, but it was shut. Fred was pleased when the knob moved under his hand. Slowly, he eased open the door.

"One minute," said a voice inside the room. A woman's voice, low and full and promising. "Then the gas will begin inside the vault. In sixty seconds you can go inside wearing your masks. After entry, you will have five minutes to empty the vault, and then another gas will be poured throughout this building. In ten minutes, the level will build up enough to penetrate this room and, shortly, into every pore in your body. Even with a gas mask, you will not be safe. You must leave before then."

Through the crack in the door, Fred could see a body on the ground. Although he couldn't be sure, it looked like Giorgio Donelli. But where were the others? Where was Taggart?

As he thought the name, a dark shape came at the door, and Fred was knocked to the tile. Taggart was on him immediately, bringing up his gun. Fred grunted with renewed pain and jabbed his own gun in the man's face. "Hold it!" he growled.

Alberto also put the nuzzle of his borrowed gun next to Taggart's cheek. "Even I couldn't miss at this range."

Taggart looked surprised. His gun lowered and he gave a rough chuckle. "Hey, it's you. FBI. I didn't know. I'm FBI too. I thought—"

Fred shoved the man off with his sore arm, feeling a gush of blood under his new bandage. "Save it," he ordered. There had been no mistaking the murder in Taggart's eyes. The belated recognition wasn't going to save him.

"They only have a minute left," Taggart rushed on. "I can't find a way inside the vault."

"Are Cassi and Jared inside?" Sampson asked.

Taggart nodded.

Fred wasted precious seconds tying Taggart's hands and feet with his shoelaces, as the man continually professed his innocence. "Too little too late," Fred said. "Alberto, if he makes a move, shoot him. Preferably in the heart, if he has one."

"You won't make it without me," Taggart said. "They're all going to die."

Fred debated. "Bring him just in case, Alberto. But keep a close eye on him." He turned into the large room with its dimly lit interior and ran to the shiny doors of the vault. He punched a few buttons on the pad beneath a square black plate.

"Jared, do you hear me?" he yelled. No answer, but he thought he heard scraping noises.

"Ten seconds," said a sultry voice. "Nine, eight . . ."

In desperation, Fred raised his gun and shot at the plate. It shattered. He shot again, and the door mechanism gave a groan and released. Fred pulled at the steering wheel handle. A sword poked out first, followed by Jared and Cassi.

". . . six, five . . ."

"Fred!" Jared said. "Thank heaven!"

"Where's Brooke?" Fred asked.

"Who?"

"The woman who looks like Laranda."

Cassi gasped and glanced back into the vault. That told Fred all he needed to know. "The masks," he grunted, and plunged inside. He found Brooke easily enough. She was lying on the marble floor in the vault, moving slightly as though trying to wake from a deep sleep. He swept her into his arms.

". . . two, one . . ."

He dived for the entrance, feeling his right shoulder hit the edge of the solid door. Pain exploded through his body, but he kept his footing. Then Brooke was lifted from his arms and a gas mask shoved on his face. Behind him, Jared was slamming the vault shut, but it wouldn't latch. Clouds of fumes escaped from the edges.

"Get back," Fred heard himself say. He had no idea how deadly the gas was, but knowing Laranda and seeing her work with Holbrooke, he wasn't taking any chances.

The others needed no warning. They already wore masks, and Cassi and Sampson were dragging Brooke back from the vault, holding another mask over her face. Fred stepped away from the door, felt his legs buckle. Jared caught him and helped him join the others.

"Is this a safe distance?" asked Cassi, her voice muffled by her mask.

"It should be . . . with the masks."

They waited for a minute that seemed an eternity. Then a terrible voice broke the silence. "Well, now that wasn't too long. I am vindicated. Jared Landine and his precious Mormon wife are dead." Laughter permeated the room as the gas had done moments before. "Now remember, you have five minutes until I release the other gas, ten before you have to be out. When you go into the vault, use your mask just in case the gas hasn't cleared enough. Oh, and thank you. It was so nice doing business with you."

"She's still going through with it!" Jared said, his voice muffled by the mask. "Of course she would."

"What's going on?" Fred asked.

"She's going to kill everyone in the building with another gas," Jared said. "We can stop people from entering the building, but there are bound to be some people inside right now who will be affected. And from the way the recording sounded, I think it lingers around for a good while. We have to stop her!"

Fred looked at Alberto. "Go try to get everyone out of the building. Quickly!"

"What about him?" Alberto pointed to Taggart, who sat on the floor with his tied hands holding a gas mask to his face.

"I'll take care of him." Cassi took Alberto's gun and pointed it at Taggart. "Move," she said to him. "You don't know how much I want to shoot you." Knowing Cassi as he did, Fred doubted she wanted to kill the man, but her act was certainly convincing. And Fred knew that her brother, a policeman in Utah, had taught her to shoot well. Taggart was secure in her hands.

"Any ideas?" Fred asked Jared.

"The electricity!" Jared shouted. "That has to be it. If we shut it off, it'll have to stop. It's all computerized. We have to find the wires. But there might not be time. I know! The breaker. We have to find the breaker."

They separated, searching for the box. Fred found himself praying they would find it in time.

* * * * *

Brooke had just started to wake when a man took her in his arms. He seemed comfortable and familiar, so she didn't struggle. At least it wasn't Giorgio. But he was dead. Or was he? Had she killed him? Her memory was fuzzy, but she distinctly remembered shooting at him.

Two others took her from the man and placed a mask on her face. They half-carried, half-dragged her across the floor. She vaguely recalled the gas masks. *My plan is working*, she thought, lapsing into a moment of triumph.

But was it? Looking around, she saw Jared alive and well, and Cassi too. The man who had carried her, and another man she didn't recognize, were also present and free. And a boy—Sampson, she remembered. They had wanted him dead. Why? Oh yes, he was Big Tommy's son. *I must get rid of him.* The thought repelled her. He was only a child.

The one man in the room not free was Taggart, whose hands and ankles were tied. Brooke watched from the corner of her eye as Cassi took a gun from the man Brooke didn't recognize and pointed it at him. That wasn't right. It should be Cassi under the gun, not Taggart. And Jared should belong to Laranda. Shouldn't he? Trying to think was like trying to walk through a thick fog. For once, she wished the doctor was here to give her an injection. The presence she had buried deep in her mind was struggling to get out.

I am in control. She took a deep breath.

The boy holding Brooke's mask fastened the straps around her head. "I'm going to help them find the box," he said.

What box? Brooke thought. Then she remembered the safe inside the vault, and the numbers the woman on the video had taught her. *I'm the woman on the video.*

Are you?

That last came from the presence she thought she had vanquished. *Shut up! I won't listen. I have to get to my safe.*

Brooke sat up, the mask still in place on her face. She inched away from Cassi, whose side was toward her. Taggart's eyes met Brooke's, but he didn't give her away. Instead, he threw his gas mask at Cassi and began to move across the floor in the opposition direction, toward the outer apartment and the street.

"Stop!" Cassi said, kicking at the mask as it flew toward her.

"Shoot me, beautiful," he challenged.

Cassi put her foot on his chest and pushed him roughly to the carpet. "Unless you know where the box is, sit still and keep quiet."

Under this distraction, Brooke had moved farther away, closer to the vault. She rose shakily to her feet. The man who had carried her from the vault was checking a wooden panel built into the white wall. Jared and Sampson were nowhere to be seen. Were they already in the vault? Brooke forced her unsteady legs to go faster.

She caught sight of Giorgio sprawled on the ground. *I killed him,* she thought.

No, said the other voice. *Taggart killed him.*

That much was true, Brooke remembered. She had tried to shoot Giorgio, but for some reason her hand kept jerking at the last moment.

I did that, said the voice.

Go away! thought Brooke. *I'm in charge.*

The voice silenced. Brooke entered the vault, relieved to see no one inside. Jared and the boy must be checking the outer apartment for the box. Strange, when he knew the safe was in here.

Opening the safe took more time than expected. Her hands rebelled at the precise movements. *Like they had when she'd tried to kill Giorgio?* At last she got it open. There was a small semiautomatic pistol inside. Brooke was sure she should have known the make and size since she had put it there, but those details escaped her now.

It didn't matter. What mattered was to stop Jared. To teach him a lesson. *He should never have refused me,* she thought.

Brooke walked slowly out of the vault. Jared was in the big room now with Sampson, helping the other man check out more wooden panels spaced at intervals along the walls. Inside them, she glimpsed video and sound equipment.

"One minute," said a voice. Her voice. It was soft and seductive, but filled every part of the room.

Brooke smiled. She took aim at Jared and fired. At the last minute her hand wobbled, sending the shot wide.

"Brooke, stop!" shouted the man who had carried her from the vault earlier.

Brooke turned the gun in his direction. He had a gun in a holster under his arm, but she saw with satisfaction that he didn't draw it. He was a man and therefore weak. He seemed familiar. Perhaps she had known him before the accident.

"Brooke, put the gun down." He removed his face mask. Nothing happened, and she assumed the gas from the vault must have dissipated to nontoxic levels.

She pulled off her own mask. "Don't call me that."

"That's your name."

"I'm Laranda."

"No, you're not. You're Brooke Erickson. I don't know what they've done to you, but I know who you really are. You used to work for a paper in Salt Lake City. Lately, you've been writing freelance articles for the San Diego Union-Tribune. And when you disappeared, I did some checking. I found your family in Indiana. They're worried about you."

"No. I don't know who Brooke is."

He took a step toward her. She kept the gun pointed at his chest.

"Fred," Jared said. "Be careful. I think they've hypnotized her and given her drugs. Look at her eyes."

Fred. That was the man's name. Thinking it made Brooke's heart feel warm. He was a good man. He had been nice to her. She wanted him to ask her out.

With a gasp, Brooke backed away, swinging her gun toward Jared. "Don't move, Fred, or I'll shoot him. I shot Giorgio, you know. I'm not afraid to shoot Jared. This is all his fault. He wouldn't love me."

"Love you?" Jared said. "Laranda never wanted love, she wanted my soul. She wanted to destroy me. But you aren't Laranda."

"I am!" Brooke's finger tightened on the trigger.

"Thirty seconds," said the voice that filled the room.

Brooke's heart began beating wildly. She didn't know what would happen in thirty seconds, but she knew it wasn't safe to be there without her mask. She had to leave.

"He's a Mormon." Fred's voice came clearly through the fog in Brooke's brain. "He was baptized, same as you. He doesn't smoke or drink or fool around. Just like you. Come on, Brooke. Put down the gun."

"No." She tried to pull the trigger, but staring into Jared's eyes above his mask, she found she couldn't. He had been nothing but kind and honest with her. She knew what Laranda had seen in him.

I'm Laranda, she reminded herself.

"Brooke," Fred pleaded.

"The real Laranda would love it that you are a member, Brooke," Jared said. "She would love to destroy your life for that reason alone. Please, don't let that happen. And please let us stop her before she poisons more innocent people."

Brooke fought an inner battle. The scene of Giorgio hitting the small man who had opened the door to them flashed into her mind. And another of the way Giorgio had treated her.

"I found it!" Cassi's voice cut into Brooke's thoughts. "It's right here behind the door. In just a minute, I'll have the electricity off."

At that moment, Brooke's desperation had a focus. She swivelled toward Cassi, who held the gun over Taggart with one hand while furiously flipping switches in a metal box with the other. The lights began to blink out.

She's ruining everything! Yes, it was Cassi all along, not Jared who was the problem. *Without her, he will turn to me. This time there will be no last-minute wavering.* She carefully locked the annoying inner voice deep in her mind.

Both Jared and Fred dived toward her. Jared reached her first. Before she could pull the trigger, she felt the prick of a needle in her arm, and her body relaxed. Someone caught her as she fell.

"I used the ring you gave me," she heard Jared saying from a distance.

It was Fred who cradled her body in his strong arms. She felt safe and protected. "Sleep, Brooke," he said. "I'll be here when you wake."

Brooke closed her eyes.

* * * * *

Cassi had felt helpless when she had heard the shot and seen Brooke with the gun, but she dared not leave Taggart. She had caught him several times biting at the shoelaces that tied his hands.

"You've got to let me out of here," he insisted.

"No," Cassi told him. She noticed that he had stopped calling her beautiful. "We have to stop the gas. Those are innocent people."

"Who cares about them?"

"I do." She looked away in disgust.

Brooke had paused now and appeared to be listening to Fred. They knew each other. Maybe he could reach her. But then the gun had turned toward Jared, and Cassi's heart felt cold. Would she lose Jared now?

No!

She stepped away from Taggart, heading toward Brooke from behind.

"Wait!" Taggart said. "Look, there it is!"

Cassi spied the breaker box behind the open door leading into the small outer apartment. She called to Jared and Fred, grateful to see Brooke's attention diverted.

Quickly, she began to shut off the switches, one by one. The lights went out. She heard Taggart moving and shoved her foot at him, forcing him to be still. "Don't tempt me."

"I'm on your side," Taggart said. "How many times do I have to tell you that?"

Cassi ignored him.

"Are you all right?" Jared appeared next to her. He had taken off his mask.

"Yes, and you?"

"Fine."

"Brooke?"

"She's out," Jared said. Cassi could see his grin by the light coming from the window in the outer apartment. "I used the ring

Fred gave me. The stuff worked fast—probably more so because of the drugs already in her system."

"Poor girl."

Jared's arms went around her. Cassi felt her knees go weak at the sudden release of tension. "Some honeymoon," Jared whispered. He released the strap on her gas mask and let it fall to the floor.

"It's over now," she sighed.

But as she spoke, the dim lights overhead flickered on, and an all-too-familiar voice spoke. "Ten, nine, eight, seven . . ."

Taggart struggled to his feet, which were still tied together. "We've got to get out of here!"

Cassi looked at Jared. "She must have a backup. Oh, yes! The generator! I noticed it when we came in."

But it was on the other side of the room. Could she make it in time? For all those innocent people, she had to try. Shoving the gun into Jared's hand, she sprinted across the floor.

". . . three, two . . ."

There was no way. *Please, help me!* Cassi prayed.

The lights abruptly went dark again, and the voice was silenced. Cassi came to a stop near the generator. Sampson smiled up at her in the dark. "I think I found the problem."

Tears ran down Cassi's face, but she laughed. "Oh, Sampson, you are one incredible boy."

"I saved everyone, huh?" He looked pleased.

She put an arm around him. "Yes, I'd say you did more than your share of saving today. Come on, let's get out of here."

They were a sorry-looking lot that came out of the building and into the small crowd of people on the sidewalk—a bloodied Fred carried Brooke in his arms, Taggart shuffled out with Jared holding a gun at his back, and Cassi and Sampson came out last, close on Jared's heels. Sampson held the samurai sword in his hands.

"Is this like the sword Nephi used?" he asked.

Cassi shook her head. "No. It's from Japan, I think. And from a later date. Still, it's very valuable."

"Cool, can I keep it?"

"Probably not," Jared said with a grin. "I'll bet it belongs to someone—or in some museum." He gave his gun and care of Taggart back to Alberto and put an arm around each of them. "But I'm sure we can find something for you that you'll like even better."

Sampson smiled. "I guess I can wait." For a moment he was silent, and when he spoke again his voice was hesitant, his face earnest. "I'm sorry I've been such a pain. But do you think you two might come see me sometime—wherever I am?"

Cassi turned to Jared. Without words, an understanding passed between them. "Well, we were kind of hoping you'd like to stay with us," she said.

Sampson's eyes widened. "Really?"

"Yeah," Jared said. "You know, just to see how you like it. I think we all make a great team, don't you?"

"Of course, our house isn't like the one you're used to," Cassi added. "It's small. But we can all choose a new one together, if we decide we need more space."

"Okay," Sampson agreed with a forced casualness, as though it was difficult for him to speak. His eyes glimmered. "I could come for a while, I guess."

Cassi smiled. What she and Jared planned for Sampson was a lot longer than "a while."

"But what about your honeymoon?" Sampson asked.

"Well, right now I think we would rather just stay home, wouldn't we, Jared?"

"That's right. Unless you know of any deserted islands available—and even that might be too much adventure. But we could go camping together sometime. If I remember correctly, we owe you some marshmallows."

Sampson grinned, shifting the sword in his hands. "I could go for that."

Sirens filled the streets. Cassi leaned her head against Jared and sighed. It really was over. *Or maybe,* she thought as she watched Sampson, *it has just begun.*

EPILOGUE

Fred looked at his watch. It was time to meet Brooke at the clinic where she would be checking out for the last time. He had been to visit her almost every day for the past five months. With each visit he became more involved.

Justin came into the room. "I've been talking with the locals in Portugal again," he said. "They still can't believe the intricacies of Garrettson's setup. We all agree that we're glad she didn't have another failsafe planned."

The idea that Laranda could have set up an automatic poison release if the generator was turned off still haunted Fred's dreams. He believed only God had prevented her from coming up with such a plan.

"According to the tapes and the computer programs, Laranda would have killed everyone, regardless of the choice Jared and Cassi made in the vault," Justin went on.

Jared had mentioned as much when they had gone to the morgue one last time to check Garrettson's death information. Fred had believed him even without Justin's proof. "Well, it's over now." He pushed his chair back from the desk and stood. "She's dead and gone."

"A good thing, too. She took too many with her as it was. But at least Agent Worthington survived, thanks to you." Justin looked at his watch. "Hey, aren't you going to be late?"

Fred found his keys. "Only if I drive slow."

"Tell her hi for me, okay?"

"I will."

When Fred entered Brooke's room, she was ready to go. "Hello," she said, a bit breathlessly. She was as beautiful as ever, but the confidence that had once shone in her eyes had dimmed. The doctor said she had made a full physical recovery from the high dosage of experimental drugs given her, but the mental recuperation would take more time. "It's nothing physical," the doctor had said, "but more a coming to terms with what happened and the role she played. But she's a very strong woman, and I believe she'll soon be fine." Fred thought so, too.

"You didn't have to come," Brooke said to him now. "I could've taken a taxi."

"I wouldn't make you do that." There were unspoken words in his heart, but he didn't know how to get them out. He took her suitcases, and together they walked to his car.

"What now?" he asked when they were inside.

She didn't meet his gaze. "I don't know. I've been thinking about going home for a while."

"What about being a reporter for the San Diego Union-Tribune?"

She grimaced. "Sorry about that. I just knew that if I could do a big story, they'd take me on full-time. I'd done well enough in Salt Lake. Will you ever forgive me?"

"I already have." They had talked about this several times over the past months, but she obviously felt the need to explain again. In his mind, Brooke hadn't lied about writing for the paper. The paper had picked up a few of her articles, and he had no doubt that her story about Big Tommy and the Donellis would have secured her a permanent position—if she had been in any condition to write it. But that honor had gone to another, more fortunate reporter. "You could still work for them."

"I guess I could try. But I already blew the big story, perhaps the biggest of my career. I'm finding it a little difficult to start over." She wrung her hands, now absent of any ring, though Fred had already returned the band he had found at Donelli's.

"Yeah, but I have an idea."

She leaned forward in her seat, looking at him with much of her former enthusiasm. Fred ached to take her in his arms and hold her, to tell her how much she meant to him. "What? Tell me, Fred!"

"I have a story that I think has headline potential. But it does involve a little trip to Brazil. Do you think you're up to it?"

"I don't know." The hesitation was back.

"I'll be going, too," Fred said. "It's FBI business. And while it's not in my jurisdiction, this is something I don't want to trust to any messenger. In fact, I'm taking a vacation just for the job."

"You, a vacation?" Her pale eyes twinkled. "Then it must be important."

"Well, I had so much fun on the last one." He meant it as a joke, but Brooke frowned. "I guarantee you'll have a good time," he added quickly. "Brazil has wonderful beaches."

She didn't reply.

"Please, Brooke. I want to be with you." He held his breath.

"Oh, Fred." She put a soft hand on his arm. "I like you so much. Sometimes I can't tell you how much. And then all at once the memories come back and make me feel so odd. I remember Giorgio, and how part of me thought to use him and the other part shrank in terror when he so much as touched my arm. I don't know how I got out of that business without ending up in his bed. And that frightens me. I don't know that I'm ready for a relationship right now. I was before, and I was attracted to you, but now . . ."

"I'm not in a hurry." Fred put his hand over hers. "I've waited a long time to find a woman like you."

"I was so weak!" She tried to pull away.

"No, you were so strong. Not once did you hurt someone. The doctors told me what a miracle that was. You held onto yourself and to your faith. I admire you so much. I want to be your friend, Brooke. Well, not only your friend. I want much more. But I'm willing to keep it at that until you're good and ready."

She stopped trying to free her hand. "It's a good story, huh?"

"Yeah. It has real human appeal."

"Beaches?"

"The best."

"Separate rooms?"

He laughed. "Of course. I wouldn't have it any other way." He might have once, but not now.

"Okay," she said. Her smile melted his heart. "I'll go on one condition. That you'll read the Book of Mormon. Not for me, but for yourself."

"Deal." They shook on it. Fred didn't tell her that he had already read the Book of Mormon Jared had given him, and that he had agreed to see the missionaries. He intended to search for the real truth he believed had to exist somewhere on earth. If the Mormons had it, he would soon know. If they didn't, he would keep searching. Either way, he knew Brooke would be part of his future. A vital part.

Without warning she leaned over and kissed him. Given their conversation, the action took Fred by surprise. "I always wondered what your moustache would feel like," she whispered.

He chuckled softly and kissed her back, gently, not with demand but with promise. When she pulled away, he let her go, knowing that she had already begun to trust him. It was just a matter of time until he won her heart.

* * * * * *

Dennis Faron opened the door to his rented cottage door. His heart sank as he saw the couple outside, both obviously American. He stepped out into the bright Brazilian sun, closing the door behind him.

"I wondered when you would catch up to me," he said. "Please, I won't make any fuss. Just let me say good-bye to my wife and kids." In a way, the discovery was welcome. He had moved three times in the past five months, after being sure he had been spotted. His children, uprooted once again, asked questions he didn't know how to answer, and each day the guilt ate further into his soul. No, it was better the farce ended now. He couldn't imagine living the rest of his life in this terrible limbo.

The man shook his head. "No. Look, this isn't what you think." He was a strong-looking man of average height with brown hair and eyes, and a trim moustache. He looked vaguely familiar. Perhaps he was in law enforcement. It hardly mattered.

"Who are you?"

"I'm Supervisory Special Agent Fred Schulte from San Diego, and this is Brooke Erickson."

Now Dennis remembered the man. He had come to the prison the day Holbrooke had died. *The day you killed Holbrooke,* he told himself.

"But I'm not here to take you anywhere," Schulte said. "I've just come to deliver this document. And Brooke here has a few questions. She'd like to write your side of the story."

Dennis was stunned. He had to force his hands to be still as he read the paper the agent had given him. Words jumped out of the document, disconnected and unreal—"matter of the murder of Quentin Thomas Holbrooke . . . acting under excessive coercion . . . determined innocent . . . all charges dismissed . . ."

He looked up. "But how?"

"A few people involved, myself included, have requested that the charges be dropped. Under the circumstances, those in authority agreed."

Tears sprang to Dennis' eyes. "But—but why? Why would you do this for me?"

"Because I know you had no choice."

Dennis didn't know what to say.

"I read your confession. I believed you."

"But I still did it. I deserve to be punished! I should have told the authorities."

"No. I know these people. You made the only choice you could for your family. Make no mistake; if you had refused or gone to the authorities, they would have killed either you or a member of your family, or both. You had no choice. None but the one you made."

Dennis was crying openly now. For months he had dreamed of hearing those words from someone other than his loyal wife. "I really didn't know what to do. I even liked the guy."

"He wasn't a good person." Schulte's voice was grim. "He was a murderer, and much more."

"I know. But he always talked so nice. He missed his son." Dennis closed his eyes. "Oh, his son," he moaned. "How is he?"

Schulte cleared his throat. "Rumor has it that he was murdered in Europe by an opposing cartel." He hesitated, then appeared to make a decision. "That's the official record. But I happen to know that he is safe and is being adopted by a nice couple who have no mob connections. The details are secret for his own protection."

Dennis gave a sigh of relief. "Well, thank God for that. You can be sure I won't tell anyone. Thank you both for coming."

"I'd like to talk to you about your experience," the woman said. "It's for an article in the paper, and maybe later a book. I think it'll help people understand why you had to make the choice you did. That will prepare the way for your family to go back to the States, if that's what you want."

Dennis wiped his tears with the back of his hand. "Come in, then." He opened the door and led the way inside, where his wife and his children stared at him with wide, frightened eyes. "It's okay," he said, letting the longing show in his voice. "They've come to help us go home."

* * * * *

Cassi and Sampson sat in folding chairs on the small cement patio in back of the house. Sampson pushed two more marshmallows onto the end of his metal hanger and held it over the fire Jared had built in the cut-off bottom of an old metal trash can. It wasn't exactly camping, but it was as close as Cassi wanted to get in February, when the nights were still cool in the mountains. Later on in the summer, they would do the real thing.

"Look who's here." Jared came from the house with Fred and Brooke. The couple held hands as they walked toward the chairs.

Fred smiled at Sampson. "So, the big day has finally arrived."

Sampson swallowed his marshmallows. "Yeah, can you believe it?"

"I'm glad you got back from Brazil in time for our party," Cassi added. "It wouldn't be the same without you here."

Fred grinned, seeming more relaxed than Cassi had ever seen him. "We wouldn't miss this for the world."

"Brazil's neat," Sampson said. "But I like Portugal better. We're going back to Alvito next month to see Marisa."

"Sampson and Marisa have been writing." Jared slapped thick steaks on the grill in preparation for the additional guests who would soon arrive to help them celebrate the change in their family status.

"Marisa, huh?" Fred's voice was teasing.

Sampson colored slightly. "Yeah. She's okay for a girl." He reached for another marshmallow, but Cassi grabbed the bag.

"After dinner, okay?"

He grinned. "All right." Sampson wasn't always so agreeable, but today was special and apparently he was on his best behavior.

Sampson Landine was now officially their son. The boy had agreed readily to the adoption after living only a month with them, but he had been reluctant to change his last name. In the end, Fred had convinced him that it would be safer for all of them, just in case some obscure relative came looking for him. Sampson didn't call her mom yet, but Cassi wasn't going to push him. The memories he had of his birth mother were very important to all of them. At his insistence, Cassi had already completed Maura's temple work, and felt that she had accepted the gospel. She wasn't the only one.

"Now that I have official parents to give me permission, I'm getting baptized next week," Sampson told Fred. "Are you going to come?"

"Sure, I'll be there."

"You too, Brooke. I want you to come, too."

"Thank you, Sampson. I'd like that." Brooke cast a mischievous glance at Fred. "Of course, I'd like it better if Fred here would take the plunge, but I guess we can give him a little more time."

Fred put an arm around her. "Thank you. When I'm ready, we'll have another party."

"Cool," Sampson said. His hand sneaked toward the bag of marshmallows, but Cassi pulled it out of reach and stored it under her chair.

"As soon as Sampson's baptized, we're going on splits with the missionaries," Jared said. "I'm going to show him what tracting is like. It's about the only thing he hasn't had the opportunity to do."

"It won't be easy," Brooke warned.

"I think I can already guess," Sampson said with a moan. But he looked happy at the prospect.

Cassi watched everyone with enjoyment, especially Fred and Brooke. They were obviously in love, though neither seemed to know it yet. She couldn't get over how different Brooke looked now. Without the makeup, the sleek hairstyle, and the green contacts, she no longer resembled Laranda. Her face was warm and friendly, her manner easy and likeable. Cassi hoped that given a little more time, they would become good friends.

"I'm having a little sister, you know," Sampson said suddenly.

Fred and Brooke looked to Cassi for verification. "A baby?" asked Fred.

Cassi felt her face flush. "We were supposed to announce it after everyone got here. But yes, we're going to have a baby."

"That's wonderful," Brooke said warmly. "Congratulations!"

How marvelous to hear those words! In the past months, Cassi had begun to worry that she would never have any biological children. Not that she didn't love Sampson. She did—deeply. All of the pain and trials they had suffered with Laranda and Big Tommy were nothing compared to the joy of having him in their family. She would go through it all again, and much more, to have Sampson as her son. And now this baby—the fulfillment of a lifetime desire—was icing on the cake.

Jared left the grill and came to stand beside her chair. To Cassi's delight, he placed his hands under the tight ringlets that had nearly regrown to their full length and firmly rubbed her shoulders. "We don't know if it's a girl yet."

"I do." Somehow Sampson had another marshmallow on his hanger, and the bag had disappeared from under Cassi's chair and nestled in his lap. This time she didn't object. After all, they were in the midst of a party, and a few marshmallows had never stopped Sampson from gulping down at least two helpings of whatever dinner she and Jared served. He was remarkably easy to feed, and even ate Cassi's charred attempts at food with no comment.

"My mother once promised me a little sister," Sampson continued. "I think she'll arrange it somehow."

Cassi laughed and grabbed one of Jared's hands with her own. Her heart was so full she couldn't speak. Yes, everything they had been through was worth having Sampson with them. She couldn't wait to see what other surprises life would bring.

ABOUT THE AUTHOR

Rachel Ann Nunes (pronounced *noon-esh*) is a homemaker, student, and Church worker who lists writing as one of her favorite pursuits. *Love on the Run* is her eighth novel to be published by Covenant. Her *Ariana* series has been very popular in the LDS market.

In addition to writing and family activities, Rachel enjoys reading, camping, volleyball, softball, and traveling to or reading about foreign countries. She served an LDS mission to Portugal. Rachel and her husband, TJ, are the parents of five children.

Rachel enjoys hearing from her readers. You can write to her at P.O. Box 353, American Fork, UT 84003-0353, send e-mail to rachel@ranunes.com, or visit her web site at http://www.ranunes.com.